SILENCE OF THE BONES

A MURDER FORCE CRIME THRILLER

ADAM J. WRIGHT

THE MURDER FORCE SERIES

EYES OF THE WICKED

SILENCE OF THE BONES

REMAINS OF THE NIGHT

HOUSE OF THE DEAD

ECHO OF THE PAST

ALSO BY ADAM J. WRIGHT

DARK PEAK (DCI Battle)

THE RED RIBBON GIRLS (DI Summers)

CHAPTER 1

The night was quiet.

He drove along the main road of the village with his headlights turned off. No need to wake up any curious residents or light sleepers who might be able to identify his Land Rover to the police. It was almost three in the morning, and he wanted to ensure that the sleepy village of Temple Well remained just that; sleepy.

There would be plenty of excitement here tomorrow, once someone discovered what he was about to leave in the ruined temple on the hill. Until then, the village could remain unremarkable. And he could travel through it unseen.

Turning off the main road, he drove the Land Rover up a steep incline that terminated at a pair of wrought iron gates set into a stone wall, silhouetted against the moonlit sky.

He killed the engine and got out, being sure to close the driver's door quietly behind him.

Standing on the pavement, he listened to the night. His senses seemed more alive than ever. There was a smell in the air that he couldn't describe in words, but that he knew meant it was going to rain tomorrow. He could hear the scuffling of leaves on the other side of the wall as small, nocturnal animals moved through them, searching for food.

Satisfied that there was no one else on the street, he went around to the back of the Land Rover and opened it.

The bundle lay there, waiting.

He'd wrapped the girl's remains tightly in a bedsheet to keep them all together. Looking at the result of his handiwork as it lay in the shadows in the back of the car, he could almost believe it was nothing more than a collection of sticks swathed in the sheet.

As he leaned forward and picked up the swaddled remains, they felt light and brittle inside the material, adding to the illusion that this could be nothing more than a collection of branches.

Leaving the back of the Land Rover open to dissipate the musty smell that had permeated the air in there, he carried the bundle to the gates.

The tall, wrought iron gates were closed, but not locked. A sign bolted to the wall announced that *Temple Well Chapel* lay beyond the entrance. The chapel, he knew, had been built by the Knights Templar a long time ago and had given Temple Well half of its name, the other half being provided by a sacred well on the outskirts of the village.

Pulling back an iron latch with his knee—the swaddled remains were light but required both of his arms due to their size—he proceeded through the open gate and into the car park that had been built for tourists visiting the ruins.

He crossed the car park quickly and walked up a grassy slope to where the ruins waited, their crumbling walls shining in the moonlight.

"Nearly there," he whispered to the girl in his arms. He knew she couldn't hear him—she hadn't heard anything at all for a long time—but he felt that talking to her was the right thing to do, for some reason. Tomorrow, she would be found by the police, but for now, she was in his care, and it was up to him to make sure everything was done correctly for her.

Entering the ruins through an archway in the outer wall, he searched for a suitable place to leave the girl. It only took a couple of seconds before he decided on a stone altar that stood at the far end of the ruined structure. It was perfect.

He carried her over to it and laid her down gently on the rough, stone surface. Stepping back, he surveyed the scene. Some tourist or local would stumble across the body on the altar tomorrow, and then the girl's remains would be given back to her family for a proper burial.

He retraced his steps, leaving the ruins quickly. When he got back to the Land Rover, he closed the tailgate and got in behind the wheel.

With the headlights off, he drove back down the incline to the main road that led through the village. He felt a sense of accomplishment but knew that placing the girl on the altar was simply the start of a long road. He had a lot of work ahead of him.

There were many, many more girls like her.

This was just the beginning.

CHAPTER 2

"How did you feel after your husband died?" the psychiatrist, whose name was Trudy, asked.

Detective Inspector Danica Summers, who was sitting opposite Trudy in the psychiatrist's York office, frowned. What the hell did this have to do with her getting back to work?

"I don't see how that's relevant to what we're discussing."

"Everything is relevant," Trudy said. "It's only been two years since you lost your husband. How are you coping? Do you feel you're able to handle life on a day-to-day basis?"

"Yes."

Sitting back in her chair, the psychiatrist said, "Could you elaborate on that?"

Dani sighed. She obviously wasn't going to be able to get out of this office—which felt suddenly hot and stifling—until she'd given the psychiatrist chapter and verse.

"When Shaun died, I was devastated. My entire world fell apart. But I couldn't wallow in self-pity because I had responsibilities; to my daughter, to my dogs, and to the people I work with. I had to get on with it."

Trudy nodded slowly and seemed to be considering Dani's words. Probably searching for something that would break through Dani's calm demeanour. The detective had already decided—since the moment she sat down in the room, in fact—that the psychiatrist was probing for a weakness.

"Tell me about your daughter."

"She's a smart and beautiful girl," Dani said. "She's studying for a Chemistry degree at Birmingham University."

"How has all this affected her?" The psychiatrist waved her hands in the air vaguely when she said, "all this," lending the words a sense of ambiguity. She might be referring to Shaun's death, or to the shooting that had cracked Dani's ribs, or even to life in general.

"She handles everything very well," Dani said, deciding to be just as ambiguous with her answer.

"The shooting?" Trudy asked. "How did she cope with that?"

"Very maturely."

"Her father's death?"

"The same. Look, I thought we were here to discuss my fitness to return to work, not my entire life story."

"We can't separate one from the other if we're to look at this holistically. We can't compartmentalise aspects or events of our lives. Is that what you do, Detective Inspector? Compartmentalise?" She leaned forward slightly, her eyes scrutinising Dani from behind her glasses.

That gave Dani pause. She did separate the various aspects of her life; she knew that. Everything was ordered and simple. She went to work. When she got home, she walked the dogs. Charlie visited during the holidays; well, she used to visit during the holidays, but she was growing up now and that was changing.

The only thing she found hard to disconnect from was her work. When she was working on an active case, it occupied her thoughts, no matter what she was doing. Day or night. The case bled into every aspect of her life.

There was no way she was going to tell the psychiatrist that.

"I put things into their own boxes when I need to," she said.

"When you get home, do you leave work behind?"

"Yes." It was a lie, but she told it convincingly.

"Do you think about when you were shot?"

"No." That wasn't so much of a lie; other than a couple of nightmares, she barely thought of being shot. The pain in her ribs, yes. The frustration at not being able to move without pain for six weeks, also yes. But the actual moment she was shot, no. That was in the past. She'd locked it away in its own mental box.

"You aren't reminded of it when you feel pain in your ribs?"

"I'm virtually pain free."

"When you were recovering, then."

"No. The pain simply reminded me to not stretch too far or put too much weight on my side."

"Didn't you feel anger at the man who shot you?"

Dani shook her head.

"Why not? He put you into this position. Because of him, you've missed six weeks of work already."

Dani didn't like the sound of that last sentence. The psychiatrist made it sound as if there might be more weeks at home, more long hours of boredom. She couldn't fail this evaluation; she was itching to get back to the Murder Force. Missing out on the team's formative weeks made her feel like an outsider. Working relationships would have been built, trust established between team members. All while she was absent.

"I don't feel angry at him," she said. "We were on opposite sides of the game. I wanted to catch him, and he wanted to escape."

"So, you understand his actions because you see him as an opponent. An opponent trying to win a game you were both playing against each other."

Dani nodded. "Yes, I suppose so."

"So, your job is a game?" The psychiatrist regarded her over the top of her glasses.

"No, it isn't a game. We deal with life and death every day. It's deadly serious. But each case is like a game in the way it plays out. There are players with opposing motives and ideals, strategic moves, and everyone tries to win." She paused and then added, "But, unlike a game, no one really does."

Trudy looked up from her notes. "Oh? Surely you believe you won your most recent case. The perpetrator was caught. Isn't that a win for you?"

"People died. Others went through experiences that will affect them their whole lives."

"Are you including yourself in that list? Will you be affected your whole life by what happened to you?"

"Every case affects the detectives who work on it in some way or other. We wouldn't be human, otherwise."

"What about being shot? Did that make this case affect you more than usual?"

"Only because it knocked me off my feet for six weeks. It hasn't affected me psychologically, if that's what you're thinking."

The psychiatrist consulted her notes again. That

obviously *was* what she was thinking. It was also probably what Chief Superintendent Gallow had been thinking, since he'd insisted Dani come to this psychiatric evaluation before re-joining Murder Force.

"That isn't necessarily what I'm thinking," Trudy said. "I do think that you've been reticent to speak about yourself during this session."

"I'm not really a sharer."

"Nothing you say in this room will go beyond these four walls."

"Yes, you said that when I arrived." She checked the clock on the wall. It was almost eleven. She'd been here for an hour.

"I just want to ensure that you know you can say anything here and it will remain between us. The report I send to the Chief Superintendent doesn't contain any specifics of this interview, only my evaluation of your fitness to return to work."

"And what is your evaluation?" Dani asked. She was tired of playing this particular game, and angry at herself for feeling somehow beholden to this woman sitting in front of her. Trudy held the key to her immediate future, but Dani refused to ingratiate herself towards the psychiatrist.

"Oh, you're fit to return to work," Trudy said. "I knew that after the first ten minutes. I'll send my recommendation to Superintendent Gallow that you be reinstated on the team with immediate effect."

Dani frowned, confused. If the psychiatrist knew she was mentally fit after ten minutes, then why had she sat here being grilled for another fifty?

Trudy answered the unspoken question. "I'm writing an article on the mental effects of police work. Your situation is quite intriguing, with your background of personal loss, separation from your daughter, and the shooting incident. I wanted to delve deeper, as it were, into your thoughts on those events."

Dani got out of the chair. She wouldn't be this woman's lab rat for some damned article.

"We don't have to stop yet," Trudy said. "I don't have another appointment until—"

"I don't care when your next bloody appointment is. I didn't come here to be part of your experiment."

"It's not an experiment," Trudy said, seemingly offended. "It's a peer-reviewed article."

"I don't care what it is, I'm out of here." She strode to the door, grabbing her coat from the stand as she went. Flinging open the door, she stormed past the bewildered receptionist and out into the corridor.

After pausing for a moment to try and remember if the elevators were to the left or right, she recalled that she'd come from the right and headed off in that direction.

As she was walking along the corridor, her phone, which was in her coat pocket, began to buzz.

Dani fished it out and checked the screen. She didn't know the number, but the dialling code—01904—told her the call was coming from York. She answered it. "Hello?"

"Summers, is that you?"

"Yes, who's this?"

"DCS Gallow."

"Sorry, sir, I didn't recognise your voice."

"Yes, well, no matter. The good news is that Trudy Manners has just rung me and told me I can have you back on the team whenever I want."

Dani felt herself smiling. The psychiatrist had probably been worried that Dani might let Gallow know she'd been using the return-to-work interviews for her own purposes, so she must have got on the phone as soon as Dani left her office. Case closed. Dani hadn't intended to tell Gallow anything, anyway, but the fear that she might had spurred Trudy into action, and that pleased her.

"And I want you back on the team now," Gallow continued. "So, I'm afraid your little holiday is over."

"Yes, sir." Dani had never been so glad to leave a holiday behind. She'd reached the elevators now, and was jabbing at the button to call one to this floor.

"You have the address of the new headquarters?"

"I have it, sir." During her recovery, she'd been sent a letter informing her of the new location of the Murder Force HQ. She'd placed the letter in the glove box of her car, ready for the day she returned to work.

And now, that day had arrived.

"Right. Well get over here as soon as you can. We've got a new case, and I want you on it."

"I'll be there shortly, sir."

"Excellent. I'll see you then." He hung up.

The elevator arrived and Dani got in.

She was still smiling when she exited the building and walked to her car.

Retrieving the crisp, white printed piece of paper that contained the address of her new headquarters from the glove box, she entered the postcode into her Land Rover's SatNav and waited for the mechanical voice to guide her.

While the computer was still searching for a satellite, Dani drove out of the car park and joined the traffic on the busy road.

Her recovery—or her "little holiday," as Gallow had called it—was over.

She was back.

CHAPTER 3

The SatNav took Dani through the outskirts of the city, until she found herself driving north on the A19. After half an hour of driving through villages and along lonely stretches of road, she followed the monotonic voice's instruction and turned right, heading east through the moors.

A couple of villages and miles of moorland later, she arrived at the village of Stonegrave and the SatNav sent her north again, until she arrived at her destination, which seemed to be an old school building.

The two-storey, brick structure was ringed by an iron fence which had been painted dark green at some point in the distant past and which bore no identifying signs or markings upon its paint-flaked railings.

The only thing that told Dani she was at the correct location was a number of police cars parked around the building. She drove through the open gate and parked her Land Rover Discovery in between two patrol cars.

There was only one obvious way into the building; a pair of double doors that were made from wood and glass, and looked like they'd seen better days. Dani slid out of the Discovery, crossed the car park quickly, and pushed through the doors.

A foyer, which had bare brick walls, had been turned into a makeshift reception area with the addition of a curved counter and a plexiglass screen that ran along one wall and a dozen plastic chairs that had been lined up along the opposite wall.

A uniformed officer sat at a desk behind the counter, tapping at a keyboard. When he saw Dani, he smiled and said, "Can I help you?"

"DI Summers," she said, showing him her warrant card through the screen.

"Yes, ma'am." He stood up and came over to the counter. "The squad room is on the first floor. You can take the stairs, or there's a disabled access lift." He gestured to a set of wooden and steel stairs that looked like they'd been built in the seventies, and a wooden door with a disabled sign on the wall above.

"Thanks," Dani said. She turned towards the stairs but was stopped by the man's voice.

"You'll need this, ma'am."

She turned to face him again. He was holding a

laminated ID card that had the word *Visitor* printed across it in red.

"I'm not a visitor," she told him. "I work here."

"Oh, I see. I'm sorry. So, you already have an ID card, then?"

She shook her head.

"Then you'll need this, ma'am. And if you'd just sign in, that would be great." He indicated an open ledger on the counter and a pen next to it.

She walked back to the counter and signed in before taking the proffered visitor's ID card, which she clipped to the hem of her jumper, as she returned to the stairs. She ascended them slowly. Her ribs might have recovered from the fracture, but Dani was still hesitant to push herself physically. The memories of the agony she'd experienced over the last few weeks were too fresh in her mind for her to risk any action that might bring it back.

She'd only recently been able to walk without pain shooting through her body, and she wanted to keep it that way. She wasn't going to set back her recovery by sprinting up a flight of stairs.

When she got to the top, she was faced with a double door, to which someone had taped a piece of paper bearing the printed words *Murder Force*.

Either the budget for the team hadn't arrived yet, or the builders were still on their Christmas holiday, despite the fact that it was now February.

Dani opened the doors and was greeted by the

sight of a busy, open plan office. Desks had been pushed together to form islands on the expanse of blue carpet and each was a flurry of activity, with uniformed and plainclothes officers typing into computers, answering phones, and chatting with each other.

A number of private offices and meeting rooms had been built around the perimeter of the large room. Unlike the foyer and the stairs, this part of the building had been built to house the Murder Force.

"Summers!" DCS Gallow was leaning out through one of the office doors and beckoning her over. She wondered if the uniform in the foyer had informed Gallow of her arrival while she'd been gingerly climbing the stairs.

"Good morning, Sir," she said as she approached him.

"Not for some, it isn't." He stepped aside to let her into the room, which had been set up as a meeting room, with a large table in the centre and a large whiteboard fixed to one wall. Sitting around the table were DCI Battle, DC Tom Ryan, the psychologist Tony Sheridan, and Detective Sergeants Matt Flowers and Lorna Morgan.

"Take a seat," Gallow said, gesturing to the empty chairs around the table.

Dani took a seat next to Sheridan, who whispered, "Glad to have you back," as she sat down.

"Yes, we're all glad to have DI Summers back,"

Gallow said, folding his arms and leaning against the wall. "Now, let's focus on this new case. DCI Battle will fill us in on what we know so far."

"Thank you, sir," Battle said. "He climbed out of his chair and stood at the head of the table. "These are a bit grim," he said, handing out A4 pieces of paper.

The papers were passed around the table and when they arrived in front of Dani, she looked down at copies of a number of crime scene photos that showed a badly decomposed body, wrapped in a white sheet, lying across what looked like a stone altar within some sort of ruins. The corpse was so badly decayed that barely any flesh was left on the skeleton and that which was still there had been stretched tightly across the bones. The skull, which was topped with long dark hair, and the shoulders poked from the sheet, but the rest of the corpse was covered.

"You can see right away why this one has caught a lot of media interest," Battle said. "A few hours ago, the body of a young girl was found in a ruined chapel in the village of Temple Well, Derbyshire. A family from Leicester came across the body while they were visiting the chapel. The body was completely wrapped in the shroud but the father, curious about what was inside, partially unwrapped it. He won't do anything like that again in a hurry."

Holding up a photo that showed the ruined

chapel from a distance, Battle said. "This is Temple Well Chapel, built by the Knights Templar in the 12th Century. The press have caught wind of this one and are going with the ritualistic elements on their front pages."

"We need to get a result quickly," Gallow said. "Before the public believe there are satanic cults lurking in every village from here to Land's End."

Tony Sheridan held up one of the photos. "This isn't a ritualistic killing."

"What are you talking about?" Gallow said. "The girl was found on an altar."

Sheridan nodded. "Yes, she was. But ritual murder involves the killing of a live victim, an offering to some higher power. This girl has been dead for, what, ten years? There's soil in her hair and inside the shroud. It looks like she's been dug up from somewhere else and simply placed on the altar. That isn't a ritualistic killing."

Gallow opened his mouth to speak, but Battle beat him to it. "That doesn't really matter to the media, Tony. They'll run with the ritualistic angle because it's a better story."

Sheridan nodded. "Fine, but we need to bear in mind that this girl was dead long before she ended up in this chapel. The location might have been chosen to make us think this is something it isn't."

"We'll keep an open mind," Battle said.

Gallow pushed away from the wall and said, "You

can work out the finer points when you get to Derbyshire. By the time you get there, the press will be all over this, so let's try to get a speedy resolution to this case. Work with the pathologist and identify the girl. Then find out how she ended up in that chapel. Who put her there? We're arranging accommodation for each of you in Temple Well and the surrounding district. We'll also be employing a number of uniformed officers to assist with things like door-to-door enquiries."

"Will we have a base down there, sir?" Ryan asked. "A temporary HQ?"

"We'll find somewhere suitable," Gallow said. "Everyone clear about what they're doing?" There were no murmurs of dissent, so he said, "Right, let's get this one sorted out quickly and efficiently. Dismissed." He left the room.

"Looks like you came back at the right time, guv," Ryan said to Dani. "We've been sitting on our arses for a month doing bugger all. The day you return, we land a case. You must be a good luck charm."

"Not so lucky for this poor girl," Dani said, tapping her finger on the crime photo.

One by one, the team filtered out of the meeting room. Battle leaned over the table, staring at the photo of the shrouded corpse.

"Everything all right, guv?" Dani asked.

He looked up and paused for a fraction of a second before saying, "Yes, I think so. I'm just thinking of a missing persons case from fifteen years ago." He jabbed a finger at the photo of Temple Well Chapel. "Not too far from here."

"Do you think this is the missing girl?"

He shrugged. "It could be. I hope not. I promised her family I'd find her, but the case hit a dead end. If this is her, I'm going to have to go back to her parents and tell them I failed. Their daughter is dead."

"You haven't failed, guv. I'm sure you did everything you could at the time."

"I did," he said. "But if the girl on that altar is Daisy Riddle, then I didn't do enough."

CHAPTER 4

Dani got to her neighbours' house an hour later. She needed to sort out the dogs before she made the long drive to Derbyshire. Thanks to her neighbours, Elsie and Bob Carmichael, the dogs were always cared for when she spent too long away from the cottage.

Elsie and Bob, who lived less than a quarter of a mile up the road, knew that if Dani's car was gone for long, it meant she was probably stuck at work. That sent them into action, and the elderly couple would use the key Dani had given them some time ago to let themselves into the cottage and take Barney and Jack for regular walks until Dani returned. They'd also cared for the dogs while Dani had been in recovery.

Their own dogs—a French poodle named Bella and a shitzu called Alfie—were friends with Dani's German shepherds, and she'd looked after them while Elsie and Bob had been on holiday in Spain last year.

As she pulled up onto the drive of the Carmichael house, she saw Bella and Alfie leaping up at the living room window, triggered into a paroxysm of barking and tail wagging by the arrival of Dani's car.

By the time she got out of the Discovery, the house's front door was already open, and the poodle and shitzu were bounding up her legs.

"Alfie! Bella!" Bob Carmichael called from the open doorway. "Behave!" He smiled at Dani and said, "Don't tell me; you're going away for a while."

"I'm afraid so," Dani said, approaching the doorway with the two dogs still circling excitedly around her legs.

"I suppose it's something to do with that girl they found in that ruined church." Elsie appeared behind her husband, a mixing bowl beneath her arm and a wooden spoon in her hand. She wore a floral-patterned apron, and the smell of something sweet and delicious drifted out of the house.

"It's been on the telly," Elsie said, "and I said to Bob, that's the kind of thing that Dani's team deals with."

"Sounds like a job for the Murder Force," Bob added with a wink.

"Yes, I'll be driving down there as soon as I've packed a bag."

"Well, don't worry about Barney and Jack," he said. "We'll take good care of them."

"Thank you, I know you will. And they'll be happy to see Bella and Alfie again."

He grinned. "Of course they will."

"Ooh, before you go, I've got something for you," Elsie said, before disappearing into the house. She returned a minute later with a large Tupperware container, which she gave to Dani. "I cooked those ginger biscuits half an hour ago. They're still nice and warm. They should keep you going during the drive."

There must have been at least two dozen biscuits in the container, separated into layers by neat folds of baking parchment paper.

"Thank you," Dani said. "Now, I'm afraid I really must go. I'll let you know when I'm back."

"You take as long as you need," Bob said. "Just make sure you catch whoever needs to be caught."

She smiled and walked back to the Discovery, still being followed by the dogs. "I will." She reached down and stroked Bella and Alfie before climbing into the car. As she reversed off the drive, the elderly couple waved to her from the doorway.

She pulled up on her own drive a minute later and got out of the car. Unlike the Carmichaels' dogs, Jack and Barney didn't make an appearance at the window. The two German shepherds preferred to lie in wait inside the door and ambush her when she entered the cottage. God help any burglar who managed to get inside.

As she put her key into the lock, she heard scrabbling inside, and when she pushed open the door, the two big dogs leapt up and moved in tight circles, their huge tails pounding on the floor.

"Hello, you two," she said. "It isn't long since I left, is it? You're probably wondering what I'm doing here." It was only a couple of hours ago that she'd left the house for her appointment with the psychiatrist.

"Uncle Bob and Auntie Elsie are going to take care of you for a little while," she said, making her way to the kitchen and opening the cupboard where she kept the dog treats. "I'll be back as soon as I can." She hugged the big dogs and gave each of them a bone-shaped treat before heading to the bedroom and taking a large black suitcase from the top of the wardrobe.

She placed it on the bed, opened it, and began filling it with items she'd need in Derbyshire such as underwear, jeans, trousers, T-shirts, and tops. After filling a toiletry bag with various items from the bathroom, she packed that into the case, along with the clothes. She threw her laptop and charger on top of everything and added two paperback thrillers she'd been meaning to get around to reading.

During her recovery, she'd devoured a huge number of books and had reacquired a love of reading that she'd lost at some point during the past couple of years. Now that she'd rediscovered the lost passion, she couldn't imagine travelling without taking a book.

As an afterthought, she added a third novel to the suitcase; she had no idea how long she'd be in Derbyshire.

She doubted this case was going to be concluded quickly. The girl had been dead for over a decade at least, which meant trails would have gone cold, witnesses could have moved away or even died, and memories would have become dulled.

If the girl on the altar was the missing girl Battle had referred to—Daisy Riddle—then they would at least have a starting point for the investigation, but Daisy's case hadn't been solved when her disappearance had been fresh in the memory of everyone involved. Getting those same people to remember details from fifteen years ago would be an almost impossible task, which meant a killer could escape the net simply because of the passage of time.

The only advantage to finding the body now rather than a decade ago was that methods of detection, particularly in the field of forensics, had advanced over time, and the body would probably contain evidence, particularly DNA, that could bring a swift conclusion to the case.

The only thing Dani knew for sure at this moment was that the girl on the altar—whether she was Daisy Riddle or not—deserved justice. And it was Dani's job to help her get that.

She zipped up the suitcase and took it to the front door.

Barney and Jack, having finished their treats, watched her with sorrowful eyes from the living room rug.

She felt a pang of guilt at leaving the dogs, who had become used to her constant company during the last couple of months, while she went away, but knew she had no choice.

Crouching down, she held her arms out, and the dogs came over to her, resting their heads on her shoulders. "I'm going to miss you two," she said. Now that Shaun was gone and Charlie spent most of her time at uni, the dogs were her only real company, other than her work colleagues.

Jack's ears pricked up and he turned his face towards the front door. His tail began swishing over the floor.

A moment later, Barney was doing the same thing.

Dani heard voices outside. She went to the window and saw Bob and Elsie out there, being led across the drive by Bella and Alfie, who were pulling against their leads in an attempt to get to the cottage faster.

Jack and Barney were going crazy now, bounding up at the front door and yapping excitedly.

Dani got their leads from where they hung by the door and attached them to the dogs' collars. She opened the door, and now all four dogs were barking at each other.

"We thought we'd take them all for a walk on the moors," Bob said. "Let you get on with packing."

"Thanks," she said, stepping out onto the drive and trying to keep Jack and Barney in check. That wasn't an easy task; each dog weighed in excess of seventy pounds. She handed the leads to Bob.

"Don't you worry about them," he told her. "They're in good hands. They'll be glad to see you when you get back."

She gave the dogs a final stroke and the elderly couple led them away. Anxious to get onto the moors, Jack and Barney barely looked back.

Dani grabbed the suitcase from the hall, loaded it into the back of the Discovery and climbed behind the wheel. She typed *Temple Well* into the SatNav and waited for the computer to find a satellite.

Her phone buzzed. She checked it and found a text that read, *Chapel View Guest House B&B, Temple Well*, and a postcode.

The SatNav connected and planned out the route to the Derbyshire village. Apparently, it was going to take almost three hours to get there. Dani didn't bother changing the destination to the address she'd just been texted; she'd find the B&B when she got to there. The village wasn't that big, after all, so she shouldn't have any problem.

She wondered how big the Chapel View Guest

House was; surely the whole force wouldn't be staying there. If everyone was going to be spread out in and around the village, it would create logistical problems, unless they had a central base to work from.

She reversed off the drive and headed towards Tollby. The route would eventually lead her to York on the A64, and then south on the A1 to Derbyshire.

Clicking on the radio to keep her company, she heard the tail end of a drama about a violinist and then the news came on.

The female newsreader's voice filled the car. *"Derbyshire police still haven't identified the body of a young girl found in the ruins of Temple Well chapel this morning..."*

CHAPTER 5

"James Gibson was a private man," the vicar said from the pulpit. "That is reflected by the small number of people here today, but he left behind his loving son Robert and his grandchildren, Sam and Olivia."

Sitting in the front pew, Rob Gibson turned his head slightly so he could see his wife, Sonia, who was sitting next to him. She was staring straight ahead, her emotions unreadable. She knew as much as he did that the vicar's words were bullshit. The man lying in the coffin in front of them had never even seen his grandkids. Rob had made sure of that. And as for "loving son," it was the most ridiculous thing he'd ever heard.

His father had been disliked by everyone. That was why the only other people who had bothered to turn up to his funeral were a couple of distant cousins, sitting stony-faced across the aisle, and Eric, his father's brother. Eric had moved away from the area years ago, probably to get away from his older sibling, and now lived down south somewhere.

Rob was surprised his uncle had bothered to make the drive up to Derbyshire to attend the funeral at all. Probably wanted to make sure James was actually gone.

Rob didn't blame him. The only reason he was here himself was to make sure the old bastard was buried deep in the ground. Even James Gibson couldn't hurt anyone from six feet under.

The pallbearers—all provided by the funeral director because there weren't enough family or friends willing to carry the coffin to its final resting place in the churchyard—walked to the front of the church and manhandled the coffin onto their shoulders. As they carried it back along the aisle, sombre organ music filled the air.

Rob got up, glad to stretch his legs. His arse had gone numb after sitting in the pew for the short service; God knew how churchgoers could stand that kind of torture every Sunday.

As he fell into line behind the coffin, he felt a smile play over his lips and hoped no one would notice. His father had been an avowed atheist. The recipient of a strict, religious upbringing—thanks to the fact that Rob's grandfather had been a Pentecostal pastor—his father had railed against religion of any kind. So, the fact that his body had spent its last moments above ground level inside a church, was an irony that was not lost on Rob.

Outside the church, a light rain had begun to fall. Sonia took hold of Rob's arm and whispered, "Are you all right?"

"Never better," he said in a low voice. She knew there was no love lost between him and his father. She didn't know the whole story, of course, but she should realise that today was a day of celebration, not mourning. James Gibson had shuffled off this mortal coil, and the world was a better place for it.

"Bloody hell, my phone's ringing," she said, holding up her handbag, from which an insistent buzz could be heard. "I'll ignore it."

"No, go ahead and answer it," he told her. "It might be important." The more irreverence he could bring to this funeral, the better. The sheen of respectability that this occasion afforded his father galled him. If they only knew who James Gibson *really* was, they'd be chuck him unceremoniously into an unmarked grave.

But they didn't know what he knew; they hadn't been brought up by the mean old fucker in the coffin. As far as they were concerned, they were simply burying a lonely old man who had lived a quiet life and was leaving behind a loving son.

As he passed beneath the doorway and out into the churchyard, Rob shivered slightly. The damp, drizzling rain was cold, and managed to soak through his suit jacket and shirt, chilling his skin.

"All right, I'll be right there," Sonia was saying into her phone. He'd been so lost in his thoughts that he hadn't noticed her answering it.

She put the phone back into her handbag. "That was Emma. Sam is throwing some sort of tantrum and has locked himself in his bedroom."

He frowned, confused. "How can he? His bedroom door hasn't got a lock on it."

"He's pushed his bookshelf behind the door, or something. Look, I'm going to have to go and see what's up." She cast a glance at the pallbearers and the coffin. "I can't stay, I'm sorry."

"Of course, love, it's fine. You go, and I'll be there later."

"All right," she said with a relieved sigh. "Are you coming straight home after this?" She gestured at the churchyard.

"I'd best go and check his house."

"Again? You were there last night."

"I know, but it's out there in the middle of nowhere, standing empty. Anyone could break in."

"You said yourself, there's nothing valuable inside."

"I said I don't think there is, not at first glance, anyway. Who knows what the old sod has got squirrelled away in his cupboards?"

She sighed again, this time out of frustration.

"The sooner we sell that place and get it off our hands, the better. I suppose I'll have to walk home, then, since you're going to need the car."

"No, you take the car. I'll walk home after this is done and take the Land Rover up to the house."

The Land Rover he was referring to was a blue Defender that had been his father's but which he'd inherited, along with the house. It was old and clanky, but Rob actually liked it, or, rather, the freedom that came with it.

Until now, he and Sonia had shared a car; their five-year-old Ford Focus. Because they worked opposite shifts—she as a teaching assistant during the day and he as a security guard at night—they'd never needed a second vehicle. But shortly after his father's death, Rob had felt a desire for more freedom. He needed his own space, and his father's house and car fulfilled that need.

Besides, now that his father was gone, he might be able to find the answer to a question that had been eating away at him from the inside since he was a child; he might be able to find out what had happened to his mother.

"All right, I'll see you in a bit." Sonia planted a brief kiss on his cheek and then made her way to the car park at the front of the church.

Rob watched her go, wishing he was also leaving. But there was something he had to do before the first clumps of dirt were thrown onto his father's coffin.

In his trouser pockets were two notes. In his left pocket, a neatly folded piece of lined paper contained the words, *I hope you rot in Hell for what you did*. He'd written that a couple of nights ago, with the intention of throwing it into the old man's grave before the hole was filled in.

The note in his right pocket had been written last night, while he was at his father's house. The words he'd written on the yellowed piece of paper he'd found in his father's bureau were, *I'm sorry I couldn't be the son you wanted me to be. I'm sorry I was a disappointment*.

He only intended to throw one of those pieces of paper into the grave, and that was the *rot in Hell* one. He wasn't even sure why he'd brought the other one along with him to the funeral. In fact, he wasn't even sure why he'd written it in the first place.

Yes, he had been a disappointment to his father, he knew that, but being a disappointment to a man like James Gibson wasn't necessarily a bad thing.

"Robert."

He turned around to see Eric walking towards him.

"Uncle Eric. I'm surprised you came."

"I felt it was my duty." He gestured to the coffin, which the pallbearers were laying over the open grave. "Not to him, but to you, I suppose."

"Me?" Rob was surprised.

Eric nodded. "Is everything all right, Robert?"

Assuming his uncle was asking if everything was all right now that his father was gone, Rob nodded. "Yes, everything's fine. We weren't close, you know."

"I know. He was never close to anybody. That isn't what I mean. What I'm trying to say is..." he paused, as if trying to formulate his next sentence carefully. "You've inherited his house. I assume you've been to it. Is everything all right? At the house?" He gave Rob a knowing look, as if his nephew should know what he was talking about.

Rob nodded slowly, but he felt a sudden tightness in his gut. Did Eric know something about what Rob had discovered at the house? No, he couldn't; it wasn't possible. "Everything's fine," he repeated, but this time his voice cracked in his throat.

Eric looked at him closely, with narrow eyes.

"They're lowering the coffin," Rob said, striding away to the graveside and leaving his uncle standing on the path. Despite the chilly rain, he felt sweat break out all over his body. What the hell did Eric know? Had he put two and two together regarding the girl?

The coffin was lowered gradually into the grave. When it reached the bottom, Rob reached into his left pocket and took out the note he'd written at home, telling his father he hoped he'd rot in hell. He tossed it into the hole. It landed on the casket and lay there against the wood.

Watching the paper as it became soaked by the

rain, Rob absent-mindedly reached into his right pocket and took out the other note. He held it over the gaping hole for a moment before releasing his grip on it. The piece of paper fluttered down to join the other. Rob sniffed, grabbed a handful of dirt, threw it onto the coffin, and turned away.

He was almost at the car park when he heard Eric coming up behind him.

"Robert, wait!"

He paused and waited for his uncle to catch up with him.

"I'm sorry if I seemed a bit vague," Eric said. "It's just that I think I knew your father better than you do. I grew up with him. I know what he was capable of. When I heard you had the keys to his house, I was worried about what you might find there."

Rob knew exactly what his father was capable of. A childhood memory crept into his mind, but he pushed it away.

"What do you mean, exactly?" he asked, deciding to see just how much his uncle knew.

Eric shrugged. "Look, can we meet up for a drink and a proper chat?" He reached into his coat and produced a business card, which he handed to Rob. "My mobile number is on there."

Rob looked at the card. It seemed Uncle Eric was the director of a construction company based in Plymouth. The mobile number was indeed printed on the card, but Rob doubted he'd use it. If he waited long enough, Eric would eventually return down south, and leave him alone.

Or perhaps he should find out just what Eric knew—or suspected—regarding his father's house.

"Right, I'll give you a ring sometime, then," he said, noncommittally. Waving the hand that held the business card at Eric, he turned and headed for home.

As he strolled through the village of Hatherfield, where he'd lived almost all of his adult life, the residents who were out and about greeted him with a cheery wave and a smile. Some addressed him by name and asked him how he was doing. Everyone in the village knew everyone else. Sonia loved that aspect of village life; being part of a community. Rob wasn't so sure anymore.

He'd never really thought about it until recently, but the idea of everyone in the village knowing the ins and outs of each other's lives put his nerves on edge. What if he wanted to do things that he didn't want anyone else to know about? What if he wanted to live his life without having to worry about curtain twitchers watching his every move?

That was why he wanted to hang on to his father's house for as long as possible, despite Sonia's desire to sell it. He had a bolt hole he could retreat to, away from the busybodies and gossips. Somewhere he could do whatever the hell he wanted without having to keep up appearances.

He frowned at his own thoughts. He hadn't questioned village life in all the years he'd lived in Hatherfield, so why now?

Because last night, he'd done something that no one else must ever know about, and he liked having a secret. Something that was his and his alone. As he exchanged greetings with the locals on his way home from the church, he felt a kind of superiority to them. They were going about their dull lives while he was doing things that they wouldn't dream of doing in their darkest nightmares.

He got to the house and decided not to go inside. Whatever crisis was happening in there, Sonia and Emma, the babysitter, could handle it. They'd probably coaxed Sam out of his room by now and were having a cup of tea together. No need for him to interrupt.

Taking the Land Rover's keys out of his pocket, he unlocked the vehicle and climbed inside. He turned the key in the ignition and was rewarded with a low growl coming from the Defender's engine.

He put his foot down and headed out of Hatherfield, driving north towards Buxton, but heading east long before he got anywhere near the town. After passing the village of Miller's Dale, he turned onto the road that led to his father's house.

The old house sat nestled in the foothills of a range of peaks that cut off the view of the horizon and made the world seem small. Rob parked the

Land Rover outside and got out, noticing tyre tracks in the gravel. He was sure these weren't the tracks he'd made when he'd come here last night. Had Eric stopped by, hoping to find him at the house, perhaps?

A sudden panic welled within him, and he fumbled the house keys out of his pocket. There was no indication that Eric—or whoever had been here—had gone inside, but the thought of someone being in the house, of seeing what was in the cellar, made him almost vomit with fear. A coppery taste flooded his throat, and he swallowed it down as he turned the key in the lock.

As soon as he was inside the house, he strode along the hall to the kitchen, and the cellar door. The door was closed, and there was no sign of it having been opened by anyone. Still, he was going to have to get a lock for it. He couldn't risk a burglar or a squatter finding what was down there.

Opening the door, he clicked on the light and descended the wooden steps that led down to the dirt floor. The cellar, like the house above it, was expansive.

If Rob hadn't found the folded piece of paper with a crude drawing of the cellar and various areas marked with an X, he'd never have known where to dig last night.

He walked over to the hole he'd dug and stared

down into it. He'd dug down at least five or six feet before he'd found the bones.

The square hole, now empty, reminded him of his father's grave.

He turned away from the hole and surveyed the rest of the cellar. He'd have to fill in this grave and continue his search.

He hadn't been looking for the girl.

He'd been looking for the body of his mother.

CHAPTER 6

When Dani arrived at Temple Well, she felt weary from the long drive. A heavy rain had begun to fall as soon as she'd got onto the A1, and that had meant lorries spraying up water and reduced visibility.

Now, at least, the rain had stopped, and the sun was attempting to show itself from behind the clouds.

Temple Well's main street had a Post Office, two pubs, a corner shop, and a gift shop. Dani could see a Norman church on a hill set back from the road.

A large village green sat in the centre of everything, bisecting the main road. One part of the road led up a small incline and a brown sign proclaimed that it led to *Temple Well Chapel, National Heritage Site*.

Dani followed the route indicated by the sign. Might as well get a look at the crime scene before she went in search of the Chapel View Guest House.

As she'd expected, Temple Well was a hive of activity, thanks to the grisly discovery this morning. News vans were parked along the road leading to the chapel, and groups of journalists milled about, some with cameras and sound equipment, while others were drinking coffee from Styrofoam cups and chatting. A burger van was taking advantage of the sudden influx of people and was serving fast food from the kerbside.

Driving past the throng of reporters, Dani came to a stone wall and a closed wrought iron gate. A uniformed police officer stationed at the gate came forward when she saw Dani's car. She shook her head and made a whirling signal with her right hand, that Dani assumed meant, "turn around."

Her warrant card was in her handbag, in the passenger footwell. She leaned over to get it.

The officer tapped on the window and made another whirling motion with her hand that this time obviously meant, "wind down the window."

Fishing the bag off the floor, Dani pressed the button that lowered the window. It buzzed down slowly.

"Sorry, you can't stay here," the officer said. "You need to go back down the hill with the rest of the media."

"I'm not with the media," Dani said, pulling out her warrant card and holding it up. "DI Summers. Murder Force."

"Oh, sorry, ma'am. I'll just get the gate for you." She hurried to the gate, unlatched it, and swung it open. As Dani drove through, she waved her thanks.

A tarmac path led to a car park, which was full of police vehicles and congested with officers, both uniform and plainclothes, chatting among themselves and loading evidence bags into a van. The ruins of the chapel sat quietly beyond the activity in the car park, crumbled walls and stone arches framed against the grey clouds.

Dani parked the Discovery on a patch of grass near the car park and got out, looking for a familiar face in the crowd. She spotted Tony Sheridan's blue Mini but there was no sign of the psychologist himself. Probably up at the ruins. Ryan's Aston Martin wasn't anywhere to be seen, nor was Battle's Range Rover.

She walked towards the chapel, which was encircled by blue and white crime scene tape and a number of officers. Showing her warrant card to the nearest uniform, she was nodded through the perimeter. Stepping over the crime scene tape, she stopped for a second to take in the sight before her.

Despite being in a state of ruin, the old Templar chapel still held an aura of mystery and a sense of grandeur. The walls that had stood the test of time held carvings of knights on horseback and faces that could only be described as gargoyles. Ornate fleur-de-lis decorated the buttresses that supported the walls, and the high arched windows, although devoid of glass, were magnificent.

Stepping through an archway and into the interior of the structure, Dani nodded a greeting to half a dozen SOCOs, clad in white Tyvek, who were dismantling a tent that had been erected around a stone altar at the far end of the building.

Tony Sheridan stood with his back to Dani, staring at the altar, hands in his pockets, seemingly in quiet contemplation. She went up to him and tapped him on the shoulder. "Penny for 'em."

He jumped, then quickly regained his composure. "I was just wondering, why here? Why leave a body at this site? Is there a religious connection? Or is it some sort of statement regarding repentance? But if that's the case, why not leave the body in the church?" He turned and pointed through an archway, where the distant Norman church could be seen on the hill.

"I suppose there's less chance of being seen here than there is at the church," Dani suggested.

"That make sense." He craned his head to look at the carvings on the walls. "Still, does this mean something? Is he trying to tell us something?"

"That's your department," Dani told him.

He nodded and pursed his lips. "Hmmm, yes, I suppose it is. We'll probably know more when we find out who she is, and what happened to her." His stomach rumbled audibly, and he grimaced.

"Have you eaten? I came straight here from the briefing."

"I've got some biscuits in my car."

He looked at her expectantly.

"Yes, you can have one."

"Do you know where we're supposed to meet up?" he asked, as he followed her out through the archway. "I came to the chapel because this seemed like the logical *rendez vous* point. Nobody told me to go anywhere else."

"The only address I got is a B&B," Dani said.

"Me too. They texted it to me before I drove down here." He frowned, as if trying to remember something. "The Chapel View Guest House."

"That's what mine said as well."

"Oh, so we're staying at the same place? Cool."

Dani had no idea what "cool" meant in this situation, so she didn't reply. They reached her Discovery, and she opened the passenger door, taking out the Tupperware container of Elsie Carmichael's ginger biscuits. She handed it to Sheridan.

He opened the lid and took out a biscuit before snapping the lid closed again and giving her the container. "Thanks." He bit into the biscuit and, while his mouth was still full, said, "Wow! Did you make these?"

"No, my neighbour did." She took out another biscuit and gave it to him before putting the Tupperware container back onto the passenger seat.

"Want to get a coffee?" he asked. "We could probably both do with the caffeine."

He wasn't wrong about that; the long drive from Yorkshire had made Dani tired. And there was no telling when the others would get here. "Sure, why not?"

"There's a van serving food and drink out there," he said, pointing at the gate.

She shook her head. "There's also a flock of journalists hanging around it. I'm sure we can find somewhere quieter in the village."

He nodded. "Sure. Shall I follow you, or you follow me?" He pointed at his Mini.

"Follow me," she said, going around to the driver's side of the Discovery and getting in. She started the engine and waited for Sheridan to get into his own car. When she saw him lever his tall frame into the small car, she inched slowly towards the gate. The female uniform opened it and gave Dani a short wave.

Dani drove through, checking in the rearview mirror that Sheridan was following before setting off down the hill. When she got to the main street, she spotted a place called the Sacred Spring Café, and drove into a small car park across the road from the establishment.

Sheridan parked next to her and arched his eyebrows at the building across the street. "It looks a bit New Age."

"Well, that'll keep the journalists away."

He shrugged. "Okay."

They crossed the road and entered the Sacred Spring. As Sheridan had guessed, the café was indeed based on a New Age theme, with soft pan pipe music floating from an unseen source, and posters of witches and elves on the walls. Decks of tarot cards and books on witchcraft, presumably for sale, sat on a bookshelf near the counter, and a faint smell of patchouli hung in the air.

There were people seated at some of the tables, drinking hot drinks and eating sandwiches, but the place wasn't full by any means. Dani and the psychologist sat at a table close to the window.

"Hi, guys, what can I get you?" A girl in her twenties with dreadlocks and piercings came over to the table and looked down at them with an expectant smile.

"Just a coffee for me, please," Dani said.

"I'll have a coffee as well," Sheridan said, grabbing a laminated menu from its wire holder on the table and quickly perusing it. "And a cheese and tomato sandwich, please."

"Great," she said, "Coming right up." She disappeared behind the counter and relayed the order to a clean-cut young man who was manning a coffee machine.

"It's all very Americanised now, isn't it?" Sheridan said. "Even here in a quaint English village."

Dani wasn't sure what he was talking about. "Americanised?"

He gestured to the dreadlocked girl, who was now stationed behind the counter making his sandwich. "Calling us guys. Hi instead of hello."

"I hadn't really noticed."

He shrugged. "Perhaps I notice it more because it reminds me of my time in Canada."

"You mean the Lake Erie Ripper case?"

He nodded once, and simply made a "Hmm" sound.

The young man brought their drinks over and placed them on the table. Sheridan put milk and sugar in his and took a sip.

The girl brought his sandwich over. The psychologist took a sudden, intense interest in it and set about eating it with great gusto. "Crisp?" he asked, pointing to a handful that sat on his plate, along with a garnish of lettuce, tomato, and coleslaw.

Dani took one and popped into her mouth. The salty taste was sharp on her tongue. "You think about that case a lot, don't you? The Ripper."

He swallowed a mouthful of sandwich and nodded. "It's left me with some scars, not all of them visible." After taking another sip of coffee, he said, "You must know how that feels."

She shrugged noncommittally. Just as she'd told Trudy Manners, she didn't feel particularly affected by the fact that she'd been shot in the course of carrying out her duty. It had caused a massive inconvenience, but nothing more than that.

She wondered if her emotions had been dulled by the experience. She was sure there had once been a time when she'd experienced a more emotional connection to the world around her. Now, she sometimes felt as if she didn't belong to the world at all; as if she were dead inside. Her inner coldness hadn't been caused by the shooting; she was sure of that. Perhaps it had begun when Shaun had died. Her husband's death had definitely contributed to it, but Dani was certain that the gradual dulling of her emotions had a longer history than that.

Her phone rang. She answered it and heard what sounded like a commotion of people in the background. Voices, ringing phones, and loud clatters that sounded like heavy furniture being moved around.

"DI Summers," she said.

"Summers? Where are you? Are you still driving?" It was Gallow.

"No, sir, I'm in a café in Temple Well."

"A café? What the bloody hell are you doing there? I need you at the mobile HQ. Now."

She frowned. "I don't know where that is, sir."

"The IT people sent a text to everyone in the force, telling them to come to the HQ." There was a pause, during which Dani was about to say she'd received no such text, then Gallow spoke again. "Oh,

I suppose they haven't put your name on the list yet. There was no point sending you the group texts while you were absent. Right, I'll get them to send the message over to you. Then I need you here. There's been a development."

"A development, sir?"

He'd hung up.

Dani put the phone on the table and looked at Sheridan. "Apparently, there's a text telling us to go to some sort of mobile headquarters."

"Is there?" He rummaged around in his pocket and brought out his phone. "I turned this off to save the battery while I was driving." He turned the device on and ate the rest of his sandwich while he waited for it to boot up. When the phone had finally come to life, he checked the screen. "Ah, yes, I have the address. And a missed call from Gallow."

"We'd better get over there," Dani said. Her phone *pinged* and she looked down at the screen. She had a text from *Murder Force Information*, which she assumed was the name the IT department had given to the group they were using to get information to everyone.

"If you didn't get that text before," Sheridan asked, pointing at her phone, "how come you got the one about the B&B?"

"They'd have to send the accommodation texts individually, since we're staying at different locations. The HQ one is part of a group they've set up."

He seemed to think about that, then nodded. "Makes sense. I'd never have thought of that. That's why you're the detective, and I'm just a psychologist."

Dani thought he was putting himself down too much; from what she'd seen of Tony Sheridan, he was a highly resourceful and intelligent man.

"We need to get over there," she said, getting up from the table. "Apparently, there's been a development."

"Right, I'll just pay for this. My treat." He got up and went over to the counter. Dani pushed through the door and stepped out onto the street. A chill breeze had begun to move through the village, and dark storm clouds hung over the buildings.

Dani didn't believe in omens, but still, she hoped this wasn't one.

Sheridan came out of the Sacred Spring Café with his phone to his ear. He was saying, "Yes, okay. See you later. Bye."

Putting the phone in his pocket, he turned to Dani and said, "That was Gallow. He rang me back. I found out what the development is."

Dani raised a quizzical eyebrow. "Oh? Something interesting?"

"You could say that," he said, as they crossed the road to the car park. "They've identified the girl on the altar."

CHAPTER 7

The mobile HQ turned out to be a mobile command centre truck parked in a field just outside Temple Well. Dani flashed her warrant card at the uniform who was manning the gate and drove over the ruts and grass to where six cars were clustered together, forming a makeshift parking area.

As she got out of the Land Rover, Sheridan parked beside her and climbed out of his Mini. "Wow! What a view!"

Dani, who hadn't noticed their surroundings, turned to see what he was talking about. Beyond the farm in which the mobile command centre was located, the landscape fell away into a green valley, only to rise again in the distance in the form of rolling hills that jutted high into the pale February sky.

She supposed there was a natural beauty to it,

although the landscape seemed to be more tamed and cultivated than the wild, rugged moors back home.

"Come on," she said. "Gallow won't be too pleased if we stand here gawking at the view." She walked up the metal steps that led to the command centre door and opened it, revealing a space inside that was occupied by a table and six chairs. Two TV screens were fixed to the wall, and one of them was currently showing a news channel, while the other—which was obviously hooked up to a laptop that sat on the table, showed a photograph of a smiling, dark-haired girl. It looked like a holiday snap; behind the girl, Dani could see a caravan.

Chris Toombs, the IT technician, sat at the laptop. He waved when he saw Dani. Gallow stood at the far end of the office, tapping on his phone. He was dressed in his uniform, as always, but he looked even smarter than usual, somehow. Dani wondered if he was preparing for a press conference. That was the only reason she could see for someone in Gallow's position to come all the way here; he was going to deal with the media regarding the case.

DC Ryan was also standing at the far end of the room, deep in conversation with DS Matt Flowers.

"Ah, there you are," Gallow said when he saw Dani and Sheridan. "Thought you'd got lost."

Before they could reply, he gestured to the girl's

face on the screen. "We've identified the girl from dental records. Luckily, we had some idea about what records to check, based on missing persons from the area. Her name's Daisy Riddle. She went missing while walking home from a friend's house fifteen years ago. DCI Battle has gone to inform her parents, and then we'll tell the press." He checked his watch. "There'll be a press conference in an hour."

"Was she from around here?" Sheridan asked, pointing at the smiling girl's face on the screen. "Temple Well, I mean."

Gallow shook his head. "No, she lived in Castleton, which is about forty miles north of here."

Tony nodded. "And how old was she?"

"Fifteen when she went missing."

"And the bones they recovered from the altar. They're congruent with her age at the time of her disappearance?"

Frowning, Gallow said, "Congruent with her age? What are you talking about?"

"I'm just making sure that Daisy's remains aren't those of a grown woman. Was she taken and killed straight away? Or was she kept somewhere?" He shrugged. "Perhaps she was a runaway and met her fate years later."

"The pathologist's report isn't ready yet," Gallow said. "When it is, those questions will be answered. But, apparently, the condition of the bones is *congruent* with them being in the ground for at least ten years, so if she was alive for any period of time, it wasn't long. And the clothes she was found in, or what was left of them, are the same ones she was wearing on the day she disappeared. So, make of that what you will, Dr Sheridan, but I suggest you wait for the pathologist's report before jumping to any conclusions."

The psychologist nodded and said, "Of course," but Dani could tell, by the faraway look in his eyes, that his brain was already working on the case.

"What's our next move, sir?" she asked Gallow.

"The police in Buxton are sending us Daisy Riddle's missing persons case file. I suggest you familiarise yourself with it, even though it's fifteen years old. Until then, you might as well get settled into your new digs. It looks like we're going to be here for a while. Get a feel for the village. Try and figure out why those bones were left here, in that chapel."

He turned his attention to Sheridan. "That's your area of expertise, of course, but I want you to share your findings with DI Summers. I want both of you to take an eagle's eye view of the whole thing. She was taken fifteen years ago, so why did she turn up today? Why here? Make connections. Get us closer to an arrest."

"We'll do that," Sheridan said.

"One other thing before you go." Gallow let out a

breath before saying, "Despite the fact that she hasn't written a full report yet, the pathologist has already determined cause of death. Stabbing. Repeatedly, and quite viciously, apparently. There are numerous cuts on the poor girl's ribs."

Dani heard Sheridan mutter to himself but didn't catch the words.

"Whatever reason the killer had for giving us the body after all these years," Gallow said, "he's slipped up. We had no idea where Daisy was, or what had happened to her, but now we have evidence we can analyse. That evidence brings us closer to justice for Daisy."

Dani wondered if the superintendent was working on his speech for the press in his head. What he'd just said was a soundbite made for TV. The reality of the situation was that, evidence or no evidence, it was going to take a lot of work to find Daisy's killer. Unless the discovery of the body gave them something miraculous, like a DNA hit, they were still stumbling around in the dark.

"Off you go, then," Gallow said. "Let's get this one solved."

Dani followed Sheridan out of the truck. She wasn't sure that solving this case was going to be as easy as the superintendent seemed to think. Battle had worked on the case when Daisy had first gone missing and he hadn't been able to make an arrest, despite being one of the most diligent police officers

Dani knew. Why should anything be different now, fifteen years later?

Stop being so negative, she told herself.

"The question we need to address first," Sheridan said, "is why the killer left the body for us to find after all this time."

"Remorse?" she suggested.

"It could be remorse, yes. He buried Daisy fifteen years ago, in a secret place, and the burial could, in itself, be an act of remorse. But why did he dig her up fifteen years later? The shroud he wrapped her in also suggests remorse."

"But why now?" she asked, looking at the distant hills. "Why not leave her where he buried her in the first place?"

He let out a long breath. "I don't know. This one is complicated."

"Do you think Daisy was his only victim?" she asked, echoing a question she'd been asking herself since first learning of the body on the altar.

He pursed his lips and shook his head. "I think that's unlikely."

"I was thinking the same thing."

He nodded thoughtfully. Then he brightened and said, "Well, we can't really do much until those files get here. We might as well get settled in, like Gallow suggested. I assume the B&B is close by."

Dani wanted to get stuck into the case, but she knew the psychologist was right; until they had the case files, they had nowhere to start, no leads to follow. Getting settled in at the B&B sounded like a good idea. At least then she could think about the information she had regarding the case and explore the various scenarios that could have led to Daisy's body being left on the altar in the chapel ruins.

She was sure Sheridan had suggested finding the B&B because he also wanted time to think.

"Yeah," she said. "It shouldn't be too far." She got into the Land Rover and typed the address of the Chapel View Guest House into the SatNav. According to the map on the screen, the B&B was on the other side of the village, less than five minutes away. She started the engine and reversed out of the makeshift parking space.

Waving to the uniform at the gate, she drove out onto the main road and headed back to Temple Well.

She didn't envy Battle his job of having to tell Daisy's parents that their daughter was dead. Despite it being fifteen years since she'd vanished, they'd probably held some shred of hope that she was alive. Today, that shred would be torn away, and they'd have to face the fact that Daisy was never coming home.

As she reached the village, she spotted the upper reaches of the ruins in the distance, poking up above the trees on the hill.

Why there? Why did you leave her there?

Driving along the main street, she wondered

where the killer's other victims were. It was doubtful that Daisy had been the only one. Were the others still buried in a secret place, as Sheridan had called it, or were their bodies going to turn up as well?

How many more families would have that final shred of hope torn mercilessly away?

CHAPTER 8

As he drove into Castleton, Battle felt a pang of guilt and regret. The emotion made him feel as if his insides had been scooped out with a sharp knife, leaving only a hollow shell. Fifteen years ago, he'd made a promise to a family here that their daughter would be found safe and well.

Now, he had to tell them that had been a lie.

He still wasn't sure why he'd told Jeff and Pam Riddle that he'd find their daughter and bring her back to them alive. At the time, a couple of youngsters had gone missing for a day or two, only to return home bleary-eyed and tired after discovering that running away wasn't all it was cracked up to be.

Battle had assumed that Daisy had done the same, and that she'd be found within twenty-four hours at most. He'd asked his superintendent, Jack Powers, for the resources to get CCTV footage from the train station at Hope, the nearest station to

Castleton. Powers, also assuming that Daisy would simply return in a couple of days, had refused the request, thinking it a waste of manpower.

Battle had gone to the station, armed with a photograph of Daisy, and questioned the staff and passengers there, to see if anyone had seen the young girl getting on a train. No one had.

Forced by a lack of resources to keep his search limited in scope, he'd questioned the family who had last seen Daisy before her disappearance; the Marston family, whose daughter Sylvia had been a friend of Daisy's for years.

Because of the runaway angle, he'd spent most of his time questioning Sylvia, asking her if she knew her friend was intending to leave Castleton. Sylvia had vehemently denied that Daisy had planned any such thing, and Battle had believed her, but had still not considered the possibility that Daisy had been abducted somewhere along the short route from the Marston house to her own.

The Marstons and the Riddles lived two streets away from each other, no more than a two-minute walk. The chance of Daisy being abducted during those two minutes had seemed infinitesimally small.

Yet it was obvious, now, that Daisy had encountered someone during that tiny window of time and had been taken off the street.

Only to turn up fifteen years later, wrapped in a

bedsheet, on an altar in a ruined chapel forty miles south of here.

It didn't make any sense to Battle, but it wasn't his job to understand the dark workings of the human psyche; that was Tony Sheridan's job. All Battle had to do was catch the bastard who'd done it.

He pulled up outside the Riddle house and a flood of memories washed over him. The last time he'd stepped out of that house, he'd told Pam and Jeff that Daisy would be home soon.

Taking a deep breath and letting it out slowly, he got out of the Range Rover and pushed through the small wrought iron gate that opened onto the Riddle's front lawn. A gravel path led to the front door.

Before he'd even stepped onto the path, the door opened. Jeff Riddle stood in the doorway, looking as if he'd aged a lot more than fifteen years since Battle had last seen him. In fact, the man—who was younger than Battle—looked as if life had chewed him up and spat him out.

That was totally understandable, Battle thought. The man's daughter had vanished off the face of the earth, and he'd probably spent every minute of every day, for the past fifteen years, wondering what had happened to her.

He must have heard the news about the discovery at the chapel. He must have thought the girl could be

Daisy. And now, seeing a detective walking up his front path, his worst fears were realised.

Jeff leaned heavily against the doorframe and his eyes, which peered through the lenses of his glasses, were red-rimmed and cloudy. He shook his head weakly. "No. You shouldn't be here. Why are you here? It can't be her. It can't be."

"Can I come inside, Jeff?" Battle asked gently. "We can talk better in there."

"We don't have anything to talk about. You still haven't found her. You still haven't found her." He repeated the words like a mantra, as if to convince himself of their meaning. "You still haven't found her," he whispered again, but this time, he retreated into the hallway, which Battle took as an invitation to come in.

He stepped inside and closed the door behind him. "Come into the living room, Jeff, and have a sit down. Is Pam here?"

Jeff looked up at him and shook his head. "Pam died six years ago. Cancer."

Taking the other man by the arm, Battle led him into the living room and to the sofa. Jeff sat down heavily. "It's Daisy, isn't it? The girl on the news. The one they found."

Perching on the edge of an armchair, Battle nodded slowly, and then said, "Yes, it is. I'm sorry."

Jeff let out a breath he'd been holding in for

fifteen years. "My girl is dead. She's never coming home."

Battle said nothing, letting Jeff take his time.

"I don't know if I'm glad Pam isn't here, or if I wish she was. She died not knowing what had happened to our daughter. But at least she didn't have to face the fact that Daisy won't be coming home ever again; she may have suspected, but she couldn't be sure. Now, I'm sure. And it hurts so much." He began to sob.

"Dad?" A young boy's voice floated down the stairs.

Battle was surprised. At the time of Daisy's disappearance, she'd been an only child, so the Riddles must have had another child in the intervening years.

Jeff looked towards the stairs. "Go back to your room, Toby. We'll talk later, all right?"

"Are you okay?" Now the boy was coming downstairs. As he came into view, Battle saw a fair-haired young man who looked eleven or twelve years old. He was holding some sort of game console controller in his hand. He ignored Battle and went straight over to his father. Jeff put his arm around the boy and pulled him close, still crying but trying to put a brave face on for his son.

"I'm all right," he said, wiping his eyes. "I've just had some bad news about your sister. You go back to your games, okay?"

Toby nodded and looked at Battle. "Are you a policeman?"

"I am," Battle said.

"Was that my sister they found in that old church?"

Battle looked over at the boy's father. Jeff nodded, giving his assent for the detective to answer the question.

"It was," Battle said. "I'm sorry for your loss."

"That's okay," Toby said, shrugging. He turned to his father. "Can I go and play my game now?"

"Yes, go to your room. I'll be up in a bit."

The boy went back upstairs.

"He never knew his sister," Jeff said to Battle. "And now, he never will. How did my girl end up in Temple Well after all this time? Where has she been for fifteen years?"

"That's what we're trying to find out."

Jeff's face hardened slightly. "They said she's been buried somewhere and dug up again. So, while you were thinking that Daisy was a runaway, that she'd hopped on a train to God knows where, she was already dead and buried."

Battle sighed. "It looks that way, yes."

"You failed my daughter. You said you'd find her, that she'd be with us again. But she was already dead in the ground."

"I'm sorry, Jeff. I—"

"Just go," the grieving father said. "There's

nothing you can do to make it better. My daughter is gone. You can't change that."

"I can catch the person who did it," Battle offered. "It won't bring Daisy back, but—"

"Can you?" Jeff said, squinting at Battle through a veil of tears. "You made me a promise fifteen years ago, and you never kept it. Can you keep this one?"

Battle hesitated.

"That's what I thought," Jeff said. "Just go."

Battle walked towards the front door. He hadn't made a verbal promise to Jeff, but he made a mental one to himself; he was going to find the bastard who'd brought such misery to the Riddle family. Find him and...

"If you do find him," Jeff said from the sofa, as if he'd read Battle's mind, "I want you to kill him."

Battle stopped with his hand on the door. "That isn't my job, Jeff."

"I know what the justice system is like. People can get away with murder on a technicality. I can't risk that happening to the man who killed my daughter. Not after everything he's done. I just can't."

"I'll find him," Battle said, realising he'd made another promise he hadn't intended to. He opened the door and stepped out into the cool air. As he walked to the car and looked back at the Riddle house, saw Jeff still sitting on the sofa with his head in his hands.

Climbing wearily into the car, Battle let out a

breath that held a mixture of regret and disappointment.

Before he started the engine, he rang Gallow. The superintendent had asked to be notified as soon as Battle had told the Riddle family the news. Probably so he could announce to the press that the girl in the chapel was Daisy. The media would have a lot of questions after Daisy's identity was released, not least of which being the questions surrounding where the girl had been buried for the past fifteen years. That was a question he needed to know the answer to himself.

"Battle," Gallow said, as he answered the phone. "Have you notified the next of kin?"

"Yes, sir. I've done it."

"Good. How did it go? As well as one can expect in the circumstances, I suppose."

"Yes, as well as can be expected," Battle repeated, offering nothing further.

"All right. I'll announce her identity at the press conference. I suppose questions are going to be asked regarding the original investigation, so you need to be ready for that."

"I'll be ready."

"Excellent. Now, I have to go and face the vultures. Wish me luck."

"Good luck, sir," Battle said, but the line was already dead.

He was about to place the phone on the

passenger seat when it began ringing, DS Morgan's name appearing on the screen.

"Lorna," he said as he answered it. "Any news from the postmortem?" The DS had gone to the mortuary at Chesterfield Hospital to attend the procedure.

"Yeah, there's something interesting here, guv. When the pathologist and the forensic anthropologist were examining the bones in the sheet, they found an extra...hang on, I've written this down....talus bone."

"You're going to have to enlighten me," Battle said.

"It's a bone from a foot," she said. "An ankle bone."

"What do you mean they found an extra one?"

"As well as Daisy's bones, the sheet contained an ankle bone that belongs to someone else."

He frowned. "So, you're telling me there were more remains than just Daisy's wrapped in that sheet."

"That's right, guv. We've got more than one victim."

CHAPTER 9

When Battle arrived at Chesterfield Hospital, a quick flash of his warrant card to one of the receptionists earned him an escort—in the form of an elderly male hospital volunteer—to the basement. He'd been here plenty of times before, but he didn't want to disappoint the volunteer, who seemed pleased to have something to do.

When the volunteer left him at a door marked *Mortuary*, and disappeared back upstairs, Battle took a moment to compose himself before entering the place where the dead were stored and examined.

He was beginning to believe that the only reason Daisy Riddle was in this place was because of a bungled police investigation fifteen years ago; an investigation he'd been in charge of. True, he'd done his best, considering the limited resources he'd been afforded, and lack of interest from his superiors, but his best hadn't been good enough, and that was probably going to haunt him for the rest of his life.

Reminding himself that he at least had a chance of bringing Daisy's killer to justice, he pushed the door open and entered the morgue.

A bright white, clinically clean corridor led to a number of doors. DS Morgan was standing outside one of them, leaning against the wall, waiting for him. She gave him a brief wave as he walked over to her.

"What's this about another bone?" he asked as he got within earshot.

"Like I said on the phone, guv, there's an extra ankle bone."

"So, there's another body in whatever grave Daisy was dug out of."

Morgan nodded and pointed a thumb at the door behind her. "The pathologist has gone up to her office, but the forensic anthropologist is still in there."

"Right, I'd best have a word with her, then. Is it Alina?"

Morgan nodded.

Having worked in Derbyshire for most of his career, Battle knew Alina Dalca, the forensic anthropologist who worked on the post-mortems involving bones. A couple of years ago, he'd worked with her on a case that had involved a number of old graves dotted around the Derbyshire countryside, and he'd found her to be painstakingly meticulous in her examination of skeletons and bone fragments.

If he could choose an expert witness to give clear, concise testimony in court, then that expert would be Alina Dalca.

He went into the room and found her leaning over a desk, scribbling notes onto a notepad. The room itself was a small laboratory and was full of scientific equipment.

"Hello, Stewart," Alina said, "I'll be with you in a moment." She had an Eastern European accent. Battle knew she'd come from Romania to England while in her teens. Now in her thirties, she still retained the accent, but it had become less thick over time.

She finished writing, stood up straight, and adjusted her glasses. "What can I do for you?" she asked.

"I understand we've got an extra bone."

Alina nodded. "That's right. Would you like to see it?"

Battle, who had seen enough bodies and bones to not be squeamish anymore, nodded.

"This way." She led him into the room where the post-mortem had been carried out.

Daisy's body must have already been put into one of the storage drawers that filled one wall, because the only thing on display in the room was a single bone—shaped like a wedge—sitting on one of the stainless-steel tables.

"This is it," Alina said, pointing out the bone.

Battle bent over to get a better look at it. "What's that scratch on it?"

"Probably a mark from the spade sliding along the bone," the anthropologist said.

Aware that his back was liable to play up if he bent over for too long, Battle straightened. "So, our man was digging up Daisy, and he happened to dig this up as well. Was it on purpose, to tell us he has other bodies? Or was it accidental?"

He'd been asking those questions of himself, but Alina offered an answer. "It could certainly have been an accident. If a skeleton was lying in the dirt beneath Daisy's body, and if it was aligned so that it was on its side, the talus would be sticking up, so it could that the spade hit it when its blade passed beneath Daisy's body."

"All right." Battle made a mental note that the extra ankle bone could have been dug up by accident. It didn't tell him anything useful at the moment, other than the fact that Daisy had not been alone in the grave.

"Does it tell us anything about who it belonged to?" He pointed at the talus on the table.

Alina nodded. "I can tell by its size that it belonged to someone a little older than Daisy. Perhaps someone in their late twenties."

"And since it was probably buried beneath Daisy, I assume it's been in the ground for fifteen years, or thereabouts?"

"Perhaps longer," she said. "I will carry out some further tests."

"Thanks, Alina." He paused, and then said, "Can I see her?"

The anthropologist frowned, confused. "Her?"

"Daisy Riddle," he said. "I'd like to see her."

"Of course." She went to one of the storage drawers and pulled the handle. The drawer slid open smoothly.

Battle felt a blast of cold, refrigerated air as he got closer.

Alina reached into the drawer and pulled down the sheet that was covering Daisy's face.

The DCI looked down at the remains of the girl he'd promised to find fifteen years ago and let out a long sigh that was full of regret. Was there something he could have done all that time ago that might have meant Daisy would still be alive? She'd be thirty now, perhaps with kids of her own. Had his own failings stolen that life from her?

He couldn't allow himself to think like that. To do so would cloud his vision and affect his ability to solve the case. Daisy may have been let down by the police, but they hadn't taken her from the streets of Castleton fifteen years ago and killed her. Someone else had done that.

"I'll find him, Daisy," Battle whispered, making the same promise to the dead girl that he'd made to her father earlier. He turned away from the half-open drawer, feeling a lump in his throat.

"Are you all right, Stewart?" Alina asked, putting a gentle hand on his shoulder.

"Yes, I'm fine," he said, regaining his composure. "Thank you."

"I'll look into the ankle bone and see if it can tell us anything," she said, perhaps understanding that it might be best to change the subject.

"Great. Let me know if you find anything." He left the room and went back out to the corridor, where DS Morgan was still waiting.

"Everything all right, guv?" she asked, pushing away from the wall.

"Yes, although this case just got a lot more complicated. Alina says the extra bone belongs to an adult. That means we're looking for someone who might be killing indiscriminately. He's not just taking victims of a certain type; he's killing all and sundry."

"That's going to make finding potential victims via missing persons a lot more difficult," she said, following him along the corridor to the exit. "We'll have to look at everyone who's gone missing in the last fifteen years."

"Even longer ago than that," he told her. "The ankle bone was underneath Daisy's body, so it had been buried earlier. How much earlier is anyone's guess."

Morgan let out a sigh.

"And there's something else we need to know," Battle said.

"What's that, guv?"

"We know he's buried at least two bodies. How many more are there?"

CHAPTER 10

In the dim light cast from the naked lightbulb hanging from the cellar's ceiling, Rob could barely see what he was doing. He'd filled in the first hole and now he was digging another at the opposite end of the cellar, the location guided by an 'X' on the scrap of paper from his father's bureau.

The bottom of the hole lay in deep shadow. Rob had no idea how long he'd been down here digging, but he was almost waist deep beneath the level of the cellar floor.

"I guess this is what they mean when they say following in your father's footsteps," he mumbled to himself. His father had dug a hole in this exact location, sometime in the past.

The only difference was that his father had been burying a body, and he was digging it up.

Putting the bodies in places where the police would find them was his way of getting his father back for all the misery the old man put him through when he was alive. Wrapping the remains of the body he found last night—which he now knew from the news was a girl named Daisy Riddle--in a sheet from his father's bed and laying the corpse on the altar of a ruined chapel had been an affront to his father's atheism.

Not that Rob had any particular religious beliefs of his own, but it had still felt good to rebel against his father's lack of them. His dad had wanted the girl to be kept down here, beneath the dirt, forever, but Rob had ruined the old man's plans. And he intended to do the same with every body that was hidden down here.

Especially his mother's.

If she's here at all, he reminded himself.

He leaned the shaft of the spade against the side of the hole he was standing in and wiped the sweat off his brow with the sleeve of his shirt. Maybe he should have changed after the funeral; his suit jacket lay over the back of an old armchair in the corner of the cellar, but his best trousers and shirt were filthy from digging in the dirt.

Climbing out of the hole, he brushed himself down with his hands, but it was no good; the dirt was ground in.

He took off his trousers and shirt and, in his boxers, took them upstairs to the laundry room that was attached to the kitchen. Bunging them into the washing machine, along with his socks, and adding a scoopful of washing powder he found on a shelf, he switched the machine on. As it filled with water, he walked barefoot back into the kitchen.

His phone lay on the kitchen table. As he entered the room, the screen lit up. A text from Sonia. He picked it up and saw that he had a number of texts from her, as well as seven missed calls.

The texts were all along similar lines.

Rob, where are you?

Are you there?

Why aren't you answering?

Helllooooo!!!!!

Where the hell are you?

It was pitch black outside. How long had he been here? He'd lost track of time while he'd been in the basement.

Returning Sonia's call, he braced himself for the tongue-lashing he was about to receive.

"Rob? Where the hell are you?" she said as she picked up, repeating her latest text.

"I'm at my dad's house."

"Why didn't you come home after the funeral? Sam isn't feeling very well. He wants to know where you are."

"What's wrong with him?"

"He's got a bit of a temperature and the snuffles. I gave him some Calpol and put him to bed. Do you want to speak to him? He's right here."

So that explained why she wasn't going off on one; she was in Sam's room.

"Of course. Put him on."

The next voice he heard was his seven-year-old son's. "Hi, Dad."

"Hey, Sam, what's up?"

There was no answer. Then Rob heard Sonia in the background. "He can't hear you shrugging, Sam."

"I don't know," Sam said. "I just feel poorly."

"Oh dear. It doesn't sound like you'll be going to school tomorrow."

"Probably not," Sam said. Rob detected a hint of a smile in the boy's voice.

"Well, I'm sure that's disappointing for you."

Sam laughed, then coughed.

"All right," Sonia's voice got louder as she got closer to the phone. "Give the phone back to me."

Rob heard the phone being transferred. "Are you coming home soon?"

Thinking about his clothes in the washer, he said, "Soon."

He heard her sigh into the phone. "What are you doing up there that's so important?"

"Just going through some of the old man's things. There's a lot of stuff here; he was a bit of a hoarder." That was true; most of the rooms in the house were filled with items that James Gibson had collected over the years. Rob had no idea what might be worth saving and what might be junk. He also had no idea if any of it could incriminate his father.

Until he'd sorted through everything his father had hoarded, no one else was going to get a look at what was in this house.

He asked himself why he was bothered. Why not just tell the police about his father's nefarious activities? Instead of giving the bodies back to their families one by one, wouldn't that be the ultimate "screw you?" To tell the world who his father had really been, and what he'd done?

It would, but for some reason, he couldn't bring himself to do it.

Digging up the bodies in the basement—his father's ultimate hoard—and returning them to the world from which his father snatched them was meant to be an insult to his dead father's memory, but it was a private thing between him and the old man.

The world would never know that James Gibson had been a killer because it was none of the world's business. It was a private matter between him and his father.

A secret that Rob had kept locked away since he was a young boy.

He sat at the table and pushed the phone away, closing his eyes and recalling a night more than twenty years ago, when he'd awoken to the sound of a distant scream.

The noise that woke him sounded like a distant scream. He sat up in bed and rubbed his bleary eyes with the back of his hand. He had no idea what time it was, but it was still dark outside, and the moon was high in the night sky, making the distant hills and the woods near the house glow silver.

Reaching over to the bedside table, he grabbed Sam, his Action Man. Sam's presence made Rob feel better whenever he was lonely or scared, and holding the toy now made him feel brave.

"Did you hear that, Sam?" he whispered.

Sam remained stoic and silent.

Still holding the Action Man in his hand, Rob slid out of bed. The wooden floor was cold beneath his bare feet. He inched his way to the bedroom door, ears straining to pick up any other sounds in the house and opened it quietly before peering out at the darkness beyond.

The house was quiet now, and he wondered if the scream he'd heard had been nothing more than a dream.

Leaning out of the doorway, he looked across the landing, at his father's bedroom door. It was closed, and Rob wondered if his dad was asleep, or not in the house at all.

It wasn't unusual for his dad to go out at night.

Silence of the Bones

Sometimes, Rob would be awakened by the sound of the car starting up, and he'd look out of his bedroom window to see the vehicle driving away. At first, he'd worried about being in the house on his own, but as time—and the number of night time departures—went on, he became used to it, and simply went back to sleep.

His father would always be in the kitchen in the morning, making Rob's breakfast, and that was all that mattered, really.

He never raised the subject of the night time journeys with his dad, and his dad likewise never mentioned them.

But tonight was different. He hadn't just heard the car driving away; he'd heard a *scream*.

Or he'd dreamt it. He wasn't sure.

He crept to his dad's door and opened it as quietly as he could. A sliver of moonlight coming through the window illuminated an empty bed.

Rob swallowed nervously. Had his dad gone out, leaving him alone in the house, and had someone broken in? Was there a burglar downstairs?

Don't be silly, he told himself. *Why would a burglar scream?*

Holding Sam up in front of his face, he whispered, "We should go back to bed. Dad will be here in the morning, and he'll probably make pancakes for breakfast, like he did today."

He wondered if his whispering was too loud and

might be heard by anyone else who happened to be in the house.

He braced himself, ready to run back to his room if he heard footsteps on the stairs.

But no sound reached his ears.

Breathing a sigh of relief, and telling himself he'd just had a bad dream, Rob padded back to his room, yawning as he went.

As he reached the doorway, a sound from downstairs stopped him in his tracks.

He'd heard a voice. And he was sure it had been his dad's. The words had sounded distant, but Rob was sure his dad was downstairs.

Was it morning already? He didn't think so, because it was still dark outside.

He went to the top of the stairs and looked down at the shadowy hallway below. If his dad was up, why weren't the lights on?

Stepping tentatively onto the top stair, he listened, hoping some further sound would let him know what was happening. But silence had descended over the house.

"Do you hear anything, Sam?" he breathed into the Action Man's plastic ear.

Sam didn't reply, of course, and Rob hadn't expected him to, but he did hear his father's voice again. His dad was speaking to someone, but the other person didn't seem to be replying.

Overwhelmed with curiosity, Rob descended the

stairs and stood in the hallway. He was sure his dad's voice had come from the kitchen, so he went in there, expecting to find his father sitting at the table reading the paper or, better yet, standing at the cooker, making pancakes.

But there was no one in the kitchen. The door that led to the cellar was open, and the light was on down there, because some of it spilled out of the open doorway and onto the kitchen floor.

Rob never went into the cellar. His dad kept the door padlocked and had explained that by saying it was dangerous down there, and full of rats. That had been enough to satisfy the young boy's curiosity, even though he walked past the locked door every time he was in the kitchen.

Now, the padlock sat on the kitchen table, and the light beyond the open doorway seemed to beckon him.

Squeezing Sam tightly in his hand, Rob walked over to the doorway and looked inside. Wooden steps led down to a dirt floor. The lights were on down there, but Rob couldn't see anything other than the floor from his vantage point.

"Dad?"

There was no reply, but Rob heard scuffling from somewhere down there. He hoped it wasn't a rat, because if it was, it was a really big one.

"Dad?" he repeated.

More scuffling, and now he knew it wasn't a rat

because he heard someone trying to say something, but their voice was muffled.

Then his father's voice drifted up from the cellar. "Don't come down, Robert."

"I can't sleep," Rob said. "I heard a noise."

"It was nothing. Go back to bed."

He heard the muffled voice again. It sounded like someone who couldn't open their mouth. But was trying to scream.

"What's that?" he asked.

His father appeared in the section of the cellar Rob could see from the top of the stairs. He was wearing a red and black checkered shirt that Rob was sure he'd never seen him wearing before. He looked hot and sweaty. His hair was plastered to his forehead, and he was breathing hard. In his hand was a knife. Rob had never seen that before, either. It looked like a hunting knife.

"You go back to bed," he said. "And we'll have pancakes in the morning, with maple syrup."

Rob didn't move. He wanted to go back to bed, because he felt tired, but he also wanted to know what was going on in the cellar. Who else was down there with his dad?

For one fleeting moment, he wondered if it was his mother. He could barely remember his mother; she'd left when he was just six years old, abandoning him and his dad in the middle of the night and going to live somewhere else. Maybe she'd come back.

He wasn't sure why that thought had crossed his mind. Surely, if his mum had returned, she'd want to see him. She'd be in the kitchen, hugging him, not hiding in the cellar.

"Rob," his father said in a warning tone. He glanced to his right, at a part of the cellar Rob couldn't see, then looked back at his son. "Actually, perhaps you should come down. Come and look what I've got down here."

Now that he'd been invited, Rob hesitated. Something in his father's voice sounded odd. He couldn't put a finger on it, but it sounded as if his dad had kept his true voice caged up in his throat all this time and was only now releasing it.

"Come on," his dad said. He beckoned for Rob to come down the stairs, but the hand he beckoned with was the one holding the knife, which made the gesture a lot less inviting.

When Rob didn't move, his dad sighed with frustration. "Either come down or go to bed. The choice is yours."

Rob looked down at Sam, as if the plastic doll could offer some guidance. When none was forthcoming, Rob's curiosity won out over his tiredness. He moved forward and descended into the cellar.

~

~

His phone beeped, drawing him out of the memory. Reaching for it, he noticed that his hands were trembling.

It was another text from Sonia. *Sam asleep. Please come home as soon as you can.*

Rob hadn't realised until now that he'd named his son after the Action Man he'd played with as a child. He remembered that when they were expecting Sam, Sonia had suggested that they each write a list of names, which they would then narrow down. The only name he'd put on his list had been Sam. Since the same name had appeared on Sonia's list, their son's name had seemed like destiny.

Rob hadn't thought about Sam the Action Man since that night in the cellar—and he hadn't seen the toy since then, either—but the name must have been floating around in his subconscious or something.

He wasn't ready to go home yet. The memory of waking up on that fateful night and being invited into the cellar by his father had made him determined to find another body and remove it from the old man's buried hoard.

Still in his boxers, he went back down to the hole he'd been digging and climbed back into it. The air in the cellar was cold against his dry skin, and he shivered as he picked up the spade. After a couple of minutes of striking the blade into the soil, he began to feel warmer.

It wasn't long before he felt the spade strike

something hard in the ground. Getting to his knees, he scraped the dirt at the bottom of the hole away to reveal denim. Someone was buried here, and they were wearing jeans.

He began to dig with his hands, uncovering more of the remains. At times, he had to use the spade to lever parts of the body out of the ground. It took at least an hour, but he finally revealed what the dirt had been hiding. Climbing out of the hole, he examined the result of his labour.

At the bottom of the hole lay the body of a dark-haired girl. She was curled into a foetal position, and Rob could almost imagine that she was simply asleep. She wore jeans and a faded grey T-shirt. The exposed parts of her skin—or what was left of it—were leathery and stretched tight over the bones beneath.

Rob needed something to wrap her in. He'd used one of the sheets off his old man's bed the last time, and that had worked well enough to keep the body intact while he'd taken it to Temple Well. He went back up to the kitchen, then upstairs to his father's bedroom, where he pulled another sheet off the bed.

Back in the cellar, he got into the hole with the corpse and carefully wrapped it in the sheet. By the time he was done, he was sweating and breathing hard. He was also covered in soil. Tightening the wrapping, he lifted the body out of the hole and climbed out after it.

Standing with his hands on his hips while he got his breath back, he wondered how many bodies there were down here. The scrap of paper had seventeen Xs marked on it, but that didn't mean there couldn't be more graves.

He wondered if his mother's resting place was marked with an X, or if her grave was unmarked.

He no longer believed the story about his mother leaving them one night when he was little. He'd woken up one morning and his father had told him that she'd left the previous night, without so much as a goodbye.

As a child, Rob hadn't questioned it, but even then, he already knew the type of person his father was. He'd seen the rage in the old man's eyes—although his father hadn't actually been old then—the evening before the morning when he'd been told the story about his mother leaving.

He'd never believed she'd leave him here, in this house, with his dad. And later, when he'd discovered what his father was doing in the cellar, he'd put two and two together and begun to suspect that his mum had met a gruesome end and had been buried somewhere beneath the house.

He picked up the swaddled body of the girl and took it upstairs, lying it on the kitchen floor.

His phone began to ring. It was Sonia again.

Gingerly pressing the screen with his soil-covered finger, he said, "What is it?"

"You said you were coming home." The frustration was clearly audible in her voice. "Where the hell are you?"

"I had an accident," he said, thinking on his feet. "I had to put my clothes in the washer."

"What? Why?"

"There was a tin of paint. I didn't realise it was open, and it spilled on me."

She sighed. "That won't come out easily."

"It'll be fine. I chucked my clothes straight into the washer."

"Well, can't you find something else to wear? Some of your dad's clothes? You can't spend all night there; you've got work tomorrow."

"Yeah, I'll sort something out." He looked over at the body on the floor. "I've just got a few things to do, and then I'll be there, okay?"

"Yeah, okay. I can't promise I'll still be awake."

"Don't wait up. You go to bed."

She hesitated, and then said, "All right. Be careful what you touch in that house. I dread to think what your father might have stashed away."

A slight smile played over Rob's lips. She didn't know the half of it.

"See you later," he said, and hung up.

He went upstairs to his father's room and opened the wardrobe. The hangers mostly contained old jackets and coats, crammed together in the available space. Trying a chest of drawers by the bed, Rob found trousers and shirts, which he scattered over the bed.

One shirt in particular caught his attention; it was checkered red and black and looked exactly like the shirt he'd seen his father wearing over twenty years ago in the cellar. Surely it couldn't be the same shirt.

But judging by his father's hoarding ways and the fact that some of the other clothing on the bed looked at least twenty years old, it probably was.

This was the shirt his father had worn when he went out at night.

When he went hunting.

Rob touched the sleeve of the shirt with his fingertip. Last night, when he'd taken Daisy Riddle's body to the old temple ruins, he'd experienced a heightened awareness. Every one of his senses had been dialled up to maximum, and he'd felt almost high. He knew it was the danger of the situation that had caused that, along with the chance of getting caught.

How must his father have felt when he'd hunted those girls and taken them off the streets? That had been infinitely more dangerous than dumping a corpse in a ruin.

Rob had to admit that, in some ways, he respected the old man.

Picking up the checkered shirt, he put it on and found a pair of jeans that had the right length in the leg but were too tight around the waist. He remedied that by leaving the top button undone. That made them fit snugly, if a little uncomfortably, around his belly.

Dressed in his father's attire, he went downstairs and opened the front door before lifting the wrapped body over his shoulder and getting it into the Land Rover. He laid it across the back seat and used the seatbelts to keep it in place, the same as he'd done with Daisy Riddle's body.

But, unlike Daisy Riddle, he couldn't leave this girl in the chapel; there was bound to be a police presence there.

After getting his phone from the kitchen, and locking the front door of the house, he got in behind the wheel and considered where he could leave this one. Temple Well had been perfect because it was a sleepy little village but also popular with tourists because of the ruins. He'd known someone would stumble across the body soon after he'd left it there.

The Templar chapel wasn't the only location in the village that attracted tourists; there was also a spring there that had once been considered sacred by the Romans. The village was named Temple Well because of the temple and the sacred spring.

There might be police stationed at the ruins, but they had no reason to interested in the spring, which he knew was on the other side of the village and tucked away in the woods.

It was perfect.

Nodding to himself, he started the engine and set off down the track that eventually led to the main road.

He put the radio on, and grinned when the song *Wrapped Around Your Finger* by *The Police* filled the car. The song was about an apprentice who becomes powerful and destroys his master, just like he was doing to his dad.

Staring into his own eyes in the rearview mirror, Rob told himself, "I'm tearing down his work, piece by piece."

In the darkness, the image in the mirror seemed to flicker and change. Rob averted his eyes and concentrated on the road ahead.

He had thought, for one fleeting moment, that it hadn't been his own face staring back at him, but his father's.

CHAPTER 11

When Battle arrived home, it was almost midnight. He'd spent most of the evening in the mobile headquarters, poring over every report he could get his hands on from the officers who were investigating the Daisy Riddle case, from the original enquiries and interviews to the newly reincarnated investigation now that Daisy's body had been found.

There was little of any substance, and certainly nothing that was even remotely like a lead. He knew how these things worked, was acutely aware that it would probably be a long time before the work done by the team uncovered something useful, but he'd felt it his duty to personally review everything.

He owed it to Daisy.

He pulled up outside his house and got out of the Range Rover, closing the door quietly in case Rowena was in bed.

Unlike the other members of Murder Force, he was able to stay in his own house while in Derbyshire. It was on the market but hadn't sold yet, which meant Battle spent Mondays commuting to York—where a small flat had been provided for him from the force's budget—and Fridays driving back home to spend the weekends with his wife.

He was slightly concerned that the house hadn't sold yet. It was a pleasant 4-bed in a good location for schools and shops, but so far, no one seemed interested. Until the house was sold, he and Rowena wouldn't be able to search for their dream house by the sea.

So, for the last two months, Battle had been living in a transitory existence. He didn't feel as if he belonged in Derbyshire anymore, because he would hopefully be leaving it behind soon, but Yorkshire didn't feel like home either, because he was simply existing in a police flat there and hadn't had a chance to put down more permanent roots in the area.

He unlocked the front door and went inside. Expecting to find the place quiet, he was surprised to hear the sound of the television in the living room.

He poked his head around the door and saw Rowena on the settee, legs tucked beneath her, snuggled under a tartan blanket that was usually draped over the armchair as a decorative throw.

The glowing television screen threw a blue hue

over the living room walls. A late night talk show was on. Half a dozen people sat around a table in a studio, discussing the health care system.

Not wanting to wake his wife, Battle went into the kitchen to make a cheese sandwich. The loaf he found in the bread bin was wholemeal, another sign that he wasn't here often. Rowena had switched to healthier options like wholemeal bread and oat milk a couple of years ago, but there'd always been white bread in the bread bin, and cow's milk in the fridge for him.

He placed a generous slab of cheese in between two buttered layers of the brown bread and added a spoonful of Branston Pickle. When he bit into the sandwich, he was shocked to find that the bread wasn't so bad, after all. Then he wondered if his tastebuds were fooling him. Because he hadn't eaten anything at all for hours, and even a piece of cardboard would taste good right now, if it had cheese and pickle on it.

He ate the sandwich slowly, reflecting on the fact that the person he was after—Daisy's killer—was probably a serial killer. The discovery of the extra ankle bone seemed to point in that direction.

How many more girls had vanished from the face of the earth, only to end up in a grave dug by their killer?

Battle had tackled this kind of thing before. A

number of young women had gone missing in the Dark Peak area over the years, and had been buried in graves marked with wildflowers. The Press had had a field day with that case. They'd called the victims the Wildflower Girls and had printed lurid details—both factual and fictional—of their deaths and subsequent interments in various places dotted around the Derbyshire countryside.

He didn't want this case to reveal yet more victims whose families he was going to have to face and tell them that their loved one was gone forever, crushing all hope—however slight—of a reunion someday.

He'd seen the look on the faces of families and friends when that moment of realisation had struck. He could only imagine the emotion churning beneath the surface that caused that expression of hopelessness.

It wasn't an emotion anyone should have to experience.

He finished eating and washed the plate and knife in the sink, putting them back in their respective cupboard and drawer after drying them on a Chatsworth House tea towel. He and Rowena had visited the house a number of times over the years, he enjoying the old paintings hanging on the wall while she took in the gardens and grounds.

They'd always done things independently, had their own interests. Before they'd got married, some people had thought they were too different to make it work for long. Some had even voiced that opinion. But that had been a long time ago, and he and Rowena were still together when many of the naysayers had split from their partners.

Perhaps it was their differences that kept them bonded. If not that, then it was certainly a *respect* for each other's differences.

"You're home." Rowena was standing at the kitchen door, the tartan blanket draped over her shoulders. "Have you been back long?"

"Just long enough to have a sandwich."

She put a hand to her forehead. "Oh, I forgot to get some white bread. I'm sorry."

"Don't worry about it, love. You didn't know I was coming back mid-week."

Still, I could have nipped to the shops."

He put his hands on her shoulders. "It's fine. I had some of that wholemeal rubbish."

She smiled. "It's better for you, anyway."

"So you keep telling me."

"Well, you should get to bed. No doubt you'll be having an early start tomorrow."

"Sounds like a good idea." He suddenly realised how tired he was.

They went up to the bedroom together and changed into their nightclothes before getting into bed and turning the lights off.

Battle felt weary, but he was loathe to fall asleep

without talking to Rowena. He was aware of how much he'd been absent from her life lately, and it rankled him.

"No more interest in the house, then?" he asked.

"There's a couple coming to look at it on Saturday," she said.

"Well, that's something at least."

"Yes, I suppose so."

He was sure it was more than just tiredness in her voice; she sounded deflated.

"At least I'll be here on Saturday," he said. "You won't have to show them round."

"The estate agent does that, anyway."

"What's wrong then, love?" In the dark, he could see that she was facing away from him. He reached out and touched her shoulder.

She rolled over to face him. "Stewart, what am I going to do in North Yorkshire?"

"What do you mean?"

"Our plan was to retire to a house by the sea. I know you're not ready for retirement yet, so perhaps we should put the dream of living on the coast on hold for a while. What am I going to do in a place where I don't know anyone, while you're at work all day?"

"It won't be all day. I'll take on less hours. Make sure I'm home at a reasonable time."

"Like tonight? You didn't come through the door until midnight."

"That's different. I'm working on the Daisy Riddle case."

"And I know how much that means to you, but after that, there'll be another case. And another after that."

"So you want me to give up work?"

She shook her head. "No, I'm not saying that. But perhaps while you're still working, it would be better if we didn't sell this house. At least I've got a job here, and friends I can visit, or go out with, when you're not around. Up there, I'd be on my own."

He had no idea she felt this way, but now the he did, he realised he hadn't even thought about her own job when he'd been transferred to Murder Force. Rowena worked at a leisure centre in Derby, on the management team. She enjoyed her work, but Battle had simply assumed that she'd find a similar job when they relocated. He hadn't known she was reluctant to do so.

"Why didn't you say something earlier? Before I joined Murder Force?"

"Murder Force was a great career move for you," she said. "I could see how much you wanted it, and I didn't want to get in the way of that. By the time I was beginning to have doubts, the house was already up for sale."

"I'll ring the estate agents in the morning and have them take it off the market."

She let out a sigh that he thought might be one of relief. "I feel terrible," she said.

"Nonsense. I'm the one who didn't think. I'm sorry, love."

"You have nothing to be sorry for. I should have said something earlier. I'm going to make the commute easier for you; I'll come up there more often, so you don't have to drive every weekend. Who knows, perhaps I'll fall in love with the place and move up there."

Battle gave her a thin smile. He didn't believe that any more than she did. Realising she couldn't see the smile in the dark, he said, "We'll see."

It took him a while to get to sleep.

* * *

He was awoken by the strident ringing of his phone on the bedside table. Reaching out with his eyes still closed, he grabbed the damned thing and answered it.

"Battle."

"Guv, it's Lorna. We've got another body."

He opened his eyes, squinting against the daylight filtering in through the curtains. "Where."

"Temple Well again. Not at the chapel this time, though. A dog walker stumbled across it at the well."

"Bloody hell. Who's over there?"

"The pathologist and her team are there already, and I think some Derbyshire uniforms are there as well. But no one from our team."

"Why not?"

"The 999 call went to the Derbyshire station, and they mobilised their officers before telling us anything about it."

"Right. I'll get Summers and Sheridan over there. They're closest."

"Want me to ring them, guv?"

"No, I'll do it. Thanks, Lorna."

He ended the call and gave himself a couple of seconds to become fully awake before ringing DI Summers.

She answered after a few rings. "Morning, guv."

"Are you in Temple Well at the moment?"

"Yes."

"I need you to get over to the sacred well. It's just outside the village. Apparently, a member of the public has found another body there. Take Sheridan with you, and see what's what. There are already Derbyshire uniforms there, but you need to get over there quickly. It could be another one of ours."

"Okay, we'll be there right away."

"I'll let the pathologist know you're on your way over." He hung up and found Alina Dalca's number in the phone.

"Hello, Stewart," the pathologist said cheerily when she answered.

"Alina, are you at the well?"

"Yes, we are putting up the tent now."

"Is it one of ours?"

"I can confirm that the body here has been previously buried and disinterred, so, yes, I would say it is one of yours."

He sighed. A part of him had hoped it might be some random dead person, an accidental death, perhaps. But no, he wasn't that lucky. "Okay. I've sent DI Summers and Dr Sheridan over. They should be there shortly."

"Very well. I shall talk with them when they arrive."

"Thanks, Alina." He ended the call and put the phone back on the bedside table before getting out of bed and stretching his stiff back.

"Another body?" Rowena asked, propping herself up on her elbow.

"Yeah, it sounds like it. I'm going to have a quick shower and get over to headquarters. Once the Press gets wind of this, it's going to be a circus."

"I hope you catch him soon," she said.

As he left the bedroom and made his way to the bathroom, he nodded. He hoped they'd catch the bastard soon, as well. It felt like the killer was toying with them.

Battle wasn't in the mood to play games, but he made a silent vow to himself as he turned the shower on and stepped into the hot spray.

This was a game he was going to make sure he won.

CHAPTER 12

When Tony Sheridan woke up, he experienced a moment of panic. The room that slowly came into focus around him was unfamiliar. Sitting bolt upright in bed, he searched the area for something familiar—a technique he'd been taught in a mental health facility in Canada—and his eyes came to rest on his open suitcase, sitting on a chair by the window. Tony recalled sitting in that chair last night and looking out at the ruined chapel beyond the trees.

Remembering that he was in a B&B in Derbyshire, he got out of bed and went into the bathroom. He emerged forty-five minutes later, shaved, showered, and ready for breakfast. He hadn't eaten anything last night, electing to spend the evening sitting in the chair by the window while making notes about the case. He'd written less than a page before weariness had crept over him and he'd been forced to crawl into bed.

Peeking through the curtains at the weather outside, and seeing a grey, drizzly view through the window, he dressed in corduroy trousers and a heavy, knitted green jumper before leaving the room and heading downstairs in search of something to eat.

The Chapel View Guest House was a large Victorian house that had been converted into a B&B sometime in the past half century. Its bedrooms—Tony wasn't sure how many there were in the house—occupied the upper two floors, while the ground floor housed the kitchen, dining room, and a communal lounge.

The elderly couple that owned the establishment, whose names were George and Janet, had proudly shown the place off when he and DI Summers had checked in. And they were right to be proud; the guest house was neat and tidy, and well located with—as its name suggested—a view of the ruined Templar chapel.

When Tony reached the ground floor, the smell of toast and fried bacon greeted him like an old friend. Following his nose, he found the dining room.

Half a dozen small tables, with white cotton tablecloths, had been set along the walls of the long, but narrow, room. At one of these tables sat a man and a woman drinking coffee, their plates with the remnants of their breakfasts on the table between them.

At a table at the far end of the room sat DI Summers. She was also dressed for the inclement weather. Her attire consisted of boots, jeans, and a cream-coloured roll neck jumper.

She waved at him. He went over to her table, noting the lack of a plate in front of her.

"Not eaten yet?"

She shook her head. "I ordered some eggs on toast a minute ago. You can join me, if you like."

"Thanks," he said, pulling out the chair on the side of the table opposite to her and dropping into it. "How did you sleep?"

"Surprisingly well. I usually have trouble getting to sleep in strange places, but yesterday's travelling must have caught up with me."

"Same here. I barely had time to make a few notes before I found myself climbing into bed."

Janet, the B&B owner, appeared next to the table with a pot of coffee in her hand. "Good morning," she said to Tony. "Would you like a full English, or something else?"

"Full English, please." His stomach rumbled at the prospect.

"And would you both like coffee?" She flipped over two upturned cups on the table and poised the pot over them.

He and Dani nodded, and the landlady poured

out the dark, steaming liquid. "I'll just get some milk for you," she said, before disappearing through a door that obviously led to the kitchen. Tony could hear food sizzling in a frying pan, and the mouth-watering smell of bacon drifted through the doorway.

She returned a moment later with a small, china milk jug that was decorated with a floral design. She set it on the table, along with a matching china dish that was laden with various packets of sugar and sweetener.

As Janet went back to the kitchen, Tony looked at Dani. "What do you think we should do today?"

She added milk to her coffee and said, "Well, Gallow said we should take an eagle's eye view, so I was thinking we might go to Castleton, where it all started. Then we'll have more of an idea of the distances involved, see the surrounding area, that sort of thing."

He nodded. "Sounds good to me."

She grimaced. "Does it? It doesn't feel to me like we're doing much."

"Gallow said we should take an eagle's eye view of everything, remember?"

"Which, in practical terms, amounts to not doing much." She sighed, and looked out through the window, at the rain. "I wonder if he thinks I'm still finding my feet."

He looked at her over the rim of his coffee cup as

he blew on the drink to cool it down. "Are you still finding your feet?"

"No, I don't think so. It's just Gallow; he seems to be handling me with kid gloves."

"I'm sure that's not the case, Dani," he said, truthfully. "Taking an overview of what's going on is an important part of the job. We're not directly chasing down the killer, but we might find something useful that helps the investigation."

"I suppose so," she said.

Janet returned with two plates. She placed a full English in front of Tony, and two slices of toast, topped with scrambled eggs, on Dani's side of the table.

"Is there anything else I can get you?" she asked.

"We're fine, thanks," Dani told her.

"Enjoy!" Janet went back to the kitchen.

Tony looked down at his plate and felt his stomach grumble in anticipation. The smell of bacon, fried bread, tomatoes, eggs, and black pudding assailed his senses as he picked up his knife and fork and tried to decide where to start.

Cutting into a rasher of bacon, he said, "You can't be a hero all the time. Leave that to someone else this time."

"I don't want to be a hero," she said. "It's just that when I think of that poor girl dumped on that altar like a bag of kindling, I want the person who did it to be brought to justice."

"And they will be." He took a bite of fried bread, and decided he might have discovered heaven on earth, despite what it might do to his arteries.

Dani nodded. "I just want to be a part of it, that's all."

They ate in silence for a couple of minutes, during which time, Tony put himself mentally in Dani's shoes. He didn't try to psychoanalyse her, but he tried to empathise with her.

"Do you feel like you're not part of the team?" he asked.

Her eyes had been focused on her breakfast. Now, she looked up at him. "What? What do you mean?"

"You've been out of action for a while, and the team has grown during that time. Perhaps you think it's left you behind."

Her shoulders lifted as she took a deep breath, then lowered again as she sighed. "Maybe. I don't know. I just feel...disconnected. I don't really know how to describe it."

"It's totally understandable," he told her. "I felt the same way after spending a long time out of the game. You'll soon get back into the swing of things."

She gave him a thin smile. "I hope so." She started to take another forkful of breakfast, but stopped, put her knife and fork down, and pulled her phone out of her jeans pocket. It was vibrating in her hand.

"It's Battle," she said to Tony, as she put the phone to her ear. "Morning, guv."

Tony continued eating, trying not to eavesdrop on the conversation, but finding it difficult not to do so, since Dani was sitting only a few feet from him. He couldn't hear the DCI's voice on the other end of the line, but it sounded like he was giving Dani instructions.

Her end of the conversation was simply, "Yes," and "Okay, we'll be there right away."

She ended the call and looked across the table at Tony. "We've got to go. A member of the public has just found another body."

That surprised Tony. He'd wondered if more bodies might turn up but hadn't reckoned on one materialising so soon. "In the chapel?"

Dani shook her head, pushing her chair back and standing up. "At a sacred well just outside the village."

Leaving his unfinished breakfast, Tony got up and followed her to the dining room door.

Janet appeared from the kitchen, a worried look on her face. "Is everything all right? Only I noticed you haven't finished your breakfasts."

"Everything's fine," Dani said. "We have to go, that's all. Can you tell us how to get to the well?"

"Of course," Janet said, brightening. "Just go out the front door and turn left. It's only a two-minute walk from here. You can't miss it."

"Thanks."

"Breakfast was lovely," Tony told the landlady as he stepped past her and followed Dani out of the room.

They went out into the rain and turned left, following the pavement past houses and the village's few shops.

When they reached the end of the pavement—and the edge of the village—a green sign with white writing told them that the "Sacred Well" was a little farther along the road.

Keeping on the grassy verge, they trudged along the narrow, winding road until they came to an even narrower track that led through a hedgerow towards the woods. Three Derbyshire Police patrol cars, and two police vans, were parked in a small, circular parking area at the edge of the woods. Beyond the vehicles, a uniformed officer was stretching blue and white crime scene tape between the trees.

Another uniformed officer was talking to a white-haired man holding a lead. On the other end of the lead, a small, white poodle sniffed at the ground disinterestedly.

The ubiquitous dog walker, Tony thought to himself. *The backbone of the British criminal justice system.*

They showed their credentials to the officer with the crime scene tape, ducking under it as he waved them through. A dirt path cut through the trees to a clearing which was bustling with activity.

In the centre of the clearing sat a small dome-like structure made of rocks, with a roughly hewn square shaped opening. Tony presumed this was the well that had given the village half of its name.

A white tent had been erected by the side of the rock structure. As Tony and Dani approached it, a petite woman emerged, dressed in a white Tyvek suit with the hood pulled up and a mask over her face.

She pulled down the hood and removed the mask, revealing long brown hair pinned back into a ponytail, and a pretty face.

Tony found himself standing straighter and running a hand through his hair, wishing he'd taken more care while brushing it this morning. He hadn't expected to be running out of the door before finishing breakfast. But then, he hadn't expected to be meeting a woman like the one standing in front of him, either. Something about her stirred a sense of attraction in him that he hadn't felt in a long time.

"Hello," she said, removing her gloves. "I am Alina Dalca, the forensic anthropologist." She had an Eastern European accent. "Are you DI Summers and Dr Sheridan? DCI Battle told me to be expecting you."

"That's us," Dani said, shaking the anthropologist's hand. "And, please, call me Dani."

"You may call me Alina."

"And I'm Tony," he said, reaching out his right hand.

Alina shook it and looked at him with deep brown eyes. "Hello, Tony. Nice to meet you."

"What do we have?" Dani asked, indicating the tent.

"Much like the body from yesterday. Skeletal remains wrapped inside a sheet. There are also remnants of clothing. The skeleton is female, and I would say from the cranial sutures that she was less than twenty years old at the time of her death. It appears she has been buried for many years."

"And she was beside the well when she was found?" Tony asked.

"Yes, where the tent is."

Dani looked at him. "You have some thoughts about that?"

"Only that he wanted her to be found. He could just as easily have pushed her into the well, where it would take longer for her to be discovered. But he didn't. He put here there, in plain sight."

"Similar to Daisy Riddle," Dani said. "Placed in full view, on the altar."

"If he wanted them to remain hidden," Alina offered, "he would leave them in the place they have been buried for all this time."

Tony nodded. "So why now? Why is he revealing them to us all these years later?" He looked around the clearing, hoping to receive some flash of inspiration but instead drawing a blank.

"That is your department, Tony" Alina said, with a smile. "As for mine, I will try to find out who this girl is. One thing I have already checked is that she has both ankle bones. The one we found with Daisy Riddle does not belong to this skeleton."

"So, there are more," Dani said with a sigh. "He's got the remains of at least one other victim hidden away somewhere."

The anthropologist nodded. "It would seem so, yes."

Dani nodded slowly and gazed at the sacred well, seemingly lost in thought. Tony wondered if she was weighing up the chances of finding the secret burial place and cracking the case. Perhaps she thought that by doing so, she would earn her place on the team.

Not that she had anything to prove to anyone; she'd been the driving force in solving the case that had landed in their laps at Christmas. But Tony knew how the mind worked. DI Summers was wondering how she could reaffirm her place among the members of Murder Force.

She turned to Tony and said, "Come on, we need to get to Castleton."

"All right." To Alina, he said, "Thanks for your help. I'll be in touch. I mean, we'll be in touch." Mentally reprimanding himself for acting like a flustered schoolboy, he followed Dani out of the clearing and back along the path through the woods.

"She seems nice," Dani said, matter-of-factly.

Tony wondered if she'd noticed his lack of composure in the clearing. Of course she had; she didn't need to be a detective to see that he was attracted to the forensic anthropologist.

"She does," he said, noncommittally.

"Any thoughts?"

"About Alina?"

She let out a short laugh. "No, about the discovery of a second body."

"Umm, yes, actually. He seems to be undoing the work he did all those years ago. It doesn't make any sense."

"Of course it doesn't make any sense. Taking those poor girls in the first place doesn't make any sense."

"It made sense to him," Tony said. "Which is why uncovering the bodies now, and leaving them in places where they'll be found, is so baffling." He let his thoughts go deeper, trying to put himself inside the head of the killer, trying to understand why the person who took these girls from the world was now giving them back.

He couldn't come up with any compelling reasons; at least not any that would account for this profound transformation of behaviour.

A thought struck him, and he explored it further

as they passed beneath the crime scene tape and stepped into the parking area.

"He didn't do it," he said, suddenly understanding.

Dani looked at him and frowned. "What?"

"He didn't do it," he repeated. "The person who took these girls buried them, hid them from sight. He probably kept them close, or at least in a place where he could visit their graves and relive his experience with them in his mind. He'd never dig them up and give them away. He simply wouldn't do it."

"So, what are you saying?"

"It's someone else. Someone else is putting the girls where we can find them."

CHAPTER 13

"What do you mean it's someone else?" Dani asked. They were in her Land Rover now, driving north through the rain to Castleton, the wipers humming across the windscreen every few seconds.

Tony had mentally picked through his theory during the walk back from the sacred well to the guest house car park. The more he thought about it, the surer he became that his assertion was correct.

"It's the only thing that makes sense," he said. "The person who took those girls would never let them go. He had Daisy Riddle's body buried in an unknown location for fifteen years. There's no logical reason for him to dig up her remains and leave them somewhere they'll be found."

"Who says he's logical?" Dani said. "He kidnaps and kills young women."

"Yes, he does, and that seems crazy to us, but we're talking about someone who is methodical, and intelligent. He got away with taking Daisy and those other girls for years. One of the main reasons for that was the lack of evidence. The police didn't have the bodies. Some of the people he took were most likely assumed to be missing, not necessarily dead. Keeping the bodies hidden was the smartest thing he did. And now he's handing them over to the police? I don't buy it."

"Perhaps he's had enough of running," she suggested. "Or he's had a change of heart."

"Then why not just hand himself in? He's got fame and recognition for what he's done. That's what a lot of serial killers crave, especially once they think they've achieved all they're going to."

The DI shrugged. "I don't know. But if it's someone else digging up the bodies, then how did they find them? And why haven't they come to us to report them, instead of digging them up and dumping them in public places? It doesn't make any sense."

She was right, and that was the part of Tony's theory he was struggling with the most. If someone had found the girls' graves, why not report the finding to the police? Digging up the bodies one by one and leaving them out in the open suggested a complex psychology at work in the person who was doing such a thing.

"I don't know exactly what's going on," he said, "but I do know that the person who took those girls is not the person who is digging them out of their graves. The man who took the girls is a collector. Their remains were part of his collection. He'd never willingly give them up."

Dani was silent for a while as she digested the information, then said, "A lot of killers leave the bodies of their victims on display."

"Not him. Not after all these years."

She sighed. "You're saying it doesn't make sense for him to do this, but it doesn't make sense for anyone else to do it, either. If it *is* someone else, then they're just as warped as he is."

"Maybe they are," Tony said. "It's certainly someone with deep psychological issues, perhaps related to the abductions, or the killings. He—and I'll refer to him as a man, but it could just as easily be a woman—has a need to protect the killer, but also a powerful, conflicting desire to undo his work. That's why he's breaking up the collection and sending it to us but hasn't told the police where the rest of the collection is, or who killed the girls."

"Please don't refer to it as a collection," she said. "It sounds creepy."

"You have to understand that that's how the killer sees it. With every abduction, he was adding to a collection that he probably built over a long time. It was his secret, his prized possession. He'd never give it away."

"All right, we'll keep in mind that it could be

someone else digging up the remains. At least that might double Forensic's chances of getting some usable DNA from the victims."

He nodded. "Hopefully."

Although Dani had agreed to consider the possibility of another person being involved, Tony could tell she wasn't sold on the idea. She had to keep an open mind, he understood that, but in his own mind, he was certain that the person who was digging up the bodies wasn't the same person who had buried them.

They continued in silence for a while, during which time, Tony watched the wipers sluice rainwater from the windscreen, and tried to figure out who the person digging up the remains might be and what connection they had with the killer.

Dani brought him out of his thoughts by saying, "So, the anthropologist. What was her name, again?"

"Alina," he said, trying to sound offhand about it. "Alina Dalca."

Dani nodded slowly, as if she'd just been reminded of the name, even though he was sure she'd remembered it perfectly well by herself. She was a detective, after all, and recalling details was part of her skillset.

"Very pretty," she said.

Tony tried to read her face, but she was staring intently at the road ahead. Was she teasing him?

"Yes, I suppose so." He tried to sound disinterested.

"Oh, I thought you noticed." She turned her head slightly towards him, and he noticed a slight smirk play across her lips.

Before he could answer, his phone rang. The screen told him it was DCI Battle.

Saved by the bell, Tony thought as he answered the call. "Good morning, boss, what's up?"

"Where are you?" Battle asked. His voice was always gruff, but today it seemed to have become even more of a growl than usual.

"On our way to Castleton," Tony said. "We're going to have a look at the place where Daisy Riddle lived."

"Never mind that. I want you to get over to Bakewell. There's a Mrs Colleen Francis there who rang the incident room this morning. She thinks the body at the well might be her sister, Mary. Colleen was with Mary when she was taken. I want you to have a word with her. I assume DI Summers is with you?"

"She is."

"Right, both of you get over there and see if she's got anything useful for us." He gave Tony an address in Bakewell.

"Has she been interviewed before?" Tony asked. "Colleen Francis, I mean. Have we got that interview on file?"

"Yes, she's been interviewed before. Twenty-two years ago. She was twelve years old. I want you to have a word with her today. See if she remembers anything she didn't tell the police at the time."

Tony let out a breath. "Seems like a long shot."

"Yes, it's a bloody long shot but we have to follow up every lead. Now get over to her house and talk to her." The line went dead.

Tony checked the screen. It said *Call Ended*. He put the phone on the dashboard.

"What was that about?" Dani asked.

"There's a woman in Bakewell who thinks the body we found this morning might be her sister. Battle wants us to talk to her. Then he hung up on me."

"You sure he wasn't cut off? The reception around here is a bit spotty."

"Maybe. He was shouting at me at the time, though, so I'm going to go with hung up."

"I think it's this case," she said. "It's getting to him a bit. He was the investigating officer when Daisy went missing, and now she's turned up dead. It's understandable that he's feeling a sense of regret."

"Of course." Tony tried to imagine what the DCI was going through. It must be a blow, both on a professional level as well as personal one, when a girl you'd tried to find many years ago, a missing person who'd slipped into the shadows, suddenly emerged from those shadows as a corpse.

"What's the address in Bakewell?" Dani asked. "You'd best put it into the SatNav."

Tony leaned forwards and tapped on the SatNav screen, cancelling the current route, which had been taking them to Castleton, and replacing it with a new destination; Wyedale Crescent, Bakewell. The computer calculated a route, and the display told Tony that the Bakewell was fifteen minutes away. The female voice told them to stay on the road they were currently on.

"We should be there in no time," he said, sitting back. "Although I doubt Colleen Francis will remember anything useful. Her sister was abducted twenty-two years ago, apparently."

"That time frame fits with the condition of the body at the well." Dani looked at him. "Alina said the body had been in the ground for many years."

"Well, many doesn't necessarily mean twenty-two. I'm afraid Colleen might want us to tell her what happened to her sister, and the truth is, we don't know whether the girl at the well is her or not."

"Even if it isn't her sister, the person who took her might be the same one who took Daisy. Colleen might have seen the man we're looking for. It's a lead."

Tony wasn't so sure. Memories didn't age well, and if Colleen Francis had seen some useful detail over two decades ago, it was unlikely she'd recall it now, at least not without some sort of help like hypnotic regression.

He knew it was a lead they had to follow, and he hoped he was wrong, and that Colleen would give them some clue that would lead them to the killer, but he was nothing if not a realist.

That was why he was trying to push thoughts of Alina Dalca out of his mind; he knew he didn't realistically have a chance with such a woman. The opposite sex tended to see him as a geek, a weirdo even. The few relationships he'd had in his life had usually ended with him being given some version of the "it's not you, it's me" speech, but he'd known every time that it was indeed him who'd been the problem in the relationship.

Part of it was his obsessive approach to his work. Once he got his teeth into a criminal case, or even his clinical work, he found it hard to think about anything else. Everything else felt like a distraction, and unfortunately, this meant he neglected communicating with people who weren't part of his work.

To someone who didn't understand this type of professional passion, he appeared detached and distant. The few women who he'd had a relationship with took his attitude towards them as a rejection, and a break-up would soon follow.

Tony didn't blame them at all; he knew the fault was his.

And, knowing that, he tended to avoid romance altogether.

He hadn't had a romantic relationship since well before he went to Canada and ended up in the house of the Lake Erie Ripper. He'd been so mentally scarred by that particular experience that he'd barely even thought about close connections with the opposite sex since.

Until this morning.

To drag his mind away from such thoughts now, he picked up his phone again and searched for the name *Mary Francis*, hoping to find details of the girl's disappearance. None of the results that appeared on the screen had anything to do with a missing person. Then Tony remembered that Battle had said *Mrs Colleen Francis*. Her surname had probably changed.

So, he typed the words *Colleen*, *Mary*, *missing person*, and *Bakewell* into the search box.

This time, he got more relevant results, including an article entitled *Young Girl's Horror as Sister Disappears*.

Clicking the link and reading the article, he discovered that Colleen's and Mary's surname had been Harwood, and that the abduction hadn't taken place in Bakewell, but somewhere called Miller's Dale.

"Do you know where Miller's Dale is?" he asked Dani.

She shook her head. "No idea."

He read on. It seemed that Colleen, 12, and her older sister Mary, 14, had been playing together on a riverbank near their home in Miller's Dale during the evening of January 13th. Not the most sensible thing in the world, Tony thought. If he had children of that age, there was no way he'd let them play by a river unsupervised.

"What are you reading?" Dani asked.

"An article about Mary Harwood's disappearance." He read it out to her, up to the point where it mentioned the girls were by the river.

"We should probably let Colleen tell us the rest," she suggested. "The press get things wrong all the time."

Tony nodded. She was right about that. He'd experienced that first-hand. When he'd been recovering in a mental facility in Toronto, there'd been a headline in the *Star* that had read *British Psychologist Loses Mind After Encountering Ripper*.

The story had been overblown, an exaggerated account of his mental state. Anyone reading it, and not knowing the truth, could be forgiven for thinking Tony had been trussed up in a straitjacket and locked away in a padded cell. That story probably sold papers, but it wasn't true.

And when he'd finally recovered and been released, the press hadn't wanted to know. There were probably some tabloid readers in Canada who still thought that a British psychologist was being kept under lock and key in a high security mental hospital because he'd gone crazy after encountering the Lake Erie Ripper.

"Bakewell," Dani said, as they passed a sign announcing their arrival at the town that was famous for having a pudding and a tart named after it.

Shortly after passing the sign, two left turns took them to Wyedale Crescent.

The house they were looking for was a neat little semi with a red Volkswagen Passat on the drive. Dani parked the Land Rover by the kerb and she and Tony got out.

After a short dash down the drive to avoid the rain, they knocked on the door.

The woman who answered was in her thirties—thirty-four, Tony told himself, after doing a quick mental calculation—and wore a baggy grey hoody and blue jeans. Her black hair was scraped back into a ponytail, and in her arm, she held a blonde-haired boy who couldn't have been more than two years old. The child had a wide smile as he looked from Dani to Tony. The woman holding him had a less pleasant disposition. Her lips were slightly pursed, her eyes narrowed. She looked suspicious of the two people standing on her doorstep.

"Colleen Francis?" Dani asked, showing the woman her warrant card. "I'm DI Summers and this is Doctor Sheridan, from the Murder Force. I believe you wanted to talk to us."

"Yes, come in." She stepped aside. Tony followed Dani inside.

"The living room's just in there," Colleen said, indicating a room on the left with a nod of her head.

The room was furnished with a plush sofa that looked like it was made from silver coloured crushed velvet. A matching armchair sat next to it. The television was on, and a cartoon pig was talking to a cartoon rabbit about jumping in puddles. Lego littered the floor, along with a number of dolls scattered here and there, staring at the ceiling with wide eyes, as if they'd become lost in the landscape of plastic.

"Take a seat," Colleen said, indicating the sofa. She sat in the armchair and placed the child on the floor. He began picking up Lego bricks and throwing them at the dolls.

"Lucas!" his mother said. "Don't do that!"

Chastised, the boy settled into a cross-legged position and stared at the television.

"What did you want to talk to us about, Mrs Francis?" Dani asked, taking a notebook and pencil out of her pocket.

"That body you found." She nodded at the telly, as if the News was on the screen and not a cartoon menagerie of animals. "I think it might be Mary, my sister."

"And what makes you think that?"

Colleen narrowed her eyes even further. "You know she went missing, right? Nobody was bothered then, but I thought you might be more interested now you've got a body."

"Are you saying no one believed you when Mary went missing?" Tony asked. He'd seen this before. Witness statements from children were taken with a pinch of salt by some police officers.

"That's right," she said, turning her attention to him. "They all thought she'd drowned in the river and I was telling tales. The river had broken the banks, you see, and we probably shouldn't have been down there in the first place, but our mum didn't mind." She paused and then let out a short breath through her nose. "We went there all the time. We knew to be careful, and we stayed away from the water."

"Tell us what happened," Tony said, leaning forward slightly and giving her his full attention.

She sighed. "Well, like I said, we were down by the river."

"In Miller's Dale."

Colleen nodded. "Yes, that's where we lived. My dad had a little farm there. Harwood Farm. That's my maiden name. Harwood. Mary and I used to go wandering all over, climbing trees and hiking along the river. Proper little tomboys we were, both of us. I looked up to Mary because she was two years older than me. And I always felt safe with her. I always felt like she'd protect me from anything."

Her face darkened and she looked at the Lego-strewn carpet, her eyes drawn to one of the lifeless dolls.

Tony could see she was drifting into a memory.

"What was the weather like that day?" he asked gently.

"Miserable," she said, still looking at the doll. "Like I said, the river had broken its banks. There'd been a lot of rain. It was muddy, and there was a light drizzle. A fine mist hanging in the air."

"But that didn't put you or Mary off. You went playing by the river, anyway."

She nodded slowly. "We weren't afraid of rain, or mud, or anything, really." Her eyes drifted from the doll up to Tony. "Perhaps we should have been."

She was getting into abstracts. Tony needed to keep her attention fixed on the details of that day. "What time was this? Morning? Afternoon? Evening?"

"Evening. It was getting dark. We weren't bothered, though. We didn't have a care in the world. We were throwing sticks into the river and chatting about anything and everything. Mary fancied a boy called Peter Trent at school. She was going on about him, mostly."

"Sounds like you were enjoying yourselves," Tony said. "What happened next?"

Colleen closed her eyes for a couple of seconds, trying to remember. "There was a car. It came over the bridge. The headlights were on, and they lit up the bank where we were standing."

"Do you know what type of car it was?"

"A black Land Rover."

"Are you sure?"

She looked at him sharply. "I was twelve, not two. I know what a Land Rover looks like."

She was losing focus, and that was his fault for questioning her. He had to get her back on track. "I mean are you sure it was black? Go back to that evening. See the car in your mind."

"It was black," she said firmly.

"What else do you remember about the car?"

"Nothing much. The headlights were so bright, it was hard to see anything."

"So how do you know the car was—" Dani began, but Tony placed a hand on her arm, silencing her. Colleen was in a receptive state at the moment, and adversarial questions would only bring her out of it. She wasn't hypnotised or anything like that, but Tony could tell by her eyes and her breathing that she'd be a good candidate for hypnosis.

"What happened next?" he asked Colleen softly.

"The door opened, and someone got out."

Tony, whose hand was still on Dani's arm, felt the DI's muscles tighten beneath her jumper. This was the crux of the matter. The man who had climbed out of that black Land Rover twenty-two years ago could be the man who abducted Daisy Riddle seven years later, along with what might turn out to be countless other girls.

Colleen might have seen his face.

"What did he look like?" he asked, trying to make the question sound casual.

She shook her head. "I don't know. He was silhouetted against the lights. They were so bright."

"Was he tall or short?"

Colleen shrugged. "I don't know. Average."

"Did he walk with a limp, or stooped over? Or did he—"

"He was just there, in front of the headlights. Standing there, watching us."

"All right. What happened next?"

"I was scared. I pulled on Mary's arm, tried to tell her it was time to go home. She wasn't having any of it. She shook me off and said everything was all right, that she knew him, and he was her friend. I told her she was a liar. I didn't believe she knew him at all. I couldn't see who he was because of the lights, but I could tell he was an adult. Mary was fourteen. She didn't have any grown up friends, at least not as far as I knew."

Tony glanced at Dani, and she looked at him, nodding slightly. If Mary Harwood had known the man who'd abducted her, it was an avenue worth investigating.

"Mary went to the car," Colleen continued. "She told me that everything was all right, but I was still scared. I told her not to go. I was so frightened, I started to cry. She told me I was a baby. She kept walking towards the Land Rover, where he was waiting, framed by the headlights."

Her eyes dropped to the carpet once more, and Tony saw tears forming in them. "She was nothing more than a silhouette as she got closer to the car. Then they both got in, and I never saw my sister again."

"What did you do?" Dani asked.

"It was completely dark once the Land Rover had driven away. I ran home. On the way, I slipped in the mud and fell into the river. I managed to pull myself out, but by the time I got home, I was soaking wet and covered in mud. I told my mum and dad what had happened, and they called the police. A couple of policemen coming to the farm. They asked me some questions and I told them what I just told you. But they didn't believe me."

"Why not?" Tony asked. He'd had no reason to believe Colleen had been anything but totally honest while telling her story, so why had the police felt differently twenty-two years ago?

"While they were interviewing me, two of their colleagues went to the place where I told them it had happened and searched along the riverbank. They found the place where I'd slipped in and decided that it was Mary who'd fallen into the river, and that I'd tried to go in and save her—which was why I was soaking wet, apparently—but had failed to stop her from drowning and had made up the story about the Land Rover on my way home."

Tony frowned. "Why would they think that?"

"I don't know. Even my mum kept telling me to tell the truth, as if she thought I was lying. And then, a couple of days later, they found Mary's coat, and one of her shoes a bit further downriver. That convinced them they were right. Everybody—including my own parents—thought I was a liar."

"So, they didn't investigate the Land Rover angle at all?" Dani asked.

Colleen shook her head. "Not after they found Mary's clothes. They were sure she'd drowned. They sent frogmen down to look for her body, but they never found anything."

She wiped her eyes. "When that girl was found in those ruins, I thought it could be Mary, but then the News said it was Daisy Riddle. Now this other body has been found, and I'm wondering again if it's my sister."

"It isn't certain that she's dead," Tony said. "She might have gone off with the guy in the Land Rover, run away from home."

"No, she'd never do that. I knew my sister. She wouldn't run away with some old bloke. And how did her coat and shoe end up in the river, if that was the case?"

"She might have been covering her tracks. Making sure no one looked for her."

"He was covering *his* tracks, more like. Making sure no one came looking for *him*."

Tony had to admit that she had a point. The coat and shoe could have been tossed into the river by the killer at a later date, to make the abduction look like a drowning.

"I've not been much help, have I?" Colleen asked, looking from Tony to Dani. "I can't remember what he looked like, and it was so long ago now, that there won't be any evidence to support my story." She grimaced. "I've even questioned myself sometimes. Maybe I *did* make the whole thing up."

"You've been a great help," Dani said. "Going back to the fact that Mary said she knew the man in the Land Rover, are you sure there wasn't an adult she knew back then? Someone who was hanging around, perhaps?"

"No, there's nobody. I've been racking my brain for twenty-two years about who it could have been, but there really wasn't anyone. Not anyone Mary told me about, anyway."

"Was she a secretive person?" Tony asked.

"Not as far as I know, but there were two years between us. She might have kept something from me if she thought I was too young to understand."

"Like boyfriends?"

"I don't think so. She wouldn't shut up about Peter Trent, but he was just someone she fancied, you know? Perhaps there *was* someone else. Someone older." She thought about it, and then shook her head. "No, I don't believe it. Mary wouldn't have been so stupid."

Despite Colleen's fierce loyalty to her sister, Tony wasn't so sure that Mary hadn't somehow become involved with the man who had caused her disappearance. It was an angle that would have to be looked into.

"How can we contact your parents?" Dani asked Colleen, obviously thinking the same thing.

"My mum's still at the farm. Well, she's in the house, anyway. Most of the land's been sold off now. But mum would never leave the house."

"And your dad?" Tony asked.

"He died when I was fifteen. Heart attack. With Mary disappearing and then dad dying, Mum went a bit downhill. I still see her every week, take her shopping and things like that. But she's not the same person she used to be. I've tried to get her to sell that big house and move to one of those sheltered housing projects, but she won't do it. Says the place has got too many memories for her to leave it behind."

Dani positioned the pencil over the notebook. "Have you got a phone number for her?"

"Yes, hang on." Colleen reached over and picked up her mobile from a side table, scrolling through her contacts before reading off a number. "That's the landline at the farm. Mum hasn't got a mobile."

"Thanks." Dani put the notebook away. "I think we've got everything we need. We'll be in touch if we have any news." She stood up, and Tony followed suit.

"If it is Mary's body you've found," Colleen said, getting up as well, "you'll let me know, right? I mean, before I hear it on the News."

"Of course," Tony said. "We always try to inform next of kin before we release any names."

"But next of kin will probably be your mother," Dani said.

Colleen looked worried. "No, please, you have to tell me. She still thinks Mary drowned. It'll be a shock to her if she finds out that isn't the case. Let me break the news to her."

"Colleen," Dani said. "The body we found might not even be Mary."

"I know that." She led them to the front door. "But with all these girls turning up from years ago, Mary might be among them, you know?"

"Do you hope she is?" Tony asked, professional curiosity getting the better of him.

Without any hesitation, Colleen nodded and said, "Yes, I do. I don't like the idea that someone snuffed out her life, or that she might have gone through...an ordeal...before she died. But at least we'd finally know where she was, and we'd be able to bury her properly."

It was the kind of answer Tony had been expecting, the kind of thing he'd heard countless times in his job. Knowing what had happened to a loved one —even if that knowledge brought with it more questions—was better than not knowing. "Of course," he said with a slight nod and a tight-lipped smile. "I understand completely."

"We'll be in touch," Dani said, opening the door and stepping out onto the front step.

Tony followed her out and together, they walked quickly to the car to avoid getting too wet in the rain.

"What do you think?" Dani asked when the car doors were closed, and she'd started the engine.

"I think the police should have believed her story twenty-two years ago."

"I'm inclined to agree with you."

Tony looked back at the house they had just come from. Colleen was standing in the open doorway, joined now by her son, Lucas, who was holding his mother's hand. In his other hand, he held one of the dolls from the living room floor.

Tony gave the lad a wave. Lucas waved back with the hand holding the doll.

As they drove away, Dani tossed her notebook onto Tony's lap. "Give the mother a ring," she said. "We're going to have a word with her."

CHAPTER 14

Tony and Dani found Harwood Farm nestled against the hills Northwest of Bakewell. On the phone, Tony had managed to reach Mrs Harwood and had told her who he was and that he'd been speaking to her daughter. When he'd mentioned that he and DI Summers would like to speak to her, she'd sounded timid, almost scared, but she'd agreed.

Tony wondered if, somewhere deep inside, Mrs Harwood suspected that the story her daughter told her on a rainy night twenty-two years ago might be true. She must have heard about the discovery of the bodies on the News, and now, a police detective and a psychologist from Murder Force were coming to visit her.

She must have put two and two together, even if only subconsciously.

"She probably thinks we're coming to tell her we've found her daughter," he said to Dani, whose attention was focused on the track that led to the farmhouse.

"Well, we're not, and we can't even hint that the body at the well might be Mary. There's no point upsetting the poor woman. Mary Harwood will be a good place to start for the comparison of dental records, but I'm sure Battle has already thought of that. I'd say he's already called the odontologist to do a comparison."

"So, we're here because..." Tony said, letting his words fade away. After hearing Mrs Harwood's timid voice on the phone, he wondered if they were being premature questioning her right now.

"Because Mary said she knew the man who drove her away in that Land Rover. Her mother might be able to shed some light on that."

"Don't you think that if Mary knew an older man, she'd have kept it from her parents? I doubt Mrs Harwood knows anything about it."

Dani shrugged. "Then we'll find that out when we speak to her."

Tony didn't reply. He wondered if the DI was taking the bull by the horns because she wanted to take a more active role in this case than she'd been assigned.

Noticing his silence, she said, "Look, the man we're looking for has taken at least three girls: Daisy Riddle; the girl at the well; and whoever that ankle bone belongs to. It isn't a stretch to think he could be the guy Colleen saw in the Land Rover that night."

Tony had to agree there was a good chance that the man who'd driven off with Mary was the same man who later abducted Daisy, and an unknown number of other girls. He just wasn't sure that Mary's mother would provide them with anything useful, and interviewing her on the off chance of gleaning a useful nugget of information had to be weighed against the fact that they would be dredging up painful memories.

At least the rain had stopped. Looming storm clouds coloured the sky dark grey, but their edges were illuminated by the sun as it tried to cut through them.

Dani parked the Land Rover in the front yard of the farmhouse—a gravelled area surrounded by outbuildings—and got out. Tony followed, looking around as Dani knocked on the door.

The farm was remote, surrounded by wide expanses of fields framed by low hills. A line of trees in the distance snaked through the landscape. The trees probably grew by the river where Mary and Colleen had been playing over two decades ago.

The door opened, and a slight woman in her late fifties peered out from within the house. She wore large glasses that looked decades out of date, and an oversized grey jumper with blue jeans. Her hair was fixed into a ponytail with a rubber band.

As Dani introduced herself and showed the woman her warrant card, Tony realised how much looking at Mrs Harwood was like looking at an older version of Colleen. An older, more stooped version, anyway. The woman seemed to have all the cares of the world on her shoulders.

"Mrs, Harwood, I'm Tony Sheridan," he said, showing his identity card and an accompanying smile that he hoped looked friendly.

"Come in, both of you," she said, shuffling into the house like someone twice her age. "And call me June. Now, who wants a cup of tea?"

Dani declined, but Tony said, "That would be lovely, June. Thanks."

"Colleen rang me when you left her house," June said, going into the rustic, farmhouse kitchen and filling up the kettle. "Said she gave you my number. She also said you don't know who that girl is that was found today. I'll tell you now, it's not my Mary. Colleen might have some fanciful notions in her head, but my daughter drowned in a river more than twenty years ago."

"That may be the case," Tony said. "We've just come here to talk to you about Mary."

She took two mugs from cupboard and set them on the counter. "Because Colleen has been filling your head with stories, and you think that girl you found today might be her."

"Not necessarily. We're just covering all angles.

"Well, you'd make better use of your time looking for the person who murdered those poor girls, instead of delving into the past. Mary died by accident. It was tragic, and heart-breaking, but it was an accident. Nobody did anything to her."

Tony simply nodded. During his time as a clinical psychologist, he'd seen many people trying to convince themselves of something, to squash a nagging doubt in the back of their minds. He was seeing that now in June Harwood. On the one hand, she was telling them they were wasting their time here, that her daughter's death had no bearing on the current case, yet on the other, she hadn't turned them away, or refused to speak to them.

On the contrary, she was inviting them in and making tea. Tony was sure that even though June outwardly dismissed Colleen's story, a part of her—perhaps hidden deep inside her subconscious—wondered if it was true. If a man really had driven Mary away in a black Land Rover all those years ago.

And no matter how hard she tried, she couldn't completely ignore that niggling voice, because like any mother, she had an overwhelming desire to know the truth about what had happened to her daughter.

The rejection of Colleen's story, and the assertion that Mary had drowned in the river, was a psychological shield, protecting her from having to face the possibility that someone had hurt her daughter.

The fact that she was talking to them at all meant there was a crack in that shield.

"Tell us about Mary," he said. "What sort of girl was she?"

June eyed him suspiciously over the teapot. "I suppose you're expecting me to say she was the life and soul of the party, or she lit up the room when she walked in. That's what most people say on telly when they've lost someone, isn't it? Well, Mary was an average girl. She was special to me, of course, and to her dad, but she was an average fourteen-year-old. There was nothing special about her."

She poured boiling water into the teapot and added, "What I'm saying is, there's no reason anyone would kidnap her, or abduct her, or whatever you want to call it. She didn't draw attention to herself. What her sister says about her knowing some older bloke is a load of rubbish. Mary wasn't like that. She kept herself to herself."

Tony felt a stab of disappointment. That was that line of questioning out of the window. If Mary *had* known the man in the Land Rover, she hadn't told her mum about him.

"Do you have any of her things?" Dani asked. "Anything we could have a look at to get a better idea of who she was?"

June nodded. "I've got all of her things. Her room is still just how she left it. I never had the heart to clear it out."

Tony posed his next question carefully. "Do you think we'd be able to have a look at it? We'd really like to get to know Mary better."

The suspicious look didn't leave June's eyes. "But if she drowned in an accident, there's no reason for police to be looking through her things."

Tony hesitated before replying. She'd thrown out a logical statement that was true. If Mary had drowned, there was no reason for him and Dani to go and look at her room. By not refusing his request, but by putting out this statement, June had opened a small doorway. He knew that his reply couldn't be anything along the lines of, "But we don't believe she drowned," because then that shield would be raised again, and the doorway of opportunity closed.

Considering this, he nodded in agreement with June and said, "That's right. There'd be no need at all. If she drowned." He didn't put any particular emphasis on the word if. He wasn't implying a question mark surrounding Mary's death. He was simply replying to Mary's statement with one of his own.

He was allowing her the opportunity to allow them into Mary's room without conceding that the story she'd made herself believe for all these years might be false.

When June busied herself with the teapot and the mugs and didn't reply, Tony—remembering what Colleen said about her mother not wanting to leave memories behind—added, "I'm sure you have many fond memories of your daughter, June. We never knew Mary, so we can't share those memories. But we'd like to get a glimpse into her life."

She pursed her lips, obviously thinking. Letting them into Mary's room would be the closest she'd ever come to admitting there was a possibility, no matter how slight, that her daughter had been taken.

"All right, you can have a quick look," she said. "But don't be too long, or your tea will get cold."

"Is her room upstairs?" Tony asked, moving towards the staircase in the hall before she could change her mind.

"Yes," she said. "Last door on the left."

Tony ascended the stairs, followed closely by Dani. When they got to the top, a dim hallway—lit only by a single net-curtained window—stretched along the length of the house. There were four closed doors up here. Tony went to the last door on the left, which waited in deep shadow, and opened it.

Mary's bedroom was brighter than the hallway, thanks to a large window that overlooked the front yard, where Dani's Land Rover was parked among the outbuildings. The room was furnished with a single bed, a small bookshelf, a pine bedside table and matching dressing table, and a large, dark wooden wardrobe that looked like it could be as old as the house itself.

The walls were adorned with the usual things one would expect to find in a teenager's room in the late 90s: posters of bands that were popular at the time, including All Saints and Westlife; fashion drawings that might have been made by Mary herself; photos pinned on the wall by the dresser; and an acoustic guitar hanging from a wall mount.

A dressmaker's mannequin stood in one corner of the room, wearing a green dress that was held together with a multitude of pins, and would never be finished.

"I thought Colleen said she and Mary were tomboys," Dani said, inspecting the fashion drawings on the walls. "It looks like Mary was the opposite."

"She was fourteen," Tony offered. "Perhaps she'd been a tomboy for a while but was becoming interested in other things. Totally opposite things. Like fashion. Girls go through a lot of changes at that age."

Dani raised an eyebrow at him. "I know. I have a daughter who went from splashing in puddles to going on dates in the blink of an eye. And I was that age myself once, about a hundred years ago."

Tony laughed. "Yeah, I know how you feel." He opened the wardrobe and looked inside. Jackets, plaid shirts that fit the tomboy image, and jeans dangled from hangers. Beneath the clothing, he found a shoebox, which he pulled out and placed on the bed.

"Got something?" Dani asked. She was picking

books out of the bookshelf and flicking through the pages.

"Speed reading?" Tony asked.

"Books are great places to find things," she said, placing a stack of paperbacks on the bed next to the shoebox. "A lot of people hide things in books." Tony looked at the titles. They were romances and seemed to be about love in faraway places. *Marriage in Marrakesh. The Paris Fling. Romance in Rio.*

"Looks like she wanted to get away," he told Dani. "Her leisure time was spent dreaming of distant lands."

"That's not unusual. I wouldn't read too much into it." She continued riffling through the pages.

He opened the shoebox. Inside, he found a number of loose photographs that had been taken with a Polaroid camera, and some jewellery. The yellowing photos were of locations that Tony guessed were nearby. Fields, woods, and a river which was probably the one Mary had apparently drowned in.

One picture showed a young woman in a summer dress, sitting by the river, a brooding look on her face as she regarded the water. In another image, she was sitting in a field, surrounded by grass which had faded from green to pale blue as the photo had aged.

Tony took his phone out of his pocket and checked the photo of Mary in the article he'd been reading on the way to Colleen's house. Then he looked at the woman in the photos on the bed. She wasn't either of the Harwood girls.

"Got something?" Dani asked, watching him as he stared at the Polaroids.

"I was just wondering who this is." He held up the photo of the unknown woman sitting by the river. "It isn't Mary or Colleen."

"Perhaps June will know. Do you think it could be important?"

He pointed at the photos that were pinned to the wall by the dressing table. Some were of Mary, others of Colleen, and one of the Harwood family. Two photos showed a black and white border collie running around a field. "She displayed those, but not these. She placed these in a shoebox in her wardrobe."

"You think she didn't want anyone else to see them?"

"Maybe."

"The photos on the wall aren't Polaroids," Dani said. "Mary could have taken these without anyone knowing. No need to have them developed."

Tony placed the Polaroids in a neat row on the bed and took photos of them with his phone. He was fairly sure June wouldn't let the originals leave the house.

"Anything in those books other than passionate romances in foreign locales?"

Dani shook her head. "Nothing." She returned the paperbacks to the bookshelf.

Tony's phone buzzed. It was Battle again. Tony answered the call, "Hi, boss."

"Where are you?" Battle said. His rough manner hadn't smoothed out at all since his last call.

"We're at the house of June Harwood."

"What are you doing there?"

"She's Mary Harwood's mother. Our chat with Colleen led us here."

"Well, you can give her the good news, then."

"Good news?"

"The body isn't Mary Harwood's. The dental records don't match."

"Oh." Tony almost felt disappointed. At least if the body had been Mary's, it would have given Colleen and June some closure. "Do we know who it is?"

"No, that's going to take a bit longer to establish, I'm afraid."

"Of course." Eliminating Mary Harwood would have been simple, since they knew which records to check, but comparing the dental records of all missing persons from the area in the last two decades and hoping for a hit would be a much more difficult task.

"Anyway, that's all. I'll let you know when we have a positive ID."

"Thanks," Tony said, ending the call. He hadn't

exactly hung up on Battle, as the DCI had done to him, but it gave him an odd satisfaction exerting a little bit of control. As he put the phone into his pocket, he said to Dani, "It isn't Mary. They still don't know who the victim is, but it's not Mary Harwood."

"That's a relief. I don't fancy going back downstairs and telling June they've found Mary. She's living in her own fantasy world where her daughter died from a tragic accident. I'm not sure how she'd handle reality if it hit her head-on like that."

"She'd cope, eventually. Besides, just because it wasn't Mary at the well doesn't mean she wasn't taken by the same guy. Her body might turn up tomorrow."

"You think we'll get another one tomorrow?"

He shrugged. "Why not? Two days, two bodies. Whoever's leaving them where we can find them is trying to tell us something. If he's got more bodies to give us, he'll do so."

"That's all we need. With every body that turns up, the case will become more complex. More threads to investigate, more witnesses to interview."

"Well, you said you wanted to get stuck in." He held the photo of the girl by the river aloft. "Let's see if June knows who this is."

They went back downstairs. June was still in the kitchen, sitting at an old, scarred wooden table, drinking tea. When she saw Tony, she pointed at the other mug, which was still on the counter. "There's plenty in the pot." Turning her attention to Dani, she added, "For both of you, if you've changed your mind."

"I'm fine, thanks," Dani said.

Tony filled the mug and placed the Polaroid in front of June. "Do you know who that is?"

She squinted at the photo, picking it up and holding it close to her eyes, before shaking her head. "No. Should I?"

"She wasn't one of Mary's friends?" Dani asked.

"I don't recall seeing her before. My eyes aren't too good nowadays, but there's nothing wrong with my memory."

"Do you mind if we take the photo with us?" Tony said.

"Did you get it from Mary's room?"

He took a sip of tea. "Yes."

"Then it stays here."

He nodded. "I thought you'd say that. By the way, I have some news regarding the body that was discovered this morning."

Her face paled and some internal emotion dragged her features into a look of horror.

"It isn't Mary," he said.

June's face returned to normal, and there was only a slight quiver in her voice when she said, "I could have told you that. Saved you the journey."

Ten minutes later, as they left the farmhouse, Dani said, "Why do you think he doesn't ring me?"

"The question took Tony by surprise. He had no idea who she was talking about. "Why doesn't who ring you?"

"Battle. He's rung you twice today. He knows we're together, so why doesn't he ring me? Even once?"

"Don't get paranoid about it. He assumes you're driving."

"I *was* driving."

"He's right to assume that, then."

They got into the Land Rover. "Where to?" she asked.

"A spot of lunch would be nice. We passed a pub on the way here."

She nodded. "All right."

He took his phone out of his pocket and brought up the picture of the girl by the river.

"Who do you think she is?" Dani asked.

"I don't know. But considering the fact that Mary kept these photos secret, I think we'd better find out."

CHAPTER 15

Rob got out of bed at three in the afternoon, his usual time for rising when he was working. Sonia would be bringing the kids back from school soon, which gave him a short while to get ready for his shift before eating dinner with his family.

Before he got into the shower, though, he had to know if the police had found the girl he'd left at the ancient well.

Padding downstairs in his pyjama bottoms, he turned on the telly and found a 24-hour News channel. Sure enough, the story was about the remains of a girl discovered in the village of Temple Well, the second such discovery in two days. The footage they were showing onscreen had been taken from a helicopter and showed a glimpse of a white police tent in the woods near the village.

The report flicked back to the studio, where a neatly presented man in a police uniform was being interviewed about the find. According to the caption, his name was Chief Superintendent Ian Gallow.

Rob smiled. They'd brought out the big brass to investigate the little gift he'd given them.

He'd created quite the disturbance.

Better than that, he was undoing his father's work, piece by piece. In time, he'd empty out the entire basement, leaving nothing down there but empty graves. And that was what his father's work—if you could call it that—would amount to in the end. Nothing.

What James Gibson had taken a lifetime to build up, Rob would tear down.

Leaving the telly on, he went up to the bathroom and got into the shower. The hot water felt like tiny needles prodding at his skin. As he lathered the shower gel—something Sonia had bought that smelled of honeysuckle—onto his body, he wondered if he dared dig up another girl later.

It was too risky. After finding two bodies, the police would be on high alert.

Not only that, tonight wasn't like the last two nights; he was at work. His night watchman job at the quarry demanded that he stay at his post. He couldn't drive to his father's house and dig up the basement when he was supposed to be making sure no one robbed the quarry offices or—much more likely—broke into the place and got killed in the process.

He realised that the question wasn't did he *dare* dig up another body; it would be more honest to ask himself if he could *resist* digging up another one. There was something about his newfound hobby that thrilled him. Placing the girl by the well, unseen under the cover of night, had made his heart beat faster, pumping adrenaline through his body, bringing his senses to life. Compared to that, everyday life seemed dull and lifeless.

If he felt this way after just digging up two bodies, how must his dad have felt when he'd stolen the girls from the world and ended their lives?

He closed his eyes and leaned forward under the hot spray. His dad had offered to share that feeling with him, once. Rob had refused.

His thoughts drifted back to when he was a young boy, standing at the top of the cellar stairs, clutching his Action Man.

∼

"Either come down or go to bed," his dad said, sighing with frustration. "The choice is yours."

Although he felt more than a little trepidation, Rob moved down the stairs, holding Sam tightly in his hand.

His dad smiled and nodded. "That's right. Come down, son."

Rob stepped onto the cellar's dirt floor. The large

room was mostly in darkness, the dim light from the single naked bulb casting shadows over the walls and ceiling.

"Have a look over there," his dad said, indicating a dark corner at the far end of the room.

Overcome with curiosity, but also afraid of the atmosphere that seemed to be hang in the cellar like a cloud of dark energy, Rob moved towards the corner. He wanted to see what was there, but he also didn't want to see. Some part of his mind screamed at him that if he saw what was in that corner, his world would change, and would never return to one he'd known up to this moment.

Just turn away, he told himself. *Go back to bed and pull the covers up over your head.*

"That's right," his dad said. "Just a little further."

Rob jumped. He hadn't realised his dad was right behind him, following him.

A noise came from the dark shadows in the corner. It was the same muffled noise he'd heard earlier; like someone trying to speak. The voice sounded frightened. Rob wondered if the person in the corner felt as frightened as he did.

Something lunged out of the darkness at him. He cried out and stumbled backwards, landing on his bottom on the dirt floor.

The girl who had come out of the darkness had her hands tied behind her back. Her ankles were also tied. A piece of grey tape covered her mouth. Her blue eyes were wide and wild, staring at him through tangles of dark hair, which had fallen over her face. She wore jeans, and a white T-shirt with a pink rose on the chest. She was a lot older than Rob.

She tried to speak through the tape. Rob was sure she was trying to say, "Help me!"

His dad lifted him to his feet and pressed the handle of the knife into Rob's hand. Rob opened his palm and looked down at it, the blade shining in the dim light. The handle was made of rough wood, and had the initial *JAG* carved into it. Those were his father's initials. James Andrew Gibson. Rob got the feeling that his dad, who was a capable carpenter, joiner, and woodturner, had made this knife himself, and that no one else had seen it. He'd certainly never seen it until this moment.

"What do you want me to do with this?" he asked.

His dad grinned and nodded towards the tied-up girl. "What do you think?"

Rob looked over at her. She was shrinking back into the corner, eyes wide with fear.

"Come on, son. You know what to do," his dad urged.

Rob closed his fingers around the handle of the knife, gripping it so tightly that the rough wood pressed painfully into his palm. Did his father really want him to use this on the girl? The thought repelled him, yet he also felt a shudder of excitement run through him.

His dad knelt down next to him and put a hand on his shoulder. "You're a good boy, Rob. But now, it's time to become a man. Use the knife on the bitch."

More than anything else, hearing his father use that word brought Rob back to reality. He'd only ever heard that word before when he'd been in his room and heard his parents arguing downstairs. His father often shouted it at his mum. Or, at least, he had before she'd left.

He wavered. Did he really want to be like his dad? If he did what his father wanted him to do, he'd be setting foot on a path from which there was no return. He understood that, even at his young age.

"Come on, Rob," his dad urged. "Do it."

The girl in the corner was almost lost in the dark shadows, but Rob could see her eyes staring out from the darkness, silently pleading with him.

If he didn't do what his dad wanted him to do, what would happen to him? Would he and the girl share the same fate? Would his dad get mad at him, the same way he'd always seemed to be mad at his mum, and would Rob disappear the same as she did?

He felt warmth trickling down his leg, wetting his pyjama bottoms.

His dad stepped back, looking at him with disgust. "What the hell are you doing? Are you pissing yourself?" He laughed suddenly, an ugly barking sound. "You're pathetic, aren't you? Give me the knife."

Rob held out the knife towards his father with a shaking hand.

His dad snatched it and said, "You're a disappointment. I thought you were ready to be a real man, but you're just standing there in a puddle of your own piss. Get out of my sight. I can't even look at you."

Rob ran for the stairs, wondering with each step if he was about to feel the cold steel of the knife slice into his back. Only when he got to the top of the cellar stairs and stood in the kitchen did he dare let out a breath he hadn't realised he'd been holding in his lungs.

He went quickly up to his room and changed his pyjamas, leaving the wet ones on the floor. Then he crawled under the sheets and pulled them up over his head. Whatever was going to happen next in the cellar, he didn't want to hear it. Couldn't bear to hear it. An image of the terrified girl's eyes, pleading to him from the darkness, swam into his head.

He closed his own eyes tightly, wishing he was somewhere—anywhere—else.

At some point during the night, he fell asleep. When he awoke the next morning, he sat up in bed and it all came flooding back to him. He looked down at the floor, where he'd left the wet pyjama bottoms, but they were gone.

Getting out of bed, he listened to the sounds in the house. Someone—probably his dad—was in the kitchen. The radio was playing down there, and the smell of pancakes drifted up the stairs. Ignoring the rumbling in his tummy, Rob went to the top of the stairs and looked down at the kitchen and the cellar door.

His dad was standing at the cooker, flipping a pancake out onto a plate where at least half a dozen more were stacked.

The cellar door was locked.

Rob padded downstairs, wondering what sort of mood his dad was in.

That question was answered when his dad turned to him with a big smile, and said, "Sit yourself down, son. I've made pancakes. Your favourite."

Sitting at the table, Rob cast a glance towards the locked cellar door, and then back to his father.

"What's wrong?" His dad put a plate of pancakes in front of Rob and took the seat opposite him at the table. There were no pancakes on his own plate, just two slices of toast.

Rob shrugged. He didn't know what to say. He wanted to ask where the girl was, but he couldn't bring himself to do it, because he knew he probably wouldn't like the answer.

"You had a nightmare about the cellar last night," his dad said. "I heard you talking in your sleep, so I went into your bedroom, and you were talking about the cellar. I don't know exactly what you were dreaming about, but you were frightened." He paused while he began to butter his toast, and then added, "You even wet your bed."

Rob felt his face burning, both from embarrassment and anger. He hadn't wet the bed at all; he'd wet himself in cellar, holding a knife which his father wanted him to kill a girl with. This story about a nightmare was just that: a story.

"Anyway," his dad said, "you can forget all about it now. You don't have to think about it ever again. Aren't you going to put some maple syrup on those pancakes?"

Nodding, Rob picked up the bottle of syrup and poured a copious amount on his breakfast. If last night's events *had* been a dream, then he'd never have to wonder about the girl in the shadows. If she'd only been a dream, then he could decide, right now, that she'd escaped and gone home. It was *his* dream, after all, so he could decide what happened in it. And he decided that the girl was safe at home, and probably eating pancakes for breakfast, just like he was.

∼

Rob pulled his head back from the hot shower spray and opened his eyes. He'd been foolish, all those years ago, to tell himself the encounter with the girl in the cellar had been nothing more than a dream. Deep down, he'd known the truth, of course, even then. But it had been easier to dismiss the whole thing as a figment of his imagination than face the terrible truth.

He turned the water off and dried himself quickly before going back to the bedroom naked and picking up his phone from the bedside table. He found the number for Night Owl Security and waited while the call connected.

"Night Owl Security," said a female voice on the other end of the line.

"Oh, hi, is that Vera?" he said, putting a croak into his voice and trying to sound listless.

"Yes."

"Vera, it's Rob Gibson here. I'm afraid I've come down with something, so I'm not going to be able to work my shift tonight."

"Oh," she said. "You're at Walker and Sons Aggregates, is that right? The quarry?"

"Yeah, that's right."

"All right, I'll get someone to cover for you. Do you think you'll be back at work tomorrow?"

"I'm sure I will."

"Okay, Rob. Look after yourself. I'll put you down for tomorrow's shift, but let me know it anything changes, all right?"

"I will, Vera. Thanks." He put the phone down.

He couldn't face a night of sitting in his hut at the quarry, freezing his balls off. Not when he had more important things to do.

He usually waited for Sonia and the kids to get home from school before he left for work, but he felt a strong desire to get to the house in Miller's Dale as soon as possible. It was almost like the place was pulling him by an invisible cord, and there was nothing he could do to resist it.

Dressing quickly in the clothes he'd worn last night—his dad's clothes—and his own padded jacket, he left the house and climbed into the Land Rover.

As he drove out of Hatherfield, and headed for Miller's Dale, he caught himself grinning. The anticipation of what he was about to do excited him. Digging up bodies in a cellar might not be everyone's idea of fun, but despite the hard work, Rob enjoyed it.

It connects you with him. Your father.

"No, it doesn't," he said aloud, pushing the thought away. "I'm doing this to spite him. To destroy his legacy."

If you wanted to do that, you'd just leave the bodies where they are. No one would ever find them, and no one would ever know what he'd done. By bringing them out into the open, you're giving him a legacy.

He shook his head against his own thoughts. "He wanted them to remain buried. I'm going against him by digging them up."

That isn't why you're doing this. You want to know if she's down there.

That was true enough. He had to know if his mother was buried in the cellar. If his father had lied to him his entire life. But there was more to it than that.

"There's more to it than that," he said.

Yes, I'm sure there is. Like the fact that you like digging around in the dirt with those poor dead girls. You're just like him. And the more you do this, the more like him you become.

"Rubbish," he scoffed. "I'm nothing like him."

Probably not. He was strong. You're weak.

He gripped the wheel tightly and gritted his teeth.

He was a killer. You pissed yourself at the mere thought of it.

"Well, that isn't a bad thing. It means I'm better than him."

It means you're a disappointment to him.

He concentrated on the road, tried to ignore his thoughts. It was already beginning to get dark. He turned the headlights on and turned the radio up so loud that it hurt his ears.

When he got to Miller's Dale, he turned it down again. Thankfully, the music had kept his thoughts at bay.

But as he approached his destination, he realised he might have another problem. His headlights picked out a car parked in front of the house. A silver Lexus.

Rob parked behind it but stayed in the Land Rover, keeping the headlights trained on the other car.

The driver's door opened, and someone got out, shielding his eyes from the light. "Rob, is that you?" he said, trying to peer into the Land Rover. "I think we need to talk."

It was Eric.

CHAPTER 16

Rob felt frozen to the driver's seat. His heart hammered in his chest. What the hell was Eric doing here?

"Rob?" Eric repeated, shielding his eyes from the glare of the headlights as he approached the Land Rover. "Is that you?" He reached the side window and peered in. "Turn the engine off. I want to talk to you."

Seeing no way to avoid his uncle, Rob sighed and killed the Land Rover's engine. "What's up?" he asked, hoping to sound casual but inwardly grimacing at the frightened sound his voice made.

"I just want to talk." He moved to the front door of the house, waiting for Rob to let him in.

Did I close the cellar door when I left last night? Rob couldn't answer that question with any certainty; he'd been busy moving the wrapped-up body to the car. Had he bothered to lock the door? If he let Eric inside, and then went straight to the cellar door to lock it, he was going to arouse his uncle's suspicions. But if he didn't lock the door, the nosy bastard would be down the stairs, snooping around. There was still an open grave down there.

Reluctantly, he got out of the Land Rover, and went to the front door. He had to act normally around Eric. The old man was too nosey for his own good. The fact that he was here, at his dead brother's house—when he should have gone home after the funeral—proved that.

"Are you all right?" Eric asked, as Rob fumbled for the keys to the house.

"I'm not feeling very well. That's why I'm off work tonight." As he pushed the key into the lock, he said, "How did you know I'd be here?" He already knew the answer to that; Eric *didn't* know he'd be here. No one knew. Had he just come by on the off chance? How many other times had he driven out to the house when Rob hadn't been here? Had he looked in the windows? Tried to get inside?

"I thought you'd turn up here sooner or later," Eric said. "You're cleaning out the house, right? That must be quite a job."

"I don't mind it." Rob turned the key and stepped into the house, his gaze falling immediately on the unlocked cellar door. The padlock was sitting on the kitchen counter, next to the scrap of paper that showed the location of the graves.

He went over to them and scooped them up before pushing them into his pocket.

Eric was looking around the kitchen, wrinkling his nose. "It smells in here. Maybe you should open a window, or at least get an air freshener."

Rob hadn't noticed a smell, but he did see a scattering of soil on the floor, where he'd placed the wrapped-up body last night.

Eric noticed it, as well. He looked down and pursed his lips but didn't say anything.

"So, you said you wanted to talk to me," Rob said, trying to catch the other man's attention. "What about?"

"How about a cup of tea?" Eric said, planting himself on one of the kitchen chairs. He obviously wasn't going anywhere until Rob had heard him out.

"Fine," Rob said, going to the fridge to get the milk. He cursed himself for being weak. He should have told Eric he couldn't come in, instructed him to stay away. That's what his father would have done.

But he wasn't his father, so he put the kettle on, and got two mugs from the cupboard, throwing a teabag into each while the water warmed up.

Eric remained silent while Rob made the drinks.

Rob placed a mug of tea in front of his uncle and retreated to the counter. He couldn't sit down; he was too wound up. "All right, tell me why you're here."

"I'll get straight to the point," Eric said. "I've been

worried about you, ever since I heard that James had died."

That surprised Rob. Why should his uncle worry about him? "I don't understand."

Eric sighed. "The fact is, I think I've been a bit lax where my brother is concerned. I should have kept a close eye on him. Instead, I got as far away from him as I was able, as quickly as I could. I didn't give a second thought to the people I left behind. People like you and your mother."

"What about my mother?" Rob asked.

"I'll get to that, but I want to tell you what it was like growing up and having your dad as an older brother."

Rob rolled his eyes. Had Eric come here to recount his life story? He didn't need to hear it; he had things to do. Listening to his uncle reminisce was the last thing he needed right now.

Seemingly unaware that he was outstaying his welcome, Eric took a sip of tea. As he put the mug down on the table, he said, "I'll come right out with it, Rob. Your father was the cruellest person I ever met. I'm not just saying that because he was mean to me. Older brothers sometimes are. James thought I was mollycoddled by our mum. He called me a baby, even when I was older. But that's not what I'm talking about. James had a cruel streak that extended to just about everyone around him, especially members of the opposite sex."

"Yeah, he was a bastard," Rob said. "You're not telling me anything I don't already know."

Eric nodded. "Okay, well here's something you may not know: when James was fourteen, he did something really bad."

Rob raised an eyebrow, but he wasn't really shocked. The graves in the cellar spoke to what kind of a man James Gibson had been.

Eric drank more tea before continuing. Unlike Rob, who felt no emotion regarding this revelation about his father, Eric seemed shaken. His eyes held a glimmer of something that Rob interpreted as fear, and his hand was shaking slightly as he put the mug back down on the table.

"We lived in Matlock at the time. Our father was a pastor at one of the nearby churches. And despite James's assertion that mum mollycoddled me, she spent more time at the church, running bible study groups than she did looking after her sons. So, we were mostly left to fend for ourselves. That meant coming home from school and making our own tea before I did my homework, or watched telly, while James went out."

Eric's gaze fell to the table as he told the story, his attention obviously drawn back through the years to his childhood. Rob wondered how long this was going to go on for, and when the man in front of him was going to get to the point.

"He was always going out," Eric continued.

"Especially at night. I never did find out where he went. But the more I've thought about it over the years, the more I've come to the conclusion that he was out hunting."

"Hunting animals?" Rob asked, trying to make the question sound innocent, even though he knew exactly what Eric meant.

"No, not animals. I believe he was hunting people."

Rob tried to look shocked. He wasn't sure how long he could keep this act going.

"Our mum had a car that she never used. A little blue Mini that sat in the garage. Although he wasn't old enough to drive, James took that car when he went hunting. Our parents didn't know, and he told me that if I told them, he'd kill me. The thing is, that wasn't just some idle threat; I believed him wholeheartedly. James didn't have feelings like everyone else. He had no empathy, no sympathy. He was a psychopath."

Eric looked at Rob to see if his words were sinking in. Rob tried to look suitably shocked.

"You know what he was like," Eric said.

"Yes, I do." Rob remembered standing in the cellar, knife in hand, wetting himself while his dad laughed.

"There was a particular Friday night when I was twelve and James was fourteen. It was Winter, and it got dark early. I was walking out through the school gates with a couple of my friends and James came over to me. He told me not to come home for a while, that he was going to be busy doing something and he didn't want me in his way. I told him I had to go home to get my tea because Mum and Dad were at the church that evening. James gave me a couple of quid and told me to go to the chippy."

He took another sip of tea. His hand was shaking so much that the mug chattered off his teeth. Rob knew that living with James Gibson was an unpleasant experience, and one that he and Eric shared, but his uncle seemed to be the most affected by it.

"I wasn't going to say no to free chips, so I agreed to stay away from the house for an hour. My friends went home, and I sauntered to the chippy and then stood outside eating my chips. While I was there, I saw James walking along the street with a girl named Sarah Rundle. I think she was in one of his classes, or something, and I remember thinking, "Ah, now I know why he wants the house to himself." I had no idea why a girl like Sarah Rundle would be interested in my brother, but I didn't really question it too deeply.

"After I finished my chips, I ambled along the river for a while, and then it got so cold that I decided to go home."

His gaze returned to the scarred surface of the table. "When I got there, the house was empty. At first, I thought James and Sarah were in the house, in the dark, but I checked every room, and soon realised I was alone. I inwardly cursed James for making me stay out in the cold when he wasn't even here. The house was freezing, so I put the heating on and went up to my room to do my homework.

"About an hour later, I heard someone come through the front door. Knowing it would be James, I didn't bother leaving my room. I didn't particularly want to see him, and I was afraid that if his time with Sarah hadn't gone to the way he wanted, he'd take it out on me, and demand the money back that he'd given me for chips."

I heard him moving around in the kitchen for a while, and then he came upstairs. His bedroom was just across from mine, and I caught a glimpse of him as he walked past my door. He looked exhausted and sweaty. His clothes were covered in dirt. No sooner had I seen him, than he disappeared into his room and closed the door."

Eric paused, and looked up at Rob, as if expecting some sort or reaction. Rob didn't know exactly what reaction his uncle was looking for, so he just shrugged. "I don't really get your point."

"I didn't understand, either, at the time. And I wasn't about to question James. I stayed in my room, and about an hour later, I heard him go back downstairs. Then I heard the washing machine start up, and the sound of the hoover."

Again, he looked at Rob, and again, Rob simply shrugged.

"He was cleaning up the dirt," Eric said. "Washing his clothes. He never did that. As far as I knew, he didn't even know how to work the washing machine. I found his behaviour odd, to say the least, but I just put it down to the fact that James was odd, anyway. Things didn't take a sinister turn until Monday."

Rob knew what his uncle was going to say, but he waited patiently.

"When we got to school, we found out that Sarah Rundle was missing. She hadn't been seen since Friday."

"Okay," Rob said flatly. Did Eric suspect his brother was a murderer? That he'd killed and buried Sarah Rundle? If so, why hadn't he gone to the police, or at least told his parents? Mind you, he himself hadn't gone to the police when he'd found the bodies in the cellar.

"At first, I didn't suspect James," Eric said. "Despite the circumstantial evidence I'd seen with my own eyes—James walking to our house with Sarah, the dirty clothes, and the impromptu clean-up operation—I couldn't get my head around the fact that he might have done something so terrible. I mean, I knew he was a bad person, but to kill someone? No, I didn't believe it."

He finished the tea and placed the mug back on

the table with an air of finality. "Two weeks later, I discovered something that changed my mind. I was home alone again, watching telly in the living room. Mum and Dad were at church—no surprise there—and James had gone out in the Mini, which he seemed to do even more frequently now. I was getting bored with the telly, so I decided to go to my room and find a book to read. I read a lot of science fiction, even though Mum and Dad only allowed us to read Christian books. Every week, I'd go to the library on my own, and check out a sci fi novel. I kept them hidden under my pillow, and only read them when my parents weren't there, or at night when I was supposed to be sleeping."

Rob sighed. He was getting impatient. He had absolutely no interest in Eric's reading habits.

"I went upstairs, but as I got to my bedroom door, I looked across at James's room. The door was ajar, and I decided on a whim to have a look inside. That isn't actually true; it wasn't on a whim. I felt that I *had* to look inside. Because no matter how much I told myself that James had nothing to do with Sarah's disappearance, a little voice inside my head kept asking *what if*. What if he *had* done something terrible? Shouldn't I try to find out the truth?"

He paused, as if expecting Rob to answer the question, even though it had sounded rhetorical when he'd asked it.

"Of course," Rob said, hoping Eric would leave

soon. His eyes flicked to the cellar door. He longed to be down there, in the dim light, nostrils full of the smell of earth as he uncovered another buried girl.

"So, I went into his room. I don't know what I was looking for, exactly. I just thought that if I looked hard enough, I'd discover something that would prove James killed Sarah. Or perhaps I was hoping I wouldn't find anything, and that would quiet the voice in my head."

"And did you?" Rob asked, hoping to spare himself a retelling of Eric's search of the bedroom. Couldn't he just get to the point? "Find anything, I mean? Was there anything there?" He already knew by his uncle's shaken demeanour that the room had held some clue, something that pointed to James as the girl's killer.

"Yes. Underneath a chest of drawers, I found a blue headband. The police report had said that Sarah had been wearing it the day she disappeared. As I held it in my hands, I could see a single dark stain on the material. It was probably blood."

"What did you do?"

Eric sighed, a sound that seemed to be laced with years of regret. "I put it back. I didn't tell Mum or Dad. I didn't tell the police. I kept it secret."

"Why?" Rob asked. He realised that he should already know the answer to that question. After all, he'd found the girls in the cellar and kept that secret. But the fact that his reaction to discovering that his father was a murderer had been the same as Eric's, didn't mean he understood it.

"I was scared," Eric said.

As soon as he heard that, Rob knew that his reasons for keeping James Gibson's misdeeds a secret were different to his uncle's. He wasn't scared. He had nothing to fear; his father was dead.

"What if no one believed me?" Eric went on. "I thought that James would, quite literally, kill me. That I'd end up buried next to Sarah Rundle."

Rob nodded. "So, you never said anything to anyone?"

Eric shook his head. "Never. A couple of weeks later, Sarah's coat was discovered on the riverbank, and I think that made the police assume that she'd drowned."

"You mentioned my mother. What were you going to say about her?"

"Only that when I heard she'd left, I wondered if that was just a story James had concocted to cover what had really happened."

"You think the same thing happened to her as happened to Sarah Rundle?"

Eric grimaced, then shrugged. "I'm sorry, Rob, I just don't know. But you can see why I'd have my suspicions."

"Because you found a hairband in your brother's room decades ago?" Rob tried to make Eric's conclusions sound ridiculous, even though he shared them.

He also thought his father had killed his mother and invented the story about her running away, but he couldn't have Eric thinking that. He might go to the police. What if they decided to investigate and came to the house with a search warrant? He wasn't sure what laws he'd broken by digging up the girls and taking them to Temple Well, but he'd definitely broken some. Probably very serious ones that would involve jail time.

"Yes, I suppose it does sound silly when you put it like that," Eric said.

Rob nodded, hoping to bring the conversation to an end. "Besides, it's all water under the bridge, now."

"It it?" Eric asked. "What about those bodies on the News?"

Rob put a confused frown on his face, pretending not to know what his uncle was talking about. He had to play this carefully; feigning total ignorance of the recent events would make Eric even more suspicious. "I'm pretty sure my dad hasn't got anything to do with that; he's dead and gone."

"Yes, but those girls were killed years ago, when he was still alive. And they're from this area. What do you think of that?"

"I don't make anything of it. What do you mean?" He wasn't sure if he was being tested; if Eric already suspected him and was watching his reactions. He tried to keep his face as neutral as possible.

Eric looked at him closely for a few seconds before throwing up his hands in an exaggerated shrug. "I don't know. Maybe I'm just seeing connections where there aren't any."

"Connections? Like what?"

"Well, what if James *did* kill Sarah Rundle?"

"That's a big *if*," Rob reminded him.

"Yes, it is, but hear me out. If he killed her when he was just fourteen years old, isn't it plausible that he killed others, as well? Later in his life? I've watched enough documentaries about serial killers to know that many of them commit murder for years, and no one around them even has an inkling. Look at BTK, or the Golden State Killer."

"Wait a minute," Rob said, trying to get his uncle off this train of thought. "My dad wasn't Ted Bundy."

"See, that's what I mean. For years, no one suspected Bundy. He had a wife and a daughter. They had no idea he was a serial killer."

"This is all getting a bit weird," Rob said. "You're basing all of this on a headband you found in your brother's room years ago. It's pure speculation and, to be honest, it doesn't sound very plausible." Even as he said those words, Rob was actually impressed at how close to the truth Eric was.

"I know, and after James's death, I might have decided it was all water under the bridge, like you said. But then those two bodies turned up."

"I don't think Dad managed to dig two dead girls

out of their graves when he's in a grave himself," Rob said.

"No, he didn't. But someone did. And these bodies appeared right after James died. Don't you find the timing coincidental?"

"It's only coincidental if you believe your unfounded theory that he was some sort of serial killer. Otherwise, there's no connection between Dad's death and those bodies turning up at all."

Eric nodded slowly, but he didn't look convinced.

"Anyway," Rob went on, "who would know where the bodies were in the first place? Are you saying Dad had an accomplice?"

"No, I'm not saying that."

"So your theory doesn't really make any sense at all. If Dad killed and buried those two girls, why have their bodies only been discovered now, after all this time? Maybe a jogger or a dog walker came across them—they're always finding bodies, aren't they?—but why wouldn't they just contact the police?"

"I don't know," Eric admitted. "It's all very confusing."

"Too confusing for people like us to figure out," Rob told him. "We should just let the police do their job. It's nothing to do with us, and it's nothing to do with Dad, either." He looked at his uncle closely. The older man was nodding, his lips tight. Doubt was creeping in. Whatever notions he'd had about his brother for all these years, they were beginning to crumble, Rob was sure of it.

"Perhaps you're right," Eric said. "It doesn't really make much sense." He let out a long breath. "It's a relief, actually. I've been carrying this around for a long time."

"Well, you can return home with a burden lifted," Rob said. "Where is it you live, now?"

"Exeter, in Devon."

"Devon. Nice. Is that close to the sea?" Rob knew it was, he was just changing the subject, getting Eric off track now that he'd sown the seeds of disbelief.

"Yes, not too far. Cathy wishes we were closer, but we're only a fifteen-minute drive from the beach."

"Aunt Cathy. How is she? I didn't see her at the funeral."

"No, she didn't come."

"Well, if Sonia and I are in that neck of the woods, we'll be sure to look you up," Rob said, walking to the front with what he hoped was an air of finality that Eric would pick up on, and leave.

"Yes, do that," his uncle said, finally getting up from the table. "We'd love to see you."

"I expect you want to get on the road quite soon," Rob urged. "You've got a long drive ahead of you."

"Oh, I'm not going home yet. I'm staying at the hotel tonight. I'll probably set off sometime tomorrow."

Rob forced a smile onto his face as he opened

the door. He'd rather Eric would piss off back to Devon straight away; if he stayed around here much longer, he might get more ideas regarding his brother and the bodies that kept turning up. As it was, Rob had already decided he couldn't dig up another one tonight; if Eric woke up tomorrow and put on the News to see that yet another decades-old murder victim had been uncovered, he might decide to stick around and poke his nose in where it didn't belong.

"Well, it was good to see you again, Rob." He was out of the door now, walking towards the silver Lexus. "Give my best to Sonia and the kids."

"I will. See ya." Rob waved and closed the door. He went into the kitchen and watched as the Lexus's headlights came on, and the car turned around before heading down the road and eventually disappearing from sight.

Rob let out a breath of relief. He'd begun to wonder if his uncle was ever going to leave.

The sense of disappointment he felt at not being able to reveal another body tonight was profound. He cheered himself up by telling himself that even though it was wise to wait until Eric had gone back to Devon before giving the police another body, he could still dig one up. He could wrap it up and leave it in the cellar until he was ready to deposit it somewhere else.

When he'd started digging up the cellar a couple

of days ago, he'd found the task grisly, but now he was looking forward to getting his hands dirty.

Taking the padlock out of his pocket and replacing it on the counter, he opened the scrap of paper and examined the location of the Xs his father had drawn. There was one in the shadowy corner where he'd seen the frightened girl when he was young. He'd balked at the instruction to stab her, but he had no doubt that after he'd fled the cellar, the girl had met her fate at the hands of his father.

Was that where she was buried? In the same shadowy corner where she'd cowered?

He opened the cellar door and clicked the light switch on his way down the stairs. When he stood on the dirt floor, he felt a kind of satisfaction that he'd never experienced before. In the outside world, he was just an average person, or, if he was being honest with himself, a nobody. Down here, he was the ruler of a kingdom of the dead.

The thought surprised him, even as it entered into his head. He was beginning to think like his father. Surely that was why the old man buried the girls down here; to reign over them, keep them beneath his feet.

He instantly regretted giving the two of them away. What had he been thinking? He was an idiot to give away something so valuable. At the time he'd thought he was spiting his father, but now he felt he understood why the old man had buried the girls down here in the first place.

Crouching down, he ran his fingertips over the dirt, imagining what lay beneath. A secret collection like no other. And, now that his father was gone, he —Rob Gibson—owned this treasure. It was his. The girls beneath the cellar floor belonged to him, and to him only. Nothing could take that away from him.

Unless Eric goes to the police.

The voice startled him because, even though it was inside his head, it was his father's voice.

"He won't go to the police," he said aloud. "I convinced him it was all in his head. Nothing more than a fanciful notion."

Do you think that's how he'll see it in the cold light of dawn? You may have convinced him for now, but he's been harbouring these thoughts for years.

"What can I do?"

You know what to do. You've already seen what's on the shelf over there. You shied away from it when you saw it, but now you need to pick it up.

His eyes went to a crude wooden shelf on the wall. Sitting on the shelf were the usual items one might keep in the cellar: tins of paint, spare light bulbs, a metal toolbox.

But there was something else on there, as well. Something he'd seen the first time he'd entered the cellar and had avoided looking at since.

Take it.

He slowly walked over to the shelf and reached out for the item. Picking it up, he held it in his open palm, inspecting it in the dim light.

A knife with the initials *JAG* carved into its rough, wooden handle.

CHAPTER 17

"Her name is Joanna Delia Kirk," Battle said, standing at the front of the room. An old photo of a smiling, dark-haired girl was projected onto a screen behind him. "She went missing twenty years ago from Tideswell, which is a village north of here."

The *Emerald Room* of the Rutland Arms Hotel in Bakewell was crowded with twenty or so uniformed police officers, a dozen plainclothes detectives, and at least a dozen support staff. Sitting at the back, Tony surreptitiously slid his phone from his trouser pocket and typed *Tideswell* into the search bar. When the results appeared, he clicked on a map that showed the location of the village and the surrounding area.

It wasn't too far from Miller's Dale, where he and Dani had spoken to June Harwood about her daughter.

He scanned the room for his partner and saw her sitting a few rows in front of him, among a group of uniforms. He'd missed her at breakfast this morning, and had eaten his full English in relative silence, with only the morning paper for company. Joanna Kirk's name hadn't been mentioned, so he assumed that this briefing, which he'd been texted the details of just as he'd finished breakfast, was the first time it was being revealed.

"Her parents have been informed," Battle said from the front of the room. "Joanna was fifteen when she disappeared. She took her dog for a walk in the woods on a pleasant summer's evening, and never returned. There were no clues, no leads, no witnesses. And no body, until we recovered it from the spring at Temple Well yesterday. Tests are being carried out, of course, but the body has been buried for two decades, so we need to manage our expectations regarding good forensic evidence."

The DCI nodded to Chris Toombs, who was operating the laptop and projector. Toombs pressed the keyboard and the picture of Joanna Kirk moved to the left of the screen while a photo of Daisy Riddle appeared on the right.

"We need to know how these two girls are linked," Battle said. "Because something brought them both into contact with the same killer, five years apart. From the details on the files that were compiled at the time, there doesn't seem to be any connection. They went to different schools. Castleton and Tideswell are only eight miles apart, but each is a separate community, and we have no evidence of these girls being involved in shared activities or visiting the same locations. That doesn't mean it didn't happen, of course, so we need to revisit that line of enquiry. Where did they become noticed by our killer?"

"Perhaps it was random, sir," a uniformed officer on the front row said. "He just happened to be in the woods where Joanna Kirk was walking her dog and grabbed her."

Battle nodded. "It's possible. But it's going to make our investigation a lot harder if he was working opportunistically. I want to examine every angle on this, and the chance of some sort of connection between the girls, however tenuous, could lead us to our killer."

"What about Mary Harwood?" Tony asked, raising his voice so he could be heard at the front of the room. "A connection might be easier to find if we look at all three girls."

"Mary Harwood?" Battle asked.

"She went missing twenty-two years ago at Miller's Dale. She—"

"Yes, I know who she is. I'm just not sure why you're connecting her to this case."

"Colleen Francis, Mary's younger sister, contacted us yesterday. She thought the body at the well could be Mary's."

Battle nodded. "Yes, I know. I was the one who

sent you to interview her. But now we know the body isn't Mary's; it's Joanna Kirk's."

"Still, the person who took Mary could be the same—"

"We don't have any evidence linking Mary Harwood to this case."

"Not concrete evidence, no, but there's a good chance that the person who abducted Joanna is the same man who took Mary two years earlier."

"A good chance?" Battle asked.

"Well, unless Derbyshire was riddled with serial killers who abducted similar looking girls in the same time period, yes. A very good chance."

"Until some evidence comes to light that links Mary Harwood to this case, we can't assume she was taken by the same man. Our resources are stretched as it is. We can't investigate a third girl on a whim."

"It isn't a whim," Tony whispered to himself, frustratedly.

"What was that?" Battle asked.

"I was just going to say that there's a witness to Mary's abduction, which is more than we've got where Joanna and Daisy are concerned."

"That witness is Mary's younger sister," Battle said. "She was quite young at the time of Mary's disappearance, and the police didn't think she was credible. Even her own mother doubted the veracity of her statement."

"Mrs Harwood doesn't want to believe her

daughter was abducted. She'd rather tell herself Mary drowned, even if she knows deep down that it isn't true."

Battle sighed frustratedly. "We'll investigate Mary Harwood's disappearance if evidence comes to light that points us in that direction."

"You mean if her body turns up in a public place."

"There could be any number of things that lead us to have another look at Mary's case, but they have to be tangible and evidential. A lot of girls have gone missing from this area over the years; we can't investigate all of them just because they might be connected to Daisy and Joanna."

"But how will we get any evidence if we don't at least look—"

"We're here to find Daisy's killer," Battle said, pointing at the faces on the screen. "And Joanna's. We have their remains, which were disinterred by the same person. That means there's more than a 'good chance' that they were killed by the same person; it's almost a certainty. This is where we focus our attention; on what's in front of us."

There was a lot more Tony wanted to say, but he could see there was no point. Battle was obviously so eager to close the Daisy Riddle case—a case he'd failed to close years before—that he was blinkered to the possibility that finding the killer might mean looking elsewhere. Somewhere where there was a witness and more clues.

The best way to catch a serial killer was to investigate their first kill. That was the crime where they might have made a rookie mistake. The victim was usually someone known to them. Mary Harwood had been abducted before Joanna or Daisy; she might very well be this killer's first victim.

But Tony said none of this. As the DCI moved on and began to give various units their tasks for the day, Tony looked down at his phone and brought up the pictures of the Polaroids in Mary's room. The woman sitting by the river, and in the field, dressed in a floral summer dress, intrigued him. Who was she, and why did Mary have these photos of her?

June hadn't recognised the woman, but Colleen might know who she was. He had to ask her. He'd have to do it on his own time, of course, because Battle had closed off that avenue, as far as official lines of enquiry went.

As he put the phone back into his pocket, he told himself that he was going to *unofficially* investigate Mary Harwood's disappearance. It wasn't like he had anything else to do with his free time while he was in Derbyshire. Might as well make himself useful.

When the briefing was over and everyone began filing out through the door, Dani pushed her way through the crowd towards him.

"What was that all about?" she asked when she reached him.

At first, he didn't know what she was referring to, then he realised she was talking about his brief quarrel with Battle. "Oh, nothing. Unfortunately, the DCI is so focused on solving a case he failed to solve fifteen years ago that he's not thinking straight."

"That's your professional opinion, is it?"

"Yes, certainly."

"You have to admit that there's nothing to connect Mary with the two bodies we've just found."

"There is one thing," he said, as they moved towards the door with the others.

"What's that?"

"Common sense."

She rolled her eyes.

"What? You don't think I'm right? There's every chance that the man in the black Land Rover, the one Mary drove away with, is the same man who killed Daisy and Joanna."

"And what about all the other girls who went missing from this area in the past twenty years? Are they *all* connected?"

"Well, no, I'm not saying that."

"Good, because I did some reading last night and it seems there was a spate of abductions in the Dark Peak area spanning even longer than two decades. After the case was solved, the papers called the victims the Wildflower Girls. Battle was in charge of that case, and the perpetrator was caught, so the DCI is acutely aware that not every missing persons case is related. He's being cautious."

Tony nodded. "And that's fine, as long as his caution doesn't make us overlook something vital."

"I'm sure it won't."

They were out of the door now, walking along the corridor to the exit.

"Look," Tony said, "Colleen's house is just down the road. What do you say to us taking a stroll down there and seeing if she knows who the woman on the Polaroids is?"

"I say that's going against the guvnor's orders."

Sighing, Tony said, "Fine. I'll do it on my own time."

They exited the Rutland Hotel and stood on the pavement. "So, you're going to chase this down on your own?" Dani asked.

"What choice do I have? Battle won't see sense, but I know there's something important here." He took out his phone and showed her the picture of the woman sitting on the riverbank. "Who is she, Dani?"

"I don't know."

"But don't you want to? Aren't you curious?"

"Of course I am."

He gestured down the road, towards the outskirts of Bakewell. "Colleen's house is less than five minutes' walk that way. If anyone knows who this woman is, it'll be her."

The DI put her hands on the hips and stared in the direction Tony had indicated.

"What would we be doing otherwise?" Tony asked, sensing her resolve wavering. "Getting a bird's eye view? Reading case files that have no clues or witnesses in them? At least if we find out who this is, that's something concrete we can work with."

She came to a decision and nodded. "All right, we ask Colleen if she recognises the woman, and if she does, we'll make some brief enquiries. If she doesn't that's the end of it. Okay?"

"Of course."

They set off down the road, walking past a long line of cars bringing tourists into the small town. On the other side of the busy road, there was a park where parents—wrapped up against the cold weather in thick coats—watched their children as they swung on the swings and clambered over a climbing frame.

Beyond the park, Tony could see a river with ducks and swans being fed by yet more tightly swaddled adults and children.

"It's lovely here," Dani said.

"Yes, very picturesque." Tony put his hands in his pockets. He'd left his gloves in the car, and the air was definitely nippy.

"Something important happened today," he told Dani. "Regarding the case, I mean."

She looked at him quizzically. "Oh? What's that?"

"No one has found a body. He didn't leave one for us."

She thought about that for a moment as they strolled along the pavement, then said, "Maybe he hasn't got any more. Joanna and Daisy could be his only victims."

"No chance," Tony scoffed. "This has been going on for decades. There are plenty more where they came from."

"Well, maybe he's having a day off. The police presence might have scared him. Too risky to be carting his victim's bodies around when there are police everywhere."

"No, he's not scared. Careful, perhaps, but not scared. And besides, they're not *his* victims. I told you, it's not the killer doing this. It's someone else."

"So you keep saying." Her tone let him know she didn't believe him.

"I keep saying it because it's the only logical explanation for what's happening."

"Someone else digging up the killer's victims doesn't make much sense to me. If someone found the buried girls, they'd tell the police, not dig them up themselves and leave them in a ruined temple and by an old well."

"We can't base our suppositions on what you or I would do in such a situation. I told you, this person has a complex relationship with the killer."

"An accomplice."

"No, I don't believe they were involved with the actual killings at all."

"Then it makes even less sense."

The pavement on this side of the road ended, and they continued on the grass verge. Tony glanced across the road while he gathered his thoughts. The park was behind them now, and the opposite side of the road was lined with detached houses set back from the pavement. In front of one of them, Tony saw a man in dark blue overalls working on a Marlin kit car that was parked on the gravelled area in front of his garage.

"The person who's doing this is someone closely related to the killer," he told Dani as he looked back at her. "For example, imagine a woman discovers that her husband has been killing girls for years, and burying them in the back garden. What does she do?"

"She calls the police."

"Yes, if she's thinking rationally. But what if she's not thinking rationally? What if she has mental issues of her own? What if her relationship with her husband is more complex than that? What if there's another factor involved?"

"I'm not sure I follow you. What other factor?"

"In the scenario I just described, a woman finding her husband's victims wouldn't be able to just disinter them and leave them in public places."

"No, she wouldn't," Dani agreed. "As soon as it hit

the News, her husband would know what she'd done."

"Exactly."

She looked at him and frowned. "Still not following."

"Now, imagine the same scenario, but this time, the husband is dead."

"In that case, she could dig up the bodies without the fear of him finding out."

"Yes, she could. And now, the question of whether or not to call the police isn't so simple. She'd be besmirching her dead husband's name. The police might think she was involved somehow. And not calling the police doesn't have the same consequences it would have if the husband was alive; he can't kill again due to her not reporting him."

Dani frowned. "Is this like one of those moral problems where a train is heading towards a group of people, and you can divert it, but if you do, it kills a man on the other line?"

"I'm just trying to point out that it isn't all black and white."

"So, the wife could just leave the bodies where they are, and not tell anyone. That solves the problems of her dead husband's reputation, and the police thinking she's involved."

"Yes, it does," Tony said, nodding. "But it doesn't solve the problem of how she reconciles the discovery of the bodies with her memories of her dead husband."

"Her memories would be tainted, obviously."

"If they were good memories. But what if she hated her husband even before she discovered the bodies? What if he was abusive? Controlling? His death might have been the best thing that ever happened to her."

"So, she puts the murders down to yet another bad thing he did when he was alive and tries to come to terms with the fact that she knows where the missing girls are but can't tell anybody. It isn't what I'd do, but I can see why someone else might do that. But if she hated him so much, revealing who he really was by calling the police could give her some kind of satisfaction. A type of revenge."

"Except that the police might question her involvement. Are they going to believe that he was doing this for years and she never knew about it? That she never knew about all those dead bodies in her garden? In her mind, getting the police involved could be a huge risk. She'd be gambling a lot for that revenge."

"So, she covers the bodies over, and never tells anyone," Dani said. "Or she could leave a letter to be sent to the police after her own death, explaining everything. That way, she wouldn't put herself at risk."

"But she also wouldn't get that sweet revenge while she's alive."

Dani shrugged. "I suppose not."

"So, she digs up the bodies and gives them to the police while keeping her own identity secret," Tony said. "She gets revenge on the dead husband by revealing his crimes, something he wanted to keep hidden all his life. She also keeps herself out of the spotlight by doing the grisly work at night. By the time the bodies are discovered, she's far away."

Dani thought about it for a while, and then said, "You think the killer is dead, and it's his wife who's leaving the bodies for us?"

"It doesn't have to be his wife. It could be someone else who was close to the killer or had a reason to want to bring these crimes to light. But I do think the killer is dead, yes. Otherwise, the person revealing the bodies would be putting themselves into too much danger. The killer would find out and would do something about it."

"I don't know," The DI said. "You're making a lot of suppositions."

"They're suppositions based on facts. I've tried to work out the psychological state of the person leaving the bodies based on his—or her— actions. This person is probably suffering from a psychotic breakdown. That might have been triggered by the death of the killer—someone they probably have unresolved issues with—or something else. Digging up and transporting corpses is not normal behaviour."

"That's something we both agree on," Dani said.

They reached a street named Burton Close Drive, which led to the right. Tony pointed along it. "This is the way. This road leads to Wyedale Crescent."

They left the main road behind and walked along the quiet street. "If we don't find this person soon," Tony said, "their psychosis will deepen, and they may become a threat to others. They won't be able to separate fantasy from reality. They may hear voices, experience hallucinations. That, combined with the fact that the killer of these girls is probably consuming their thoughts, will most likely cause a descent into violence."

"So, the next body we find could have been killed by them, and not the original killer?"

Tony shrugged. He'd been formulating his theories regarding this unknown person for a while, but he didn't know anything for sure. People were too unpredictable. "It's a possibility. Everyone close to this person is in danger."

They turned left down Wydale Crescent and found Collen's house. Tony knocked on the door.

Colleen answered. When she saw Tony and Dani, her face fell. "Oh my God, you've found her, haven't you?"

"No, we haven't," Tony said. "May we come inside for a moment?"

She stepped aside and let them in. Lucas was in the living room, playing with Lego on the floor while a blue creature on the TV was singing about his name being "Iggle Piggle."

"Take a seat," Colleen said, following them into the room. "Can I get you anything? Tea? Coffee?"

"I'm fine, thanks," Tony said, taking a seat on the sofa. Dani also declined and sat next to him.

Colleen perched on the edge of the armchair. She looked tired. "I've been checking the News on my phone every five minutes. I thought they'd find another girl today. This time, it might be Mary."

"No new bodies have been discovered today," Tony said. "I would like to ask you something, though, and it does involve your sister." He took out his phone and found the picture of the woman sitting by the river. Passing the phone to Colleen, he asked, "Do you know who this is?"

She looked at the screen and frowned. "No. Should I? Who is she?"

"We don't' know. We found that photograph in Mary's wardrobe," he told her. "In a shoebox, along with some others. If you scroll, you'll see them."

Colleen touched the screen. "I recognise this area," she said, holding up the landscape shots. "This is a couple of miles from our house. But I don't recognise the woman." She scrolled back to the image of the woman by the river and frowned at it. "There's something about this photo, though. Something seems familiar."

"Could you have met the woman, and not remember?" Tony asked. "You were quite young at the time."

"No, it isn't that. It's...something else." She looked at the picture for a couple of seconds before shaking her head and giving the phone back to Tony. "No, I don't know. Sorry."

"It's fine," he said, feeling his optimism slipping away. "Totally understandable."

"Sorry I can't remember. I wish I could be more help."

"Don't worry about it," he said, getting up. He was just going to have to find out who the unknown woman was by other means, although how he was going to do that with Battle on his case, he had no idea.

"Thanks, Colleen," Dani said, also getting up. "We'll let you know if we find any more information about your sister."

"Wait!" Colleen said. "I know what it is. It's the dress! Let me see the picture again."

Tony gave her the phone. She looked at it and nodded enthusiastically. "Yes, it's the dress. Mary made that dress. She was a tomboy, but she was interested in fashion, and dressmaking. She had a dressmaker's mannequin, and I remember her making that summer dress on it."

Tony felt his optimism returning. He'd seen the mannequin in Mary's room, and this piece of information, scant as it was, might lead them to the unknown woman in the photograph.

"So, she made the dress for this woman?" he asked.

Colleen closed her eyes and put her fist against her forehead, trying to remember. "She was making the dress for a competition. I remember that. I teased her that she was making a summer dress in wintertime, and there was no way she was going to win, doing that. She had a Saturday job at a shop that sold custom dresses. The owner taught Mary sewing and stuff, and I'm sure it was her who got Mary to enter the competition."

"This shop," Dani said. "Do you know where it is?"

"It's at Ashford-in-the Water. It's called *Peak Dresses*. My dad used to drop Mary off and pick her up, and sometimes, I went in the car with him."

"Did you ever see the owner of the shop? Is she the woman in the photograph?"

Colleen shook her head. "Mrs MacDonald was a lot older than that. Well, she seemed older when I was just a kid, but I suppose she was probably in her thirties, then."

"Thanks, Colleen, you've been a great help," Tony said. "I'll keep in touch." He opened the front door and went out into the cold, followed by Dani.

As they walked back along the main road towards the Rutland Arms Hotel where their cars were parked, Tony said, "Fancy a quick trip to Ashford-in-the-Water?"

"You're convinced the woman in that photograph has something to do with Marys' disappearance, aren't you?"

"Here's what we know, Dani. Mary got into a Land Rover with someone she said she knew, but who her sister—with whom she was close—didn't recognise. The photos of the woman in the dress were hidden in Mary's wardrobe. That speaks to a secret life. This woman..." He held up his phone "...was part of that secret life. So was the man in the Land Rover. That means they could be connected to each other. If we find the woman in the photos, she could lead us to the man in the Land Rover."

"It's a long shot."

"Yes, I know that. But I don't see any harm in taking a short drive to Ashford, do you?"

She thought about it for a second, and then said, "I suppose not."

"Good." Despite the bitter cold chilling him through his coat, he smiled to himself. They were getting closer. He could feel it in his bones.

CHAPTER 18

Tony followed Dani's Land Rover into the car park of the *Bull's Head* pub at Ashford-in-the-Water, which had turned out to be only a five-minute drive from Bakewell. As he climbed out of his Mini, his senses were assailed by the smell of food drifting from the establishment.

Despite having had a full English earlier, he felt a sudden craving for a burger and chips and considered sounding out the DI's opinion on grabbing an early lunch after they'd spoken to Mrs MacDonald at the dress shop.

"That's the shop, over there," Dani said, pointing at a quaint stone building with a bay window displaying wedding dresses on stone grey plastic mannequins that would never walk down the aisle. A sign above the door read *Peak Dresses,* in flowery green script over a white background.

They crossed the road and went into the shop. As

they pushed the door open, a bell tinkled cheerily overhead.

Peak Dresses could not be described as spacious, by any means. The small room was crammed with dresses—mostly white and cream-coloured bridal gowns—on racks that occupied every available inch of space.

Two small speakers attached on the walls near the low ceiling piped out some sort of instrumental love ballad that was probably supposed to sound like it was being played on pan pipes and a nylon-strung guitar, but which Tony guessed was all computerised and played on a keyboard.

A cloying, floral scent hung in the air, making the psychologist long for the smell of food coming from the *Bull's Head*.

Behind a glass counter which held a display of tiaras, a young woman with long blonde hair looked up at them and smiled. There was no way this was the Mrs MacDonald Colleen had referred to. This woman couldn't have been in her thirties twenty-two years ago; she probably hadn't even been born then.

"Hello, can I help?" she asked.

"We're looking for Mrs MacDonald," Dani said.

"Well, I'm *Miss* MacDonald. What can I do for you?"

"We're looking for an older woman," Tony said.

Dani shot him a glare, but he had no idea why.

The young woman frowned but recovered her

composure instantly. "Oh, you must mean my mum." Turning to an open doorway behind her, she said, "Mum, there's someone here to see you." Turning back to Dani and Tony, she smiled again, and said, "She'll be out in a minute. Feel free to browse the dresses while you wait. Is there something particular you had in mind?"

"Umm, we're here on business, actually," Dani said. "Police business." She showed the young woman her warrant card.

This time, the woman's face dropped, and the smile didn't return. "Oh, I see. Mum, the police are here."

"All right, all right," said a dark-haired matronly woman as she stepped through the doorway. She was a heavy-set woman, dressed in a knitted cardigan over a white blouse and dark skirt. Her features took on the smile that her daughter was missing as she turned to Dani and Tony. "I'm Moira MacDonald, the owner. How can I help you?"

"DI Danica Summers and Doctor Tony Sheridan from Murder Force," Dani said, showing her warrant card again. "We'd like to ask you some questions, if we may."

Mrs MacDonald's face became quizzical. "What is it regarding?"

"We'd like to ask you about Mary Harwood. I believe she used to work here."

The shop owner's eyes widened in surprise. "Now

there's a name I haven't heard in a long while. Yes, she worked here. You'd better come into the back. Shona, let them through." She disappeared back through the doorway.

Shona pulled up part of the counter, allowing Dani and Tony access to the rear part of the building. "Just through there," she said, nodding at the doorway.

Tony followed Dani into the back room, which was almost as cramped as the shop itself. Most of the space was taken up by an old, scarred wooden table, upon which sat a laptop, printer, and piles of papers that were seemingly arranged into some sort of order that Tony would best be described as "organised chaos."

There were more dresses in here, hanging from metal rails that were fixed to the walls. A small kitchenette area sat on the far side of the room, with a kettle, a large box of tea bags, a small jar of coffee, and a selection of mugs. Behind the mugs sat a biscuit tin.

Two large filing cabinets dominated one wall, and Tony got the impression that despite the laptop on the table, most of *Peak Dress*'s records were stored the good old-fashioned way.

An archway revealed a set of stairs that led to the rest of the building, which Tony assumed was where the shop owner lived.

"Most of our business is online these days," Mrs

MacDonald explained. "I'm just sorting through the orders and invoices. Now, you said you wanted to ask me about Mary Harwood. She used to work here, but it was a long time ago. And, as I'm sure you're aware, the poor dear drowned when she was just a child. A terrible tragedy."

"Yes, it was," Dani agreed.

"Please, take a seat." The shop owner cleared some papers away so Dani and Tony could sit at the table.

"We understand you were teaching Mary how to sew," Tony said as he sat down.

Mrs MacDonald smiled. "Yes, that's right. She was a quick learner, and she had a real eye for design. If it wasn't for the fact that she was taken from us at such a young age, I'm sure she'd have grown up to be a designer."

"She entered a competition, didn't she?" Tony asked.

"She did indeed. One of the magazines ran a competition for young dress designers and Mary was keen to have a go. I think she designed a summer dress."

Tony took out his phone and flicked to the photo of the woman by the river. "Mrs MacDonald, do you recognise this photo?"

She looked at it for a moment and her brows met as she seemed to be trying to remember something. "Yes, that's the dress Mary designed. The competition rules said that the entries had to include photographs of a model wearing the dress, so I let Mary use my Polaroid camera. Just a minute." She got up from the table and went through the archway.

The stairs creaked as she went up them to the residential part of the house.

"What's she doing?" Dani whispered to Tony.

He shrugged. "Maybe she's making a run for it."

The DI shook her head and smiled.

Five minutes later, the creaking on the stairs resumed and Mrs MacDonald appeared through the archway. "This is what I was looking for. I knew it was here somewhere. I never throw anything away, you know."

She placed a manilla envelope on the table. It was dusty and faded with age. On the front of the envelope, also faded, an address had been written in neat black capital letters, probably with a felt tip. Tony saw the words *Dressmaking & Sewing Magazine*, and *London* before Mrs MacDonald turned the envelope over and shook its contents out onto the table.

"This was Mary's entry," she said, a hint of sadness tinging her voice. "After she...you know... there was no point in posting it, but I didn't have the heart to throw it away. So, it's been gathering dust in a drawer all this time."

Tony's eyes roamed over the items that had fallen from the old envelope. There was a typewritten letter, an entry form, and another piece of paper. The thing that caught his attention, though, was a Polaroid photograph that had fallen face-down on the table's scarred surface.

Dani must have also been drawn to that item first, because she reached for it and flipped it over.

The photo was of the same woman, wearing the same dress. In this snap, she was leaning against a tree by the river, smiling at the camera.

"That's the photo we chose to send to the magazine," Mrs MacDonald explained, "because it showed off the dress best. It may look like summertime in these photos, but it was a cold January, as I recall. Mary somehow managed to choose a glorious day to take these."

"Do you know who the model is?" Dani asked tapping a fingernail on the face in the faded photograph.

The shop owner nodded. "Yes, that's Mrs Gibson."

"Do you know her first name?"

"No, I never met her myself. But Mary was always going on about Mrs Gibson. I think she was a bit besotted with her."

"What do you mean by that, exactly?"

"Well, just that Mary seemed to be very taken with her. It was Mrs Gibson this, Mrs Gibson that."

Dani took out a notebook and pen. "Can you remember any details of what she said?"

Mrs MacDonald blew out a breath of air between

her lips. "Hmm, now you're asking. I can't really remember the exact details. It was a long time ago."

"Generally, then," Tony suggested. "You say Mary was very taken with this woman. What gave you that impression?"

"Just the way she was always going on about her."

"When was the first time she mentioned her? Was it when she was looking for a model for the competition?"

Mrs MacDonald thought about that for a moment, her brows meeting again as she stroked her chin. "Yes," she said, after a minute or so of contemplation. "It when we reopened after Christmas. I told her she needed to find a model for the competition, and she said her little sister could do it. She had a sister called Colleen who was a couple of years younger than her. I told her she had to find an adult, because that was one of the competition rules; the model had to be an adult. So, I suggested her mum. Mary didn't seem too keen on that idea and asked if I'd do it."

She chuckled. "I was no more model material then, than I am now. Anyway, I gave her the Polaroid camera so she could familiarise herself with it and told her to ask around. I didn't think she'd have much problem finding someone, to be honest. Who wouldn't want to help a young, sweet girl like her enter a competition?"

"So, she found Mrs Gibson," Tony said.

"Yes, she came into the shop the following weekend, full of the joys of spring. Said she'd met a young woman walking by the river who'd offered to model for her."

"Did she say anything else about this woman?" Dani asked. "Like where she lived?"

"I got the impression she lived somewhere near Mary's house, because I'm sure she told me later that she'd walked to Mrs Gibson's house and had tea there. If the house was within walking distance, it couldn't have been that far."

"Did she say anything about the house itself?"

"No, I don't think so. Oh, wait a minute, she said she met Mrs Gibson's husband, and her young son." She screwed up her face as she tried to remember. "Yes, I think that's right. "You're asking me all these questions about Mary, but you haven't really said what for. The poor girl drowned over twenty years ago, so what's this to do with?"

"Mary's name has come up in the investigation of an ongoing case," Dani said.

The shop owner narrowed her eyes. "Is this to do with those girls that were found at Temple Well?"

"I can't really comment on that."

A realisation dawned in the shop owner's eyes, and her hand flew to her mouth. "Oh my God, you think Mary was murdered, don't you?"

"As I said, Mrs MacDonald, I can't comment on an ongoing investigation."

Tears sprang into the older woman's eyes. "Oh no, this is terrible. I thought it was a tragedy that she'd fallen into the river and drowned at such a young age, but murdered? Are you sure?"

Pointing at the photograph on the table, she said, "Do you think this woman did it?"

Tony could see that Mrs MacDonald's mental state was worsening. Her eyes darted around the room, and then back to the photograph of the woman by the tree. She kept shaking her head, as if doing so could somehow change the past.

He knew that the best way to break her out of her flustered state was to get her to focus on something mundane, something that would redirect her attention.

"Mrs MacDonald, do you still have the camera?" he asked, in an attempt to focus the woman's mind elsewhere. "The Polaroid camera. Do you still have it?"

She nodded, regaining her composure slightly. "Yes, it's upstairs."

"Could we have a look at it?"

"Yes," she said, getting up. "I'll get it."

"Does the camera have a strap?" Dani asked, before the shop owner disappeared.

"Yes, it's got a nylon neck strap." She wiped her eyes with the back of her hand. She had something to do now, something that would keep her from dwelling on the manner of Mary's death.

"Could you just hold it by the strap when you bring it down, please?"

"Yes, all right." She went through the archway and ascended the stairs.

Tony turned his attention to Dani. "Do we actually want the camera? I was just trying to distract her."

"If the woman in the photo—"

"Mrs Gibson."

"Mrs Gibson," she said. "If that *is* Mrs Gibson. If she touched the camera at any point during the photo session, her prints might still be on there."

"After all this time?"

"It's unlikely, to be honest, but Forensics can have a look. They're more likely to get a print off the back of that photograph." She nodded at the photo of Mrs Gibson leaning against the tree. "If the woman even touched it at all."

"She might have done," Tony said. "I can imagine Mary taking the picture and giving it to her to see what she thought of it. That would transfer the woman's fingerprints to the paper."

"It's possible. Anyway, if there *is* anything there, it's going to help us identify this woman much quicker than conducting a blind search will."

"So, you *do* think that identifying this woman is important," Tony said.

"I'm open to the possibility that it might be." She took two clear plastic evidence bags out of her pocket and laid them on the table. Then she produced a pair of disposable gloves from the same pocket and pulled them over her hands before placing the photograph into one of the bags and sealing it.

Mrs MacDonald returned, with the instant camera in hand, held by the strap as Dani had instructed. She lowered it to the table, where Dani placed the second evidence bag over the device and sealed it inside.

"I suppose you'll be looking for fingerprints," the older woman said. "So that means you think this woman killed Mary."

"No, it doesn't mean that at all," Tony said. "We're just trying to find out who this woman is. Fingerprints may help us determine her identity."

"Well, if you need something she touched, take that model release form. She definitely touched that." She pointed at one of the sheets of paper that had come out of the envelope.

"Model release form?" Dani asked, putting the camera and photo to one side, and taking out another evidence bag.

Mrs MacDonald nodded. "It was one of the competition rules. The model in the photograph had to sign a release form. That's the form Mary got her to sign, right there.

The piece of paper was face down. With gloved hands, Dani flipped it over. It contained a typewritten paragraph and, beneath that, a signature that had been scrawled with a blue biro. The handwriting was small and spidery.

Tony leaned forward and stared at the signature.

P Gibson.

Dani slid the model release form into the evidence bag and sealed it. Looking at Mrs MacDonald, she said, "Is there anything else Mary said about Mrs Gibson?"

The older woman thought for a moment, then shook her head. "Not that I can remember. Like I said, she was just taken with her, and sung her praises all the time. If that woman hurt her in some way—"

"We're not saying she did," Tony reminded her. "We're just checking up on some details, that's all." He searched inside his jacket for one of his business cards and handed it to her. "If you remember anything else, anything at all, or you just want to talk, don't hesitate to ring me."

"Will I get my camera back?" she asked.

"Yes, we'll get it back to you as soon as we're done with it."

"All right. Thank you." Mrs MacDonald was still visibly shocked. She sat in the chair and stared at the tabletop.

"Shall I get your daughter to come in?" Tony asked.

She nodded.

He stuck his head through the doorway. Shona was fussing over the dresses in the window.

"I think your mum could do with a cup of tea," he said.

A concerned look darkened her face as she crossed the small floor space to the counter. "Why? Is she okay?"

"She's just had a bit of a shock, that's all." He waited for her to come behind the counter and go into the back room before he headed for the exit.

Dani followed, carrying the evidence bags.

When they were outside in the cold, Tony stuck his hands in his pockets. "Well, that was productive."

"Yeah, thank God for people who never throw anything away."

"We're getting closer, Dani, I can feel it."

"You might want to temper that enthusiasm a bit," she said as they crossed the road to the *Bull's Head* car park. "We've still got to run this past Battle."

CHAPTER 19

Rob woke up in the cellar. He was sitting on the dirt floor, back against the cold, stone wall. What the hell happened? He checked his watch and could hardly believe it when he saw the time. *11:30*. Almost lunchtime. He remembered coming down here after Eric had left and taking the knife off the shelf.

And then...what?

Had he blacked out?

He squeezed his eyes shut, trying to force the memory to come back to him, but last night's events remained a black hole in his memory.

He got to his feet, and found the knife lying in the dirt next to him. Picking it up, he felt its weight in his hand before taking it upstairs and placing it on the kitchen table. Had he really been thinking about using this knife on his uncle?

It didn't matter now; Eric would be going home today. He was probably already on his way, trundling down the motorway to Exeter. He wasn't a threat anymore.

The thing that displeased him most about blacking out—or whatever had happened last night—was that he'd missed the opportunity to dig up another girl. He didn't even want to take her anywhere, just dig her up and have a look at her, like a collector of fine wine checking that all the bottles were in the wine cellar.

That made him laugh. If a wine collection was kept in a wine cellar, then what was the cellar of this house called? A body cellar?

He chuckled to himself. The humour fled, though, when he checked his phone. Sonia's name was all over his missed calls list, and his texts. Without even looking at them, he put the phone into his pocket.

He had to get home. If he spent too much time here in the house, Sonia might get suspicious and drive up here herself to see what was going on.

He crossed the kitchen to the cellar door, meaning to lock it.

He hesitated.

Sonia would be at work, and the kids at school. If he went home now, he'd be there on his own. No one would be back for at least another four or five hours.

Might as well use that time wisely.

He opened the cellar door and went down to his little domain. His body cellar. He smiled to himself and picked up the spade that was leaning against the wall. Surveying the expanse of dirt beneath his feet, he had an idea. Instead of digging the girls up and then reburying them, why not leave them out? Eventually, he could have them all on display down here, and he'd be the only viewer. His private collection.

What had his dad been thinking, burying them under the dirt where they couldn't be seen? Yes, there was a kind of satisfaction knowing they were there, but wouldn't it be much better to see them? He could sit down here with them. Perhaps even talk to them. At least they wouldn't talk back, like Sonia always did.

Maybe he'd even find his mum.

"Mum, are you down here?" he said aloud. "Knock once for yes, twice for no."

There was no answer, of course, although Rob did catch himself listening for a knock coming from beneath the earth.

Laughing at himself, he took the spade into the shadowy corner where a teenage girl had looked at him pleadingly with terrified eyes many years ago.

Before today, whenever he'd remembered the girl in the cellar, and his dad laughing at him, he'd blamed his father for expecting him to do something so terrible.

Now, he thought that perhaps he'd been too weak as a child. His dad had been trying to make a man of him. But instead of facing the challenge, he'd pissed his pants and run away like a little baby. No wonder his dad had been mad at him.

How different would his life have been if he'd just taken that step, and done what his father had asked of him all those years ago?

Deciding he'd never know the answer to that, and he'd better get to work if he was going to get home before Sonia and the kids, he set about digging. As the spade's steel blade cut through the earth, Rob wondered if a knife passed through flesh so easily. He was sure it did. The difficulty in stabbing someone might come if—like a spade hitting rocks beneath the dirt—the knife hit bone.

Had his dad known the best places to stab someone to cause a quick death? Had he even wanted them to die quickly, or had he drawn it out, making sure they died slowly?

Those thoughts would have revulsed him a few days ago, but now he had a genuine curiosity about such matters.

He whistled to himself as he dug, feeling a sense if anticipation. He knew there was girl down here, and he would find her. The Xs on the scrap of paper hadn't let him down the last two times, and he had no reason to believe they would now.

He wondered if his dad had periodically dug the bodies up, or if just knowing that they were there was enough. Rob decided the former; why would the old man have bothered to mark the graves if it wasn't so he could bring his prizes out of the earth every now and again and look at them?

An hour later, his faith in the *X*s and his father was rewarded when the spade hit something solid.

Half an hour after that, he had revealed—through careful use of the spade and his hands—the body of a girl, lying on her back in the grave.

The long hair clinging to the skull was dark. On the chest of her T-shirt, faded but still visible, was a pink rose.

This was the girl; the one who'd lunged at him from the shadows and then pleaded with him as he'd held the knife his father had given him.

"That didn't end well for you, did it?" he said softly, reaching down and brushing a lock of hair from her dirt-encrusted skull.

It took him another half an hour to get the remains out of the hole and prop them against the wall. When he glanced into the grave to make sure he hadn't missed anything, his heart skipped a beat.

There, lying face down in the dirt, was Sam the Action Man.

So he *had* dropped Sam when he'd fled the cellar all those years ago, and his dad had buried the toy with the girl.

He dropped into the hole and grabbed his old friend, pulling him from the dirt that seemed to want to retain its grip on the plastic man.

When he turned Sam over in his hands, he felt a

jolt of shock. The Action Man was still intact, but his face was blank. The plastic facial features were still there—Rob ran his thumb over the plastic protrusions that represented the nose and mouth—but the eyes and eyebrows, which had been painted onto the plastic, were gone. The empty, shadowy eye sockets stared up at him.

"Sam, what happened to you?" he whispered.

He carefully bent the Action Man into a sitting position and placed it next to the remains of the girl.

Then he heard a knock at the door.

The coppery taste of fear flooded his mouth, and for a moment he thought that Eric had gone to the police after all, and they were at the door now, probably with a search warrant.

No, that was ridiculous. Even if Eric had gone to the police and told them about his brother, they couldn't have got a search warrant in such a short time. They'd investigate first, ask questions, take their time putting a case together.

Wouldn't they?

He had to admit that he didn't really know how the police worked. And with the two bodies that had been found recently, and the public attention they'd caused, the authorities might be quicker to act than usual. They were probably up there preparing to smash the door down, for all he knew.

If they didn't have a warrant, and they were just here to ask a few questions, maybe he could dissuade them. Perhaps he could talk his way out of it.

The sound came again. Three sharp raps on the wooden door.

Brushing the dirt off his shirt and jeans, Rob made is way to the foot of the cellar steps, where he hesitated, listening for voices outside, or the tell-tale crackle of a radio. He couldn't hear anything, just silence now that the sound of the knocks had faded away.

He went up the stairs and peered around the open cellar door.

Through the frosted glass in the front door, he could see the distorted image of a single person. He was sure it was Eric.

What the hell was he doing here? Why hadn't he gone back to Exeter?

Taking a deep breath to calm himself, Rob stepped into the kitchen and closed the cellar door behind him.

Eric must have seen him through the frosted glass, because he'd stopped knocking and was now waiting to be let in.

"All right, I'm coming," Rob said. He didn't lock the cellar door, because if Eric saw him fiddling with the lock through the glass, he might wonder what Rob was hiding was down there.

He opened the door and, sure enough, there was

his uncle, wrapped up in a thick winter coat and wearing a red bobble hat.

"Uncle Eric," Rob said. "What's up? I thought you'd be on your way home."

"I was." Eric gestured to the kitchen. "But a thought struck me while I was on the motorway, so I turned around and came back here."

"What do you mean?" Rob stood in the doorway, preventing his uncle from entering the house.

"I think we should have a look around the property," Eric said. "This property, I mean. Probably in those woods, too. You should get your coat; it's cold out here."

Rob had no idea what was going on, but at least Eric didn't want to come into the house. "All right. I'll be right out. Just give me a minute." He closed the door and grabbed his padded jacket. He was about to leave the house when he turned and, almost as an afterthought, picked up the knife from the kitchen table. He slipped it into his pocket and went outside.

Eric was waiting by his car. When he saw Rob, he opened the boot and took out a spade.

"What are we doing, again?" Rob asked.

Eric closed the boot and hefted the spade in his gloved hand as he walked towards Rob. "We're going to have a look around out there." He pointed at the fields and woods that surrounded the house.

Rob shrugged. "Okay, but what are we looking for?"

"Places where the earth is disturbed. Evidence that someone has dug up a body."

"What?" Rob tried to sound surprised, but he wasn't sure if that was going to work. Did Eric suspect him already? Was this some kind of a test?

"If I'm right, and my brother killed those girls," his uncle said, "whoever dug them up might have found them here, on this property. I'm sorry, Rob, but I'm sure I'm right."

"But who would have done such a thing?" Now he was the one doing the testing.

"I don't know," Eric said, walking towards the woods. "That's the part I don't understand."

Rob followed him, his hands in his pockets, fingers caressing the rough, wooden knife handle. "It doesn't make much sense, Eric."

"I know, but if we find something, we can tell the police, and then they can sort it out."

"So, you haven't been to the police already?"

"Not much point without evidence. Like you said last night, my story doesn't sound very plausible, and it's doubtful the police would act on it. So, we're going to find something to back it up."

"A body," Rob said, trying to sound incredulous.

"Or evidence that those two bodies came from around here, yes."

"Do you really think that's possible?" Rob looked towards the woods with a look of fear on his face, as if expecting to see a band of grave robbers in the trees. He hoped he wasn't overplaying his role as the innocent and unassuming son of a serial killer.

"I wouldn't be here, otherwise." Eric pointed at a gap in the trees, where a trail snaked through the woods. "Let's start over there."

A cold, February wind blew across Miller's Dale, making the air feel icy as it entered Rob's lungs. He huddled into his coat, wondering how long Eric's enthusiasm for this hunt was going to last before he got too cold and called it a day.

He'd have to get home to Sonia soon, before she threw a wobbly and came out here to find out what he was doing. That wouldn't be good, especially when there was a dead girl sitting in the cellar.

They walked beneath the cover of the trees, sheltered from the wind by the towering evergreens.

"What exactly are we looking for?" Rob asked.

"Signs of disturbance."

"You really believe your brother—my dad—killed those girls and buried them out here?"

"If he did, I'll prove it."

It was at that point that Rob realised Eric was obsessed with proving James Gibson was a murderer. Maybe it was a sense of guilt over not going to the authorities when he found Sarah Rundle's headband in his brother's bedroom, or a need to get back at the brother who had been so cruel to him during his childhood, but something was eating Eric from the inside, and had been all his life.

Something which he obviously thought he could make better by doing the right thing now and exposing his brother for what he really was.

The man wasn't going to stop until he'd proved his theory correct.

Rob couldn't have that. He himself had wanted to get back at his father at first, revealing his crimes to the world by moving the bodies of the two girls to a public place. But he knew now that he hadn't *really* wanted to hurt his father. If he'd been serious about destroying the old man, he'd have outed him to the police.

He'd believed he was acting out of spite at the time, but he now realised that, even then, his anger had been directed at himself, and not his father. He'd disappointed the old man, and now that he was gone, there was no way to change that. Revealing those bodies had been an act of defiance against his own weak nature. Against the little boy who had wet himself and run from the cellar.

Now, he wanted to protect his father's legacy, not destroy it. He wanted to enjoy the fruits of his father's labour. The dead girls were his now. If he wanted to dig them all up and sit them in various places in the cellar, where he could visit them whenever he wished, there was no one who could stop him. He could create a kingdom of the dead down there, over which he would rule.

"What's that over there?" he said to Eric, pointing

at the base of a tree where he didn't actually see anything out of the ordinary at all.

"What?" Eric said, peering into the gloom. "What is it?"

"Looks like the earth has been disturbed." As he said the words, he checked the woods around them. There was no one about. He rarely saw anyone on this trail.

Eric stepped into the undergrowth, stooping beneath a low-hanging branch to get to the area Rob had indicated. His back was exposed as he did so.

The knife was in Rob's hand before he even realised it. Gripping the handle that bore his father's initials in a tight, overhand grip, he raised the knife into the cold air and slashed the blade down towards his uncle's back.

He hadn't reckoned on how thick Eric's coat was. The knife tore into it but seemed to only graze the flesh beneath. Eric shouted out in pain, but it wasn't the reaction Rob had hoped for. He'd expected his uncle to collapse to the ground.

Instead, Eric whirled around to face Rob. The action ripped the knife from Rob's hand and sent it flying into the undergrowth.

Eric seemed to suddenly understand that he'd been fruitlessly searching for an unknown gravedigger when, in fact, he should have been looking more closely at his nephew.

"You," he said. "It was you all along."

Rob didn't bother answering his uncle. Scrambling through the undergrowth, he searched frantically for the knife. He had to get his hands on it and finish what he'd started. He had no choice now.

He felt a heavy impact between his shoulder blades. It knocked the air out of his lungs and sent him crashing to the ground. Winded, he managed to roll onto his back and look up as Eric stood over him, spade lifted above his head, looking like he was about to play one of the old ring the bell games at a fair. But Eric wasn't trying to ring a bell; he was aiming for Rob's skull.

"Eric, don't!" Rob cried out, raising his hands in a futile attempt to ward off the spade.

His uncle hesitated for a split second, and that was enough time for Rob to jerk his knee up with all the force he could muster and catch his attacker between the legs. Eric went down like a sack of stones, clutching himself and gasping.

Rob got to his knees and brushed aside twigs and leaves, desperately searching for the knife. He didn't have much time before Eric recovered. But the weapon was elusive. He couldn't find it.

Eric was scrambling to his feet, looking decidedly in pain, but fighting through it, probably thanks to his survival instinct and an overload of adrenaline flooding his system.

Rob couldn't waste his time looking for the knife; he had to act.

Launching himself towards the spade, which Eric hadn't picked up in his groggy state, he gripped the handle and stood up. Using both hands for extra force, he swung the spade at the back of Eric's neck.

The edge of the metal blade connected with the base of his uncle's skull, and Eric went down again. He landed on his face in the undergrowth, and this time, he looked like he wasn't going to get back up.

Tossing the spade aside, Rob searched through the piles of dead leaves on the ground. This little jaunt into the woods had turned into a disaster; he couldn't let things get worse by losing his dad's knife.

He found it lying in full view ten feet away. Picking it up, he made his way back to where his uncle lay on the ground.

There was a lot of blood. Some of it was coming from the rip in the back of the older man's jacket, staining the fabric dark red, but most of it was welling from a cut in the back of Eric's neck, where the edge of the spade had cut through skin.

But despite the blood soaking into the ground around Eric's prone body, the old man wasn't dead. He was still breathing, and it looked to Rob like he might even get up again.

Dropping to his knees, he raised the knife above his head with both hands and brought it down on the back of Eric's neck. The blade sliced through flesh buried itself all the way to the hilt. Rob's hands became slick with warm blood that was already pouring from the wound.

He lifted the knife and brought it down forcefully on Eric's back, determined to cut through the thick, winter coat the man wore. It worked, but not as well as he'd wanted, so he used the knife to cut the back of the coat away, revealing a dark green jumper beneath.

He stabbed the blade into the jumper repeatedly.

He wasn't sure if Eric was already dead, but it didn't matter. The act of bringing the knife up and down was a release. This was what he should have done to that girl years ago. This was what his father had been trying to show him, the joy of killing.

A sense of elation flooded though each time the steel cut through flesh. He kept the knife moving until, eventually, he was exhausted. Pushing himself away from what was left of his uncle, he sat on the ground and gasped icy air as he recovered.

He had some work ahead of him now. For a moment, he considered putting Eric's body into the grave from which he'd unearthed the girl earlier, but something about that didn't feel right. As far as he knew, his father had only buried girls and young women in the cellar. Putting Eric down there would taint the work his father had done. Rob couldn't put Eric's body into the collection; it didn't belong there and would ruin everything.

"I'm just going to have to bury you out here," he

said to his dead uncle. After a quick visual appraisal of the area in which he sat, he decided this was as good a place as any. It was hidden by the trees and undergrowth, and far enough from the path that a hiker or dog walker wouldn't come across it by accident. He'd cover the grave with sticks and dead leaves, and no one would be any the wiser.

"That's settled, then," he said, deciding on his course of action. He would bury Eric out here in the woods, and that would be the end of it.

But first, there was something else he wanted to do.

"Don't go anywhere," he said to his uncle's body, before striding back to the house.

Once inside, he went down to the cellar and grabbed Sam the Action Man. He took the toy back to the woods and placed it next to Eric while he used the spade to dig a grave. The pain between his shoulder blades—where he'd taken a blow from the spade—didn't help, and the cold, compacted earth wasn't as easy to dig up as the cellar floor, but after an hour, he had a hole deep enough to put Eric into.

Before he threw his uncle's body into it, though, he tossed Sam in without a second thought. The faceless toy represented the scared boy Rob had once been. No one could say that was who he was anymore. The faceless Action Man from his childhood needed to remain buried.

After throwing the toy into the makeshift grave,

he hooked his arms under Eric's and dragged the body to the edge of the hole. His uncle's corpse felt almost impossibly heavy; nothing like the lightweight girls Rob was used to carrying.

After taking Eric's car key from his pocket so he could deal with the silver Lexus parked by the house, he rolled the body into the grave, hearing it hit the earth at the bottom with a wet, heavy thud.

Rob set about filling in the hole, no easy task with painful shoulder blades and muscles that were stiff from digging earlier and fighting with his uncle.

Despite the coldness of the day, he soon began to sweat from the exertion, and by the time he was done, he'd discarded his winter jacket and shirt.

After covering over the freshly dug ground with sticks and leaves, he stepped back and surveyed his handiwork, grinning with the satisfaction of a job well done. From the trail, no one would ever guess that a hole had been dug here.

Retrieving his jacket and shirt and making sure he had the knife in his pocket, he strolled back to the house with the spade over his shoulder.

When he reached the Lexus, he opened the boot and threw the spade in. Then he went around the side of the house to the garage.

The wooden structure was in a state of disrepair, but it would serve as an adequate hiding place for the car. Rob opened the doors, making a mental note that he was going to have to get a padlock for them, and looked inside.

His father's lathe was in here, along with an array of chisels and saws hanging from pegs on the wall. Planks of wood were stacked in one corner, and a row of pine shelves held yet more tools of the woodworking trade.

This had been the place from which his father had run his business as a carpenter and woodturner. The tools and machines were arranged around the edge of the garage, leaving a considerable space in the middle where cabinets, panels, and other items had been fashioned in the past.

That space was empty now and would be repurposed as a parking space for the Lexus.

Returning to the car, Rob slid into the driver's seat and started the engine. The radio came on, the digital display reading *BBC Radio 4*. A man and a woman were discussing politics.

Rob turned it down and reversed the car into the garage. After killing the engine, he left the keys inside. No need to take them into the house.

He closed the garage doors and checked the general area in front of the house. There was nothing to indicate that Eric had ever been here.

Satisfied, he went inside. He needed to have a shower; he was covered in blood and dirt. He also needed to wash his clothes. His trousers and shirt were still in the washer, so they'd just have to be washed again, with the clothes he was currently wearing.

He stripped off in the laundry room and added a scoop of washing powder to the machine before turning it on. Naked, he went upstairs and showered, then selected more clothes from his father's wardrobe—jeans, T-shirt, and a blue shirt—before going back downstairs to the kitchen.

As he passed the closed cellar door, he was sure he heard a voice down there, drifting up the steps to the other side of the door. A man's voice. His father's voice.

He was mistaken, of course. That was impossible.

But, despite that, he pressed his ear to the painted wood and listened.

"*Rob.*"

He opened the door, expecting to discover the pipes down there making noises which he'd mistaken for his name.

But when he opened the door and a shaft of light from the kitchen illuminated the cellar floor below the steps, he saw his father standing there. The old man had a knife in his hand—*the* knife. The same one that Rob had washed under the kitchen tap and placed on the counter earlier—and was grinning.

Rob glanced over his shoulder at the knife that was still lying on the counter, where he'd put it earlier.

"Come and look what we've got down here," his dad said.

Rob knew he was hallucinating, that it was a memory come to life, and the voice was actually inside his own head, but it seemed so real.

"Dad?"

"Come on, son, we've got a lot of work to do."

"More work?"

His father nodded, still grinning. *"You didn't think all this was going to end when you killed Eric, did you? No, no, my boy. That was just the beginning."*

CHAPTER 20

"What do you mean you've been investigating the Mary Harwood case?" Battle said. Tony and Dani had managed to track him down to the police station in Buxton, where an incident room had been set up and was currently being staffed by members of Murder Force.

"I specifically told you not to do that," the DCI added.

Tony wanted to say that no such specific order had been given but felt it would be wiser to keep his mouth shut.

"The thing is, guv, we've made some headway," Dani said. "We've uncovered a part of Mary's life that she kept secret from her family. The man who abducted her, the man she said she knew, was part of that secret. If we can track down P. Gibson, we might find that man."

"And what does this have to do with Daisy? Or Joanna?"

"It's probably the same perpetrator," Tony said, unable to keep quiet any longer.

Battle narrowed his eyes. "Really? Worked that out by some psychological deduction, have you? Or have you got some evidence to show me that links Mary's case to our investigation?"

"Well, nothing concrete," Tony admitted "but you'd have to be a fool to not see the connection."

"Are you calling me a fool, Dr Sheridan?"

"No. All I'm saying is that we have a lead here that could tell us who the man on the bridge was when Mary Harwood was taken. I believe that same man is responsible for the deaths of Daisy Riddle and Joanna Kirk."

Battle said nothing, but stared at the report Dani and Tony had put together in the car park. It recorded their meeting with Mrs MacDonald at *Peak Dresses* and put forward sound reasoning—as far as Tony was concerned—as to why the camera and photograph should be examined, and why the woman in the photograph—*P. Gibson*—should be tracked down.

"It shouldn't take much in the way of resources to find her," Tony said to the DCI. She's most likely still living in this area."

Battle read the hastily put together report and

handed it back to Dani. "To be honest with you, this is the biggest lead we've got. The analysis of the remains has thrown up bits and pieces, but nothing compelling. We've got DNA from the sheet, but it doesn't match anything in the database. There are fibres, that seem to have come from a vehicle, and Forensics are trying to match them to a specific make and model, but that's going to take time, not to mention tracking down all the vehicles in the country that fit the result."

He sighed. "So, what you've got here is the only thing we have that points to a specific person. However, it may not have anything at all to do with our case. Perhaps we should hand it over to the Derbyshire Police. The Mary Harwood case is theirs, and I'm not seeing anything here that tells me we should add it to our investigation."

Tony took the report from Dani and held it aloft. "That's because the evidence isn't in these words." He pointed at his own head. "It's in here. We know from experience that serial killers don't suddenly appear fully-fledged. There are usually one or two kills, or even a spate of lesser crimes leading up to the signature that eventually identifies them. Those first kills are where we're more likely to catch them out, mainly because the killer is likely to know the victim."

He gestured to the photos of Daisy and Joanna on the board. "Those girls probably didn't know the man who abducted Mary Harwood. But *Mary* knew him. Before she got into the Land Rover, she told her sister that she knew the man driving it. And now, we have a possible link to him. The woman in those photos, Mrs Gibson, was part of Mary's secret social circle. So was the man in the Land Rover. They most likely knew each other. If we find *her*, we can find *him*."

Battle hesitated. He turned and looked at the pictures of the two dead girls.

Tony could sense the DCI was wavering. He decided to speak to the guilt that was obviously eating Battle up inside. He leaned forward and gently said, "Don't we owe it to Daisy and Joanna to investigate every lead we can?"

"All right," Battle said, turning to face him. "I'm going to approve a search for this Mrs Gibson woman. Not because of your attempt to manipulate me with that low psychological blow, Tony, but because it's the right thing to do. I'll give it to the support team to check into while you and DI Summers pay a visit to the forensic anthropologist. She left me a message earlier saying she wants to speak to someone from the team. Since you two have been hard at work this morning, following your own little leads, you can take have a relaxing afternoon in the Chesterfield morgue. At least I'll know where you are."

"Right, boss," Tony said. If the visit to the morgue

was supposed to be some form of punishment, then he'd got off lightly; he was going to see Alina Dalca again, and that made him strangely happy.

"And take that camera and photo downstairs to Forensics, so they can have a look at it."

"Will do, Guv," Dani said.

As they left the incident room, and were walking along the corridor, she said to Tony, "Well, we got our own way in the end. At least you didn't tell him your theory about the dead husband and the wife digging up the bodies."

"Oh, yeah, I forgot to tell him that. Should I go back?"

"No," she said firmly.

"I was kidding."

"I know you were. Besides, I'm sure you wouldn't want to spend more time with Battle when you could be spending it with the forensic anthropologist."

"What's that supposed to mean?" He felt uncomfortable. Was he *that* obvious?

She laughed. "Nothing. Don't worry about it. In fact, you get a head start. I'll drop these things into Forensics, and I'll meet you there."

"Are you sure?"

"Of course." They found the stairs at the end of the corridor and went down together. When they reached the floor below, where the Forensics team was situated, Dani pushed through the door and smiled at Tony. "Have fun."

Tony continued his descent to the ground floor and went out to the car park. The wind had picked up, blowing cold air into his face as he searched for his Mini among the other cars. When he found it and got in, he started the engine and turned the heater up.

He had no idea how to get to Chesterfield hospital from here, so typed his destination into the SatNav, and waited for the device to calculate the route. When it finally decided which way to take him, it told him he was only forty-three minutes away.

So, in less than an hour, he could be chatting to Alina. As he drove out of the car park, he felt a sudden, sinking feeling in his gut. Chatting to her about what, exactly? The indicators of psychological deviance? Societal catalysts for sociopathy? Jungian archetypes?

It was all he knew. The job had consumed his life. He couldn't make small talk.

"You're boring, Tony," he told himself as he joined the traffic on the road. "That's all there is to it."

When he got to the hospital, he checked his hair in the rearview mirror before going downstairs to the mortuary. At the door that led into the morgue itself, he straightened himself up and knocked.

"Come in," said a female voice from the other

side. Tony knew it was Alina's from the Eastern European accent.

He opened the door and entered the office. She was sitting at a desk, in front of a computer, dressed in a long white coat over a green jumper and tan skirt. Unlike the last time he'd seen her, she wore glasses, and her hair was loose, rather than in a ponytail. It reached down to her shoulders in gentle curls.

She smiled when she saw him. "Hello, Tony."

"Hi," he said, raising his hand in an awkward wave. "DCI Battle sent me over because you wanted to see me. I mean, because you wanted to see someone from the team. I'm not here by myself; DI Summers is here as well. Well, she's not here yet, but she's on the way. She had to drop something off at Forensics, but she'll be here soon."

"Excellent," she said, seemingly unaware of his nervous torrent of words. "I have something to show you. Shall we wait for DI Summers?"

"Umm, yes, I suppose we should."

"Can I get you anything? Tea? Coffee?"

"No, thanks, I'm fine."

"Okay. Will you excuse me while I finish this report?"

"Yes, of course." He leaned against a counter, trying to look relaxed. He felt relieved that she was focused on the computer, because that meant he didn't have to make small talk, a skill he'd already decided he didn't possess.

His phone buzzed in his pocket. He took it out, grateful for something to do. Dani was calling him.

"Hey, Dani," he said, as he answered.

"Hi. I'm still at the station. We've got a hit on P. Gibson."

"Okay. So, you're not coming to the morgue?"

"I'll leave that to you, while I sort everything out at this end. Let me know what the anthropologist says."

"All right. I will."

"When I'm finished here, I'm going to head back to Temple Well. I'll see you there, later."

"Great. See you later, then." He ended the call and looked over at Alina. "DI Summers isn't coming, after all."

"Oh, okay," she said airily. "Well, I am done with my report, so I can show you what I have found, if you like."

"Yes, of course. That would be great."

She pushed back on the chair and stood up. "I have set up what we need to see through here." She opened a door that led to the actual morgue, a large white-tiled room with stainless steel tables sitting in a neat row, and matching steel drawers set into one wall.

"What I want to show you is over here," she said,

leading Tony to one of the tables, where two skulls had been placed side by side on wire stands that raised them a foot or so above the table surface. The jawbones were missing.

"These are the skulls of Joanna Kirk, on the left, and Daisy Riddle, on the right," Alina said. "I have removed the mandibles to show you better what I found inside the cranium of each girl."

"Inside the craniums?" Tony asked. He suddenly remembered a scene from *The Silence of the Lambs*, where Agent Starling found a moth pupa inside a corpse's throat. He hoped the killer hadn't done something similar to these girls.

The anthropologist nodded. "Yes, inside the craniums. Here, let me show you." She took a small torch out of the pocket of her white coat and held it beneath the skull on the left, shining the light inside. The effect was that Joanna Kirk's skull lit up like a Halloween pumpkin, the empty eye sockets now glowing.

"What am I looking at?" he asked, unsure why she was doing this.

"Lean forward and look through one of the eye sockets, to the rear of the cranium."

He did as she asked, bending over and placing one eye near the empty socket. This position afforded him a view inside the skull, and on the back of the cranium, he noticed two marks that looked like they'd been scratched into the bone.

"They're Xs," he said, straightening.

Alina nodded. "Two Xs, to be precise. She took a pen and a notebook from her pocket and drew two Xs, in the pattern Tony had seen them inside the skull. Then she ripped out the page and placed it on the table.

    X
      X

"Now, we do the same with Daisy," she said, moving around Tony to the second skull, and shining the light in the same manner. "Have a look."

Tony bent over, and looked through Daisy's right eye socket, into the interior of her skull. He saw the marks straight away, only this time there were more of them.

"There are more of them," he said, straightening again.

She nodded. "There are eight of them." She ripped another page out of the notebook—one she'd already drawn on—and put it on the table, to the right of the other.

```
X  X    X
  X
X
            X
X     X
```

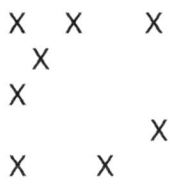

"These were made post-mortem, of course," she said. "Probably after the body had been in the ground for some time."

"So, he dug them up and made the marks."

"It seems so, yes. Some sort of sharp tool was used to engrave the *X*s into the cranium."

"These weren't done recently, by the person who dug them up and left them out in the open."

"No, the marks are many years old."

"So, they were done by the original killer."

She frowned behind her glasses. "The original killer?"

"It's a theory I'm working on. The person who's been leaving these girls for us to find isn't the same person who killed them."

"Interesting. Do you have a scientific basis for this?"

"I have a psychological basis for it, and psychology is a science, so, yes."

She seemed to hesitate, and then said, "I would like to hear more about this."

"Well, the fact that these bodies are coming to light now indicates that—"

"What I mean is that I would like to discuss this with you over...a drink, perhaps?"

"Oh, I see." Was she asking him out? "Umm, yes, of course. I'd like that."

She smiled. "Good. I will give you my number before you leave, and we will arrange something."

"Yes, that's great!" He felt suddenly elated, but he had to focus on the task at hand.

He looked at the two patterns on the notepad pages and tried to decipher them. "I don't know what this is."

"It looks like a constellation of stars," she offered.

"It does, especially the pattern with the eight Xs."

"Perhaps you have noticed that two Xs from the original pattern are incorporated into the larger pattern," she said.

Tony hadn't noticed, but now that he looked closer, he saw that the two Xs in Joanna's pattern were indeed part of the eight-X pattern from Daisy's skull.

He screwed his eyes up and put the heel of his left hand to his forehead, something which sometimes helped him think. "Why did he put this design inside their skulls? Why go to the trouble of digging up the skeletons to mark them like this?"

"It must be something very important to him," Alina said.

"Yes, very important." He tried to put himself into the killer's head. "What is most important to me? The thrill of killing? The power I hold over these girls?" The answer came to him in an instant. "The collection."

He opened his eyes and pointed at Joanna's skull. "Joanna Kirk was killed twenty-two years ago. There are two Xs." He turned his attention to Daisy's skull. "Daisy Riddle was killed seven years later, and now there are eight Xs, including the original two. It's the collection."

"The collection?" Alina asked, obviously confused.

"Yes." He focused on the patterns on the notepad pages, surer of himself now. "They're the locations of the graves. When he marked Joanna's skull, there were only two; her's and someone else's. By the time he marked Daisy's skull, there were eight. In the intervening seven years, he'd killed and buried six more girls."

"I see," the anthropologist said.

"The collection is the most important thing to him," Tony told her. "He's did this to mark each girl's place in it."

Alina pointed at the page with only two marks on it. "So, this tells us that Joanna was his second victim."

"Yes," Tony said, "One of these Xs represents Joanna Kirk."

"So, who is the other?"

He traced his finger over the two marks on the paper. "I believe it's Mary Harwood."

CHAPTER 21

"Can I take these with me?" Tony asked, picking up the two pieces of paper.

"Of course," Alina said. "I have put copies of the marks into my report, but I thought someone from the team should see these right away, in case they are important."

"They are," he said. "Thank you."

She walked back to the office, and he followed. As they entered the room, he said, "I have to go and see what Dani has uncovered regarding a person of interest. Before I go, though, you said you'd give me your number?"

"Yes, of course." She took the notepad out of her pocket, wrote on it, and tore out the page, which she then handed it to him. "We can discuss your theory," she said.

"I'd like that," he said, putting the piece of paper into his pocket.

"Then I will wait to hear from you."

"Great." He felt himself grinning uncontrollably, so he backed out of the door. "Okay, bye."

When he got out into the corridor and was walking back to the main part of the hospital, he exhaled. "You could have handled that a bit cooler, Tony." Still, he had Alina's number now. There would be an opportunity to be cool later.

He got back to the Mini and slid in behind the wheel. Already, doubts were beginning to creep into his head. When should he ring Alina? If he rang her tomorrow, would he seem too keen? If he waited until the following day, would he seem disinterested?

He gritted his teeth in frustration. He could help track down serial killers—he could even enter the house of the Lake Erie Ripper alone—so why did he find it so difficult to navigate the complexities of relationships?

He hadn't even asked Alina out. *She'd* asked *him*. So, he knew she wanted to see him in a social setting. Everything else was just details.

But it was in those details that he became lost.

He put *Temple Well* into the SatNav, started the car, and left the hospital grounds. The News came on the radio, the announcer saying that police were still searching for the killer of Daisy Riddle and Joanna Kirk. Chief Superintendent Ian Gallow had confirmed that the two deaths were being treated as the work of the same person.

"Joanna was his second victim," Tony said. "Daisy was his eighth." And he was certain that Mary Harwood had been his first. She and Joanna had both disappeared twenty-two years ago, only a few months apart, and in the same area. The *X*s scratched into Joanna's skull confirmed that the killer had dug two graves at the time he'd added Joanna to his collection. Tony was certain Mary Harwood was in that other grave.

That meant the information Dani had uncovered on Mrs Gibson could lead them straight to the killer.

"But you think the killer is dead," he told himself. "Your theory is that someone else uncovered Daisy and Joanna. Not the original killer. Because you think he's dead."

So, if his theory was correct—and he had every reason to believe it was—finding Mrs Gibson could lead them to the *dead* killer.

Where was the justice for Daisy's and Joanna's families in that? How was Colleen going to feel when she found out that the man who had driven Mary away in a Land Rover twenty-two years ago would never be punished?

At least the families would know what had happened to their loved ones, and the girls would be able to finally have a proper burial.

It made Tony wish his theory was wrong, that the killer was alive and well, so he could be put behind bars and rot in a jail cell for the rest of his days.

But he knew, deep down, that the chances of that were slim to non-existent. He was sure the killer was already dead. Daisy and Joanna wouldn't have been unearthed and left for the police to find, otherwise.

He reached Temple Well and parked in the small *Chapel View Guest House* car park, next to Dani's Land Rover. Before getting out of the car, he rang the DI.

When she answered, he said, "I'm at the B&B. Where do you want to talk? Your place or mine?" Even as he spoke the words, he cringed inwardly.

"I was thinking we might have a drink in that pub down the road," she said. "I'm starving, and they do food."

"Sounds good to me."

"I'll be down in a couple of minutes. Meet you outside."

"Okay." He ended the call. Why couldn't he be as nonchalant about going for a drink with Alina as he was about going for one with Dani? He knew the answer, of course; Dani was a workmate, a friend. He wasn't attracted to her.

That wasn't strictly true. The DI was attractive, there was no denying that. But he wasn't attracted to her like he was to the Eastern European anthropologist. That was why he had no trouble talking to Dani. That was why he could go for a drink with her and not feel like an inexperienced schoolboy who'd never been around girls before.

She came out through the door and waved at him

through the windscreen. Tony got out of the car and locked it.

"How was your meeting with Alina?" she asked. "Productive?"

"Yes, it was, in fact," he said, not sure if she was teasing him.

"Well, I've got some info about Mrs Gibson. There's one detail you're especially going to like."

"Oh? I'm intrigued."

"I need something to eat first."

"I won't argue with that." He realised how hungry he was. "I could murder some good pub grub."

"Right, let's go."

They walked quickly down the street, buffeted by the cold wind. The chapel sat on the hill to the north, silhouetted against the dark evening sky. Its towering walls and arches looked lonely and uninviting.

The Chapel Arms, on the other hand, looked warm and inviting. Tony could smell the food as soon as he could see the pub. Light spilled from the windows, and chatter and laughter came from inside. That sound was amplified as he pushed through the doors and stepped into the crowded space.

"I'll find us a table," Dani said, raising her voice so he could hear her over the hubbub.

"Right. What are you having?"

"G&T, please."

He nodded his acknowledgment, and as she went off to find a table, he fought his way to the bar. A young man in his twenties had just finished serving another customer and nodded at Tony. "Evening, sir, what can I get you?"

"A pint of bitter, and a gin and tonic, please."

The bartender rang up the sale and began pouring the drinks.

"Is it usually this busy?" Tony asked, raising his voice, as Dani had done, to be heard over the din.

"Not usually, no. It's all these journalists. The Press is everywhere. It's great for the village."

"Hmm." Tony wasn't sure how he felt about that. He was pleased that the economy of the Temple Well was booming, but disappointed that the discovery of two dead bodies could be a cause for celebration in any way whatsoever.

He paid for the drinks and found Dani sitting at a table in the corner, perusing a menu. As he sat down opposite her, he said, "Decided what you want?"

"I'm going to have the vegetarian lasagne," she said, handing him the menu.

"I don't need to look at that." He put the laminated card into its holder on the edge of the table. "They must do some sort of cheeseburger and chips."

"Right, I'll get this," she said, standing up and taking her purse out of her handbag.

"Are you sure?"

"I am. You deserve it. It seems your theory was spot on."

"My theory?"

"I'll tell you when I get back," she said. "Let's just say that it's looking more and more likely that our Mrs Gibson is the person who dug up those bodies."

Before he could get any more information out of her, she disappeared into the crowd, heading for the bar.

Now Tony really was intrigued.

When Dani came back and took her seat, he said, "So, tell me what you've found."

She took a sip of her G&T. "Mrs Gibson is Penny Gibson. According to the records the support team found, she lives at Miller's Dale with her husband James."

"So, she lives close to Harwood Farm."

"Yes, and this is the bit you're going to like. Her husband, James Gibson, is recently deceased. That makes Penny a widow, just like in the scenario you outlined to me in Bakewell. I mean, psychological insight is one thing, Tony, but being psychic is something else. Perhaps you should do Tarot readings on the side."

He gave her a thin-lipped smile. The scenario he'd described had simply been an example of how this situation *could* have played out. He hadn't expected it to be some sort of prophecy. Besides, if he looked at this rationally, there was nothing to say his off-the-cuff remark was actually correct.

"Just because her husband is dead doesn't mean I was right."

"I know, but it sounds suspicious, don't you think? This James Gibson dies and then the two bodies turn up. And the widow of the dead man is the same woman in the photographs Mary Harwood took."

He had to admit there was something going on here; there were too many coincidences for there not to be. But he wasn't ready to go pointing the finger at anyone in particular just yet.

"What else do we know about this James Gibson fellow?"

She took her notebook out of her pocket and flicked through it. "He ran a woodworking business. Died from a heart attack. He was discovered by a customer who'd gone round to see where he was after he didn't turn up at the customer's house to do some joinery work. Next of kin is his son, Robert."

"Why not his wife?"

She shrugged. "I don't know."

Tony nursed his beer while he thought about it. If Penny wasn't her husband's next of kin, that could speak to the type of fractured relationship he'd referred to in his hypothetical scenario. Perhaps it was more than hypothetical, after all. Perhaps Penny had disinterred the bodies of Daisy and Joanna due to some breakdown of the relationship between her and her husband before he died.

Everything seemed to fit into place.

So why did he think there was still a piece of the jigsaw missing?

"We need to talk to her," he said.

"We'll drive out there first thing in the morning, if you like."

The food arrived, and Tony ate his cheeseburger in silence, his mind going over the possibility that they'd cracked the case. From the look of Dani, as she happily tucked into her lasagne, she certainly thought so.

"What did you find out at the morgue?" she asked between mouthfuls.

"Hmm? Oh, yes, the morgue. Something interesting. Well, interesting from a psychological standpoint, anyway." He reached into his pocket and pulled out the pieces of notepad paper. They were crumpled from being in his pocket while he was driving. He dropped them on the table. "Tell me what you think of those."

Dani picked one up and examined it. "Looks like someone's phone number."

"Not that one," he said, taking it out of her hand and putting it back into his pocket carefully. "Those two."

She flattened them out on the table and inspected the patterns Alina had drawn. "I don't know. What are they?"

"Those marks were scratched into the inside of the skulls."

"Daisy's and Joanna's?"

He nodded and took a swig of bitter. "The two Xs were inside Joanna's skull, and the eight were inside Daisy's. They're markers of where the victims are buried. Joanna was his second victim, so there are only two marks. Daisy was the eighth victim, so eight Xs. It's an illustration of the collection."

"A collection of dead bodies."

"Yes, the killer's most prized possession."

"It's macabre."

He wasn't going to argue with that, so he went back to his burger and chips.

"That phone number in your pocket," Dani said. "Is it Alina's?"

He sighed. "Yes."

"You don't seem very happy about it."

"I'm not very good at this sort of thing. Sure, I've got her number, but when do I use it? I don't know the rules of dating. I've been out of the game for too long."

"Do you want some advice?"

He shrugged. "Sure, why not?"

"There are no rules. Ring her when you feel the time is right, not when some imagined set of rules says you should."

He put his last chip in his mouth. "Okay."

"You still don't seem very happy, Tony."

"I am. I mean, I'm glad I've got her number, and I'd like to see her outside work, but I'm just not very good at small talk. My work is my life. I know that's sad, but it's the truth."

"It isn't just the truth for you. Apart from walking my dogs, I don't do much else other than work. Do you think Battle has much of a life outside of the job?"

"Probably not," he admitted.

"This line of work isn't like a nine to five, where you get home in the evening and put your job aside for a while. It becomes ingrained into your being."

He nodded. She was right about that.

"It'll be the same for Alina," she said. "Her passion is digging around in graves and examining bones, for God's sake. You don't think she leaves work in the evening and leads some kind of normal life where she leaves all that behind, do you? Of course not. She's as geeky as you are."

"Gee, thanks."

"Not only you; me as well. Everyone in the team, probably."

"Except DC Ryan," he said. "With that flash car, I'm sure he lives some kind of double life."

She laughed. "Yeah, you could be right, there."

He finished his pint and said, "Do you want another?"

"Best not. We should get an early start in the

morning. See what Penny Gibson has to say for herself."

"Yeah, you're right."

"You're not certain it's her, are you?" she said, standing up.

He shrugged. "I don't know. Something about it just doesn't feel right."

"Well, we'll probably find out tomorrow."

They left the pub and strolled back to the guest house. Tony said goodnight to the DI and went to his room, where he put the kettle on. While it warmed up, he put the TV on low volume, for some background noise, and stood at the window, looking out at the silhouette of the old Templar chapel. The place still looked lonely, set apart from the village, partly hidden behind the trees.

On an impulse, he took his phone and the paper with Alina's number out of his pocket. He dialled the digits quickly, before he had a chance to talk himself out of it.

She answered after a couple of rings, during which Tony had forced himself to stay on the line and not hang up. "Hello?"

"Alina? It's Tony. Tony Sheridan."

"Tony, how are you?"

"I'm all right. I just thought I'd give you a quick ring. If you're not too busy to talk, of course."

"No, I'm not too busy. I was just watching television."

"Yeah, me too." He looked over at the small flatscreen. The News was on, the screen showing a reporter standing outside Downing Street. "Well, I just turned it on, actually. I had a burger at the pub earlier, and I've just got back."

"Oh, that's nice. I had a risotto."

"That sounds fancy. Microwave meal?"

She laughed, a sound that Tony found most agreeable. He found himself grinning.

"No, I made it," she said. "I love to cook."

"Really? I tend to let the supermarkets make my meals. I just heat them up."

"Well, perhaps, I shall make you risotto, one day."

"I'd like that very much."

"Good. So would I."

"I was wondering when you'd like to go for that drink."

"Well, I am free tomorrow night, if you would like that."

"I would," he said. "I'd like that very much. Umm, do you know any nice pubs?" He felt that the *Chapel Arms* was a bit too noisy for a quiet drink.

"Well, would you like to eat as well as have a drink?"

"Yes, that sounds great."

"Do you know the *Grouse and Claret*, near Bakewell?"

The name sounded familiar. Had he driven past

it on the way to Colleen's house? "I can certainly find it." Thank God for SatNavs.

"Shall we say seven o' clock tomorrow, then?"

"Yes," he said, feeling a nervous excitement run through him. He was pleased he'd called her now, delighted he'd thrown caution to the wind.

"Excellent. I shall see you tomorrow at seven. Goodnight, Tony."

"Goodnight, Alina."

She hung up, and he put his phone on the bedside table, still grinning. Talking to her hadn't been that hard, after all.

He made himself a cup of tea and sat on the edge of the bed, using the remote to surf the channels on the TV. He didn't want the doom and gloom of the News; he wanted something that matched his mood.

He settled on a rom com that starred Jennifer Lopez and caught himself grinning like a Cheshire cat through most of it.

He even began to think that maybe Dani was right, and he'd correctly guessed the scenario involving Penny Gibson and her dead husband. If that was the case, and evidence came to light to prove it, then they'd probably take the woman in for questioning tomorrow. Everything would fall into place, and the case would be closed.

Tony was positive that nothing could go wrong.

CHAPTER 22

Rob woke up in the cellar. He sat up in the dark and shivered. He felt as if his body heat had leeched into the dirt floor. His flesh was numb, and his teeth began to chatter.

Getting shakily to his feet, he picked up the knife that was lying on the floor at his feet and walked unsteadily to the steps. The door was open, but the kitchen was dark, so barely any light shone through the opening. He ascended the steps and, once he'd orientated himself in the dark kitchen, put the light on.

Checking the time on the clock on the wall, he realised his chance to get home before Sonia and the kids was long gone. It was almost midnight.

He checked his phone and found numerous missed calls and texts from Sonia. She was obviously livid. There was nothing he could do about that now.

He'd blacked out again, this time for more than

ten hours. Was there something wrong with his head?

Despite having been unconscious for such a long time, he felt tired. It would be easy to go up to his dad's bed and fall asleep, but he knew he had to go home and face the music. He wasn't really all that bothered about what Sonia was going to say to him; he felt changed now. He wasn't the man she'd married anymore; he'd felt the thrill of ending another human being's life. That was a feeling that not many people would understand.

His father would understand; he'd killed multiple times. And now, Rob knew why; the sense of elation he felt after killing Eric was like a drug coursing through his veins, but he knew it would eventually wear off and he'd have to kill again. It was who he was now.

Besides, the collection in the cellar was missing two pieces, thanks to him, and he owed it to his father's memory to replace them. And after that, he would increase the collection even further.

Wasn't that what his father had told him after he'd gone down to the cellar today? He closed his eyes and winced as a headache began to form. He couldn't remember what his father had said.

He knew it hadn't *really* been his father speaking to him; the old man was buried in the cemetery in Hatherfield. What Rob had seen hadn't been real.

Or had it? He wasn't sure anymore.

One thing he was certain of, though, was that he had to act normal around Sonia and the kids, and also around his work colleagues and neighbours. If he was going to increase the collection, then he had to make sure he didn't draw attention to himself. He had to pretend to be the same old Rob.

That meant going home for a while.

He was reluctant to leave the house, and especially the cellar, but it had to be done. Before he left, he got the washing out of the machine and hung it over the washing line his dad had put up in the laundry room. He couldn't leave the damp clothes in the machine, because they'd stink.

When that was done, he put his coat on and left the house.

As he drove away in the Land Rover, he looked at the dark woods behind the house. Eric was there somewhere, hidden in the cold ground where no one would ever find him. Rob grinned at the thought. That would teach the old bastard not to stick his nose in where it didn't belong. He'd never do that again.

He chuckled to himself and turned the radio up, singing along with it as he drove to Hatherfield. The News came on, announcing that the police still had no leads on the murders of Daisy Riddle and Joanna Kirk. Rob laughed. He was untouchable. They'd never find him.

When he got to Hatherfield, he turned the radio down and parked outside his house. There were no lights on. Sonia had work tomorrow, so she was probably in bed. Killing the engine, he slid out of the Land Rover and found his house key. He opened the front door and sneaked inside.

The house was silent.

Creeping upstairs, Rob felt like an intruder in his own home. He didn't belong here; his place was at his new house, where the collection of girls waited to be uncovered from the cellar dirt. Where they waited to have more added to their number.

He reminded himself that he had to keep up appearances so as not to arouse suspicion. For now, anyway. Maybe later, things would change.

Sneaking into the bedroom, he saw Sonia in the bed, lying on her side, snoring lightly. She was fast off. Probably tired of waiting for him. He'd have a word with her in the morning, tell her he wasn't feeling very well so he'd thought it best to stay away from her and the kids in case he was contagious. He'd also tell her the signal was almost non-existent in Miller's Dale, and he hadn't seen any of her texts or received her calls. Besides, he'd been in bed sleeping off his mystery illness. If he played this right, he might even get some sympathy.

The thought made him want to laugh, but he stifled the impulse and quickly got undressed in the dark, sliding into the bed carefully so as not to disturb his wife.

Despite the fact that his mind was whirling with plans and schemes, as soon as his head touched the pillow, he fell asleep.

～

He woke up when he heard the curtains being drawn back and felt sunlight on his face. He sat up, opening his bleary eyes.

Sonia stood at the foot of the bed. The look of anger on her face said it all, but she still decided to speak, anyway. "What the fuck, Rob?"

"What? What do you mean?"

"I mean I've been calling and calling you. You've been God knows where, and you didn't think I'd be worried? I almost called the police."

He remembered his cover story. "I've been poorly, Sonia. I had to take myself to bed at my dad's house, and there's no reception out there."

"Don't give me that rubbish! What's happening to you, Rob? You've been ignoring me and the kids for the past few days. I had to get Emma to come over last night because I was working late. She asked where you were, you know, just casually. I told her you were at work as well. I couldn't tell her the truth, could I? That I had no idea where you'd gone."

She paused, then added, "Is there another woman?"

"What? No, don't be ridiculous. Why would you think that?"

"What am I supposed to think, Rob. You disappear at all hours; you ignore my phone calls. I've got no idea where you've been."

He got out of bed and began to get dressed. Coming home had obviously been a mistake. "You know exactly where I've been. At my dad's house. Perhaps you should be a bit more compassionate; I've just had a loss."

She scoffed. "A loss? You barely knew your father. You hated him."

"Well, sometimes, when a person dies, you realise things about them. You wish you'd treated them differently when they were alive. You want to make them proud of you."

Sonia looked incredulous. "Proud of you? Do you think he'd be proud of you abandoning your wife and kids? You'd be a disappointment to him."

He turned on her. "What?"

"You heard me. A disappointment."

He felt rage suddenly flare up inside him. One wall of their bedroom was taken up by a built-in wardrobe with mirrored doors. Rob picked up his bedside table and threw it in that direction. The corner of the wooden table hit one of the mirrors and shattered it.

Sonia shrank back. "Rob, what the fuck are you doing?"

He reached into his pocket and brought out the knife. "You think I'm a disappointment to him? Maybe I should stick you with this. See how much of a disappointment I'd be, then."

Her eyes went wide with shock and her face contorted into a mask of fear. Her eyes darted to the door, but she didn't make a run for it, probably sensing that if she did, he'd catch her easily.

"Let's talk about this," she said, her voice a high-pitched whine. "You don't want to do this, Rob."

"Don't I?" he jabbed the air between them with the knife. "But you said I was a disappointment, Sonia. This could change that."

Her eyes were fixed to the blade as it glinted in the sunlight coming in through the window. "I don't know what you're talking about." Tears rolled down her cheeks. "I don't know what's happening."

"What's happening," he said, "is that I'm doing what I was supposed to do my whole life. What *he* wanted me to do."

"You're not making any sense."

He approached her slowly, ready to grab her if she made a run for it. His plan of keeping a low profile and not drawing attention to himself had gone to shit now, but that was Sonia's fault, not his. She'd provoked him. What was he supposed to do?

Let her get away with it? The old Rob might have done that, but not him. Not now.

"Think of Sam and Olivia," she said. Her pleading reminded him of the girl cowering in the shadowy corner of the cellar when he was a kid. It hadn't ended well for her, and it wasn't going to end well for Sonia, either.

He tightened his grip on the knife and moved towards her.

Then stopped.

A tinny voice came from somewhere in the room. "999, which service do you require?"

"Police," Sonia said. She brought her phone out from behind her back and showed the screen to Rob. Three digits, 999, were displayed on the screen in stark white numerals.

"Even if anything happens to me, they'll trace the call," she said quickly. "They'll be coming here, Rob."

A man's voice came from the phone. "Derbyshire police."

Rob ran. His plans had gone awry. He had things to do, and he couldn't let Sonia and the police stop him now. Fleeing from the bedroom, he half-ran, half-slid down the stairs and out of the front door.

The Land Rover waited, and as he got behind the wheel, he took a deep breath to calm himself before starting the engine.

"Where are we going?" a voice asked from the passenger seat.

He turned and saw his father sitting there. The old man had an expectant look on his face.

"We're going hunting," Rob said. "I'm going to add a new girl to the collection."

His father smiled. It was the warmest smile he'd ever given Rob. "Good. Make me proud, son."

CHAPTER 23

Tony's optimism had lessened slightly, but he was still looking forward to the day ahead as he and Dani made their way to Miller's Dale in her Land Rover. The DI had a determined look on her face as she drove, and Tony guessed that she was hell-bent on either making an arrest today, or at least cracking the case open. This was her opportunity to prove herself to Battle and the rest of the team; to show them that she hadn't gone soft during her enforced absence.

He himself didn't have such lofty ambitions. He hoped they'd uncover some evidence that would put the team's focus onto the correct individual, which at this time seemed to be Penny Gibson. That would be a step in the right direction because otherwise, Murder Force didn't even have any suspects in this case.

Gallow had put this team together to swoop in

and solve high profile cases, but in this instance, they were flailing around in the dark.

"Is it much farther?" he asked Dani.

She glanced at the SatNav. "Five minutes."

It was early morning. They'd foregone breakfast at the B&B so they could get to the farmhouse where Penny Gibson lived before she went out for the day. The details they had on the woman were scant, and there was no employment information, but that didn't necessarily mean she didn't have some sort of local job. Their hope was to catch her before she went to it.

"Did you sleep well?" Tony asked, to break the silence in the car.

"Not really. I kept thinking about this morning. How about you?"

"No, I didn't get much sleep either."

"Thinking about our meeting with Mrs Gibson?"

"Something like that." Actually, he'd been watching dating advice videos on the Internet, but he wasn't about to tell Dani that. And, although he'd spent a couple of hours watching various dating 'gurus' dispense advice about meeting the opposite sex, he hadn't really learned anything he didn't already know.

"I've got a good feeling about today," Dani said.

"Penny Gibson isn't going to break down and confess everything to us," he reminded her. "If she's suffering from psychosis, as I suspect she is, then she probably won't give anything away."

"But you'll know, right? If she's psychotic, you'll know."

"Well, there's one thing I know for sure."

"What's that?"

"We need to be very careful. If she's the person who dug up those bodies, she'll be experiencing delusions, hallucinations, and she'll probably be violent."

"I don't like that word, Tony."

"What? Violent?"

No. *If.* From what we know, Penny Gibson has got to be the person who left Daisy and Joanna for us to find. Her dead husband is probably the killer."

"From what we know, I agree. She's linked to Mary and her husband recently died, which fits my theory. But what about the things we *don't* know?"

She scowled at him. "Like what?"

"Well, by definition, we don't know what we don't know. But there's bound to be something. It can't be so cut and dried."

"You need to give yourself more credit. You had this entire thing figured out."

"Hmm." He wasn't so sure.

"Anyway, we're nearly there," she said, turning off the main road and following a narrow country road that was lined with hedgerows and trees. When gaps appeared in the hedges, Tony could see fields, and the river the police reckoned Mary Harwood had drowned in.

Following the SatNav's instructions, Dani steered the Land Rover onto an even narrower road that wasn't much more than a dirt path. The vehicle bumped over ruts and potholes. Tony was glad they hadn't come in his Mini; the exhaust would have probably been ripped off.

"Very isolated out here," Dani observed.

Tony nodded. He noticed a lot of woodland, and wondered if, somewhere among those trees was the clandestine graveyard that had been represented by the *X*s inside the skulls of the two girls they'd found.

The path led to a house that had seen better days. Tony decided that the word ramshackle described the place best. The roof looked to be in a state of disrepair and the windows were dirty. The entire structure seemed to be leaning to one side, as if its foundations were slipping.

There was no vehicle anywhere to be seen, and no sign of life.

"Dammit!" Dani said. "It looks like she isn't here." She guided the Land Rover to the gravelled area at the side of the house and cut the engine. Getting out, she said, "I'll knock on the door, you have a look around."

"All right." He got out of the car and strolled to the rear of the building, trying to look casual in case anyone *was* in the house, and was watching him from the windows.

The back garden was overgrown and unkempt. Vines and weeds had taken over and strangled the life out of everything else long ago, by the look of it. A wooden building with a sagging roof sat at the edge of the patch of weeds that might have once been a lawn.

Tony went over to it. The door didn't appear to be locked. Taking hold of the rusted metal handles, he pulled. The doors opened.

After taking a look inside, he waved at Dani, who was standing by the front door. "There is a car, after all," he told her. "A silver Lexus." He looked back at the vehicle and frowned in confusion. The car didn't fit in with the run-down house and the overgrown garden. It seemed out of place among the tools and woodworking machines in the sagging wooden building.

Tony walked over to Dani. "Any luck?"

She shook her head. "I've knocked half a dozen times. No one's in."

He went to the window and peered inside. "That's odd."

"What?" she asked, joining him and cupping her hands against the glass to see better.

The room beyond the window was a kitchen. Like the exterior of the house, it had seen better days. But it wasn't the kitchen that had caught Tony's attention. "See that open doorway?"

Dani squinted and then nodded. "Looks like a laundry room. I can see a washing machine."

"Look what's hanging on the line."

"Men's clothing."

"And it looks damp. I thought James Gibson died a week or so ago."

"It could belong to the son."

"True. Does he live here?"

"I don't know, but neither him nor Penny appear to be here at the moment," Dani said, stepping back from the house and craning her neck to look at the upper windows. "You said there's a car?"

"Yes, a silver Lexus. Looks out of place."

"All right, let's have a look at it." She went over to the building that housed the car and took out her notepad to make a note of the number plate. "I'm going to get this checked," she said, going back to the Land Rover. Her earlier enthusiasm had vanished now that it was apparent Penny Gibson wasn't here.

"Find out if the son lives here, as well," Tony said, making his way around the back of the house again. He didn't believe he possessed much intuition, and he certainly wasn't psychic as Dani had suggested, but something about this house felt off. The place felt lonely, and not just because of its isolated location. There was no life here. Everything was dead.

He found another window and peered inside. A

living room with a single armchair in front of an old television set. The rest of the room was cluttered with old furniture—such as the dusty bureau sitting in the corner—and yellowing newspapers.

Dani came around the side of the house and joined him.

"I don't think a woman lives here," he told her. "Look at the state of the place."

"Isn't that a bit sexist, Tony? You should see what my cottage looks like when I haven't bothered to clean for a week."

"This is more than a week's worth of dust and a couple of takeaway cartons on the worktop," he said. "This is real neglect. The person who lives here probably spends most of their time in their own head. Reliving memories that seem more tangible than the real world. That's why the house is the way it is; there's something more important to the occupant than keeping the place clean."

"Like killing girls, you mean?"

He shrugged. He didn't want to jump to conclusions. "It's a possibility. James Gibson probably spent most of his time in the woods, with the bodies. Or in the house itself. Dennis Nilsen did that; he used to prop the corpses of his victims up on the sofa and watch TV with them."

She leaned forward and squinted at the living room through the window. "You think there are dead bodies in there?"

"I'm not saying there are, and I'm not saying there aren't. At first, I thought those woods would make an ideal burial ground, but he might have wanted to keep them close."

Dani shook her head. "No, that can't be right. The bodies we found had been buried. So, you were probably right when you said the woods. Anyway, here's another part of the puzzle. That car belongs to Eric Gibson."

"Who's he?"

"James's brother. He lives in Exeter. Came up here for his brother's funeral. His wife rang the police yesterday. Eric was supposed to return to Exeter, but he never made it home, and she can't get hold of him."

"So, he's a missing person."

"The police were going on the assumption that he might have had an accident on his way home."

"But he can't have," Tony said, "because his car's here. He never left."

She nodded. "There's someone who might be able to shed some light on all of this. The son. Robert. Turns out he doesn't live here after all. He lives in Hatherfield, a village not too far from here."

"Maybe he'll know where his mother is."

"Let's hope so. Have you seen enough here?"

"More than enough."

"They're sending over a couple of officers to have a look at that car, since it's part of a missing persons case. I'm going to get a couple more uniforms to come over as well and have a scout around in those woods. You never know; if there is a graveyard back there, they might find it."

"Good idea."

"While they're doing that, we'll go and have a word with Robert Gibson. He should be able to tell us where we can find his mum."

They went back to the Land Rover and climbed in. Dani turned the vehicle around. As she drove past the house, and back towards the path, Tony shouted, "Stop!"

She hit the brakes and they both lurched forwards against their seatbelts. Tony unbuckled his as quickly as he could and got out of the Land Rover.

"What is it?" the DI said, following him.

He hurried back to the house to confirm what he thought he'd just seen. When he reached it, he got to his knees and tried to wipe the glass clean with the cuff of his coat.

Dani caught up with him. "What's wrong?"

"This window," he said, still trying to clean the grime off the thin oblong of glass that was set into the house just inches above ground level. "It's a cellar window."

"Okay. So, there's a cellar."

He fumbled the pieces of crumpled paper out of his pocket. He found the one with eight *X*s on it and held it so Dani could see it.

"Look at the graves. The pattern of the graves. They're in a square. If he'd buried the bodies in the woods, there'd be no need to group them together like this. They're in a square because he couldn't dig beyond the walls. The graves are enclosed. They're inside."

She pointed at the cellar window. "They're in there."

"Yes, they're in there. All of them." He'd cleaned the outside of the glass, but he could now see that the window was boarded up on the inside.

"Okay, we need to get a search warrant," she said. "But we haven't really got anything compelling that would get us one at the moment. I suggest we find Penny Gibson and go from there."

"All right," he said, getting to his feet. He looked back at the small window as he walked back to the Land Rover. If he was right, Mary Harwood was in there. The girl Colleen had told them about, the girl who had befriended Mrs Gibson, and probably sealed her fate when she visited this house for tea, and came to the attention of James Gibson, was just beyond that piece of glass.

When they were buckled into their seats again, the DI hit the accelerator and they raced towards Hatherfield.

∼

"What the hell now?" Dani said as they approached Robert Gibson's house. A police car was parked outside, and the front door was open.

Tony felt queasy. He'd feared that the person digging up the bodies could be violent, and the scene before him seemed to confirm that. He just hoped no one was dead.

Getting out of the Land Rover, he wondered what he was about to walk into. Would Robert Gibson be dead, killed by his own mother?

He followed Dani into the house. Voices came from the living room, along with the crackling static of police radios.

A woman was sitting on the sofa, clutching a balled-up tissue in her hand, tears streaming down her face. A female police officer in a hi-vis jacket was sitting next to her, comforting her, while her male colleague came into the room with a cup of tea for the distraught woman.

"DI Summers," Dani said, immediately taking control of the situation. "What's happened here?"

"This is Sonia Gibson," the female officer said. "She's been attacked by her husband."

"Is your husband Robert Gibson?" Dani asked, crouching down so she was at eye level with the woman.

Sonia nodded. "He's gone crazy. He attacked me with a knife. If I hadn't called the police. If he hadn't run away…" Her words trailed off and she began to sob.

"Sonia," Dani said, putting a comforting hand on her shoulder. "Where has he run to? Could he be with his mother?"

The tears stopped, replaced by a look of confusion. "His mother?"

"Yes. Penny Gibson."

"I know who his mother is, but she isn't around anymore. She left when Rob was just a boy."

The pieces suddenly fell into place in Tony's mind.

"What did Rob say?" he asked Sonia. "When he was here, what did he say?"

She composed herself a little and looked at the tissue in her hand as she told her story. "I was mad at him because he hasn't been home for days. He's been ignoring me."

"He was at the house, wasn't he? The house in Miller's Dale?"

Sonia nodded. "I wish I'd never heard of that place. When Rob inherited it, I thought great, we can sell it and make some money. But he seemed to want to hang onto it, for some reason. I don't know why; the house is falling to pieces."

Tony crouched down so that he too was at eye level with the woman. "Sonia, this is very important. Did Rob say anything about why he was acting the way he was?"

"He wasn't making any sense. He said he was doing what he was supposed to have been doing his whole life. What someone wanted him to do."

"Who?" Dani asked. "Did he say who?"

"His father," Tony said.

"His father's dead."

"Yes, he is, but Rob is in a psychotic state, at the moment. He's experiencing a break from reality. To him, James Gibson is still alive, probably egging him on."

The DI's expression became grim. "What will he do?"

Tony let out a breath. "He'll do exactly what his dad did before he died. He'll find a girl, abduct her, and add her to the collection."

CHAPTER 24

Rob hunkered down in the Land Rover. He'd left Hatherfield behind and driven to Bakewell. Now, he was parked in the Co Op car park, watching through the windscreen as the people around him went about their boring lives.

They were nothing to him; simply a herd of cattle from which he would choose the next to be slaughtered. She had to be right, though. Whoever he chose was going to become part of the collection, so she had to be perfect.

The girls his father preferred had been mid-teens, and dark-haired. He was sure that if he sat here long enough, the opportunity would present itself for him to pounce on similar prey.

Then all he had to do was get her to the cellar and do the thing he had fled from when he was young. It would be easy now. He was looking forward to it. After killing Eric, everything had changed. *He* had changed.

Another half an hour passed, during which time he watched pensioners feeding the ducks on the river, and mothers pushing prams towards the park.

Then he saw her.

She appeared in his rearview mirror, walking across the car park with her head down, long black hair blowing into her face. She had a rucksack slung over her shoulder, and he got the impression she was walking home from school, perhaps for lunch.

That wasn't really important; the important thing was that she was alone. And she was walking right towards the rear of the Land Rover.

He got out and walked to the same spot himself, timing his movements so that he reached the back of the vehicle a couple of seconds before she did, enough time to open the boot.

When she was within a few feet of him, he said, "Excuse me. Can you tell me how to get to—" He never finished the sentence. He smashed his fist into her face, sending her reeling. Before she staggered away from the Land Rover, he grabbed her and bundled her into the back.

There was a roll of duct tape in there, a leftover from when his dad had driven the vehicle. Rob quickly and efficiently bound the dazed girl's hands and legs and put a strip over her mouth as well, just like he'd seen on the girl in the cellar years ago.

He closed the boot and quickly got in behind the

wheel, checking all the mirrors. No one had seen him. He wasn't home free yet, but he'd done the hard part. Now he just had to get her to the cellar.

He started the engine and pulled out of the car park. In the boot, the girl was coming to, kicking at the interior of the car and trying to scream. Well, she could do that all she wanted; it wasn't going to get her anywhere.

Grinning to himself, he got onto the main road and turned towards Miller's Dale. His dad was in the passenger seat again, smiling at him with that huge, loving smile. "Well done, son. I knew you could do it."

"Thanks, Dad."

"Now let's get her home and do what needs to be done to seal the deal. Taking her off the street is one thing, but killing her is something else entirely, and I've seen you balk at that part."

"Not this time," Rob said firmly. "Not this time."

His dad looked at him with a serious expression. "Well, I'm looking forward to you not being a disappointment anymore, Rob. When you show me, you can do what needs to be done, I'll be so proud."

Rob drove all the way to Miller's Dale with a grin on his face. Even the banging in the back, from the girl kicking the back of the seats and bucking her body, didn't faze him.

The grin only faded when he was driving along

the dirt track towards his house and he saw the police cars parked there.

That bitch Sonia had sent them after him. Probably gave them some sob story about how he'd attacked her, and now they were here to have a word with him. Well, he wasn't exactly going to pull up and have a chat with them when he had a girl in the back of his car. Even he'd have a hard time explaining that one away.

He applied the brakes, turned around, and drove away. He could come back later.

"And when will that be?" his dad asked from the passenger seat. "Later today? Tomorrow? Sometime never?"

"I can't unload her from the car and take her to the cellar while the police are there."

"You don't have to kill her in the cellar, just as long as she ends up there."

"I'll do it in the woods," Rob offered.

"No, not the woods. You killed Eric in the woods. The girls are more special than that. You don't have to do it in the cellar, but it's got to be somewhere meaningful."

"I don't know anywhere like that."

"Of course you do. You're doing this for me, aren't you? To show me what a good son you are? Then there's a very particular place you can kill her. If you do it there, we can both share in the experience."

Rob knew instantly the place his father was referring to. The grin returned to his face and he headed towards the one place where he and his dad could share the experience of killing the girl.

CHAPTER 25

DS Lorna Morgan hated being cooped up in the incident room. She wanted to be out and about, doing something other than going over paperwork. She hadn't joined the police force for this, and she certainly hadn't taken the job with Murder Force to read reports.

She was back on her home turf now, the place she'd grown up and worked all her life, until joining the new team. Surely she'd be of more use to everyone if she was out in the field, using her local knowledge of Derbyshire and its people.

"Thought you could do with this," DS Matt Flowers said, putting a cup of coffee on her desk next to her.

Lorna looked up at him and smiled, appreciating the gesture. "You haven't got any chocolate have you?" she asked half-jokingly.

He smiled back. "There's a Kit Kat on my desk. Want to share it?"

"Yes, please. Anything to break the tedium of going through these reports."

He went back to his own desk and came back with the promised chocolate bar. He snapped it in half and handed her the two fingers that comprised her share. "I know what you mean. I think my vision's going blurry. The DCI is really making us go over everything with a fine-toothed comb. I heard he's looking at everything himself as well. And staying late to do it, too."

"He doesn't want to miss anything."

"I suppose he doesn't want to make any mistakes like he did last time."

"The original investigation was screwed up by the Inspector," she said. "He had a theory—that Daisy had run away—and wouldn't expand the investigation beyond that. It wasn't Battle's fault."

Matt nodded. "Yeah, I know that, but I bet that isn't how he feels about it."

Lorna nodded, but didn't say anything. She'd worked with Battle long enough to know that he blamed himself for not finding Daisy. The self-blame wasn't justified, but it was there, nevertheless.

DC Tom Ryan stuck his head around the privacy screen that separated his desk from Lorna's. "DI Summers has requested a team of officers to search some woods near the house of a suspect. Anyone up for it?"

Lorna stood up immediately, suddenly realising how stiff her backside and legs were. "Count me in. What are we searching for?"

"The gravesite where those girls came from."

"I'm in," Matt said.

Tom nodded. "All right. Let's go."

* * *

Ten minutes later, they were speeding down the A6 in DC Ryan's Aston Martin. Lorna was in the passenger seat, and Matt was in the back. Tom, who was dressed in the same black bomber jacket Lorna had always seen him wear, was focused on the road ahead.

The short, stocky man was a bit of an enigma. Lorna had heard that he'd once been a soldier in the SAS. If that was true, she wondered why he hadn't pursued a military career, and had joined the police force instead.

Of course, she wasn't going to just ask him that. Well, not directly, anyway. "I heard you were in the SAS," she said, feeling her way into the conversation.

He nodded. "That's right."

"I suppose you're not allowed to talk about it."

"No, not really. Official secrets and all that."

She nodded, understanding. She wasn't going to get much out of him. "They must pay well. Is that how you afforded this car?" She rubbed her hand along the Aston Martin's dashboard.

"No, this was a gift. I did some security work in the Middle East, and one of my clients bought her for me. What do you think of her?"

"She's lovely," she said, using the same pronoun for the car as he had. Lots of men liked to think of their cars as female. He probably even had a name for it.

"She's sweet as a nut," he said.

"Have you ever killed anyone?" Matt blurted out from the back seat.

Tom's eyes flicked up to the rearview mirror, where Lorna guessed he'd caught Matt's gaze. "Now that is something I definitely don't like to talk about."

Matt said, "I'll take that as a yes," and then fell silent.

Lorna did the same. It might not be wise to pry into DC Ryan's life too deeply; she might not like what she found.

Ten minutes later, they arrived at a remote house surrounded by fields and woods. Four police cars were parked outside and the officers who had arrived in those cars—Lorna could see eight uniformed police men and women—were all around the side of the house, inspecting a wooden structure in the garden.

The Aston Martin glided to a stop and Lorna got out, approaching the uniforms with her warrant card in her hand. "DS Morgan, Murder Force. We're here to have a look in the woods. Have you found something in there?"

"We're here to help you, ma'am," a female Asian officer said. "Well, six of us are. The other two officers are here because this car is part of a missing persons enquiry." She pointed at a silver Lexus that was parked in the wooden structure.

Lorna nodded. "All right. Everyone who's here for the search, come with me." She walked back along the side of the house to the cars. Matt was standing with his hands on his hips, staring at the distant woods, while Tom was pulling something out of the Aston Martin's boot. As she got closer, she saw that it was a spade.

"We're not even sure we're going to find anything yet," she told him.

"Better to have it with us if we do." He slung the spade over his shoulder like a rifle and waited for her to lead the way.

She did so, with the six uniforms and two detectives in tow.

As they approached the woods, she understood what a mammoth task they had ahead of them. Hopefully, she'd be able to get more officers down here, because the area they had to cover was too much for nine people to handle effectively.

"There's a trail," Matt said.

"So we know where he *didn't* bury those girls," one of the uniforms said.

"Not if he was smart," said another.

They entered the woods, stepping into the shadows beneath the tall trees. They'd hardly gone more than a few yards before Tom said, "Actually, he wasn't that smart."

Lorna turned to face him. "Why?"

He indicated an area of ground some distance from the path. To Lorna, it looked like every other piece of ground around here.

"The undergrowth has been disturbed," Tom said. "Something heavy has been dragged along there."

Lorna squinted at the ground but she couldn't see whatever Tom was seeing. "Let's have a closer look, then."

The ex-SAS soldier took the lead, stepping carefully through the undergrowth until he reached an area that was hidden from the path by trees. "The ground here has been disturbed and someone has tried to conceal it."

Crouching down, he used the spade to clear away sticks and leaves. Standing up again, he nodded to Lorna. "The earth is freshly dug."

She turned to look back across the field at the

house. This didn't seem like a location someone would choose to bury a number of bodies. It was too close to the path, too near the house. Surely a spot deeper in the woods would be more suitable.

Or maybe, like Tom said, the killer wasn't all that smart.

Don't go running away with yourself just yet, she told herself. *This might be nothing more than the place someone buried a dead pet.*

Then why try to hide it with sticks and leaves? A pet's grave would be marked, not hidden.

"Get digging," she told Tom. "Let's see what's down there." Turning to Matt, she said, "Can you take the uniforms a bit further in? See if there's anything else we should know about?"

He nodded. "All right. But I haven't got eagle eyes like Mister SAS over there."

"Just see if there's anything else of interest."

He took the officers deeper into the woods. They moved slowly, using the toes of their shoes to move the undergrowth and dead leaves aside as they inspected the ground in front of them.

It was a ten minutes later when one of the officers shouted, "Find!"

It was the same Asian officer Lorna had spoken to at the house.

"What is it?" she asked.

"Looks like blood, ma'am."

Lorna went over there to have a look. There

wasn't just a small amount of blood; there was a lot of it, staining the ground, dead leaves, and tree roots.

"We need SOCO here," she said.

"I'll sort it," said Matt.

From behind her, Tom shouted, "We're going to need the pathologist as well."

Lorna walked carefully over to the DC, trying not to disturb the undergrowth too much. This entire area would soon be a crime scene.

Tom was leaning on the spade handle, sweating from his exertion. The ground in front of him was dug to a depth of a few feet, and Lorna could see a man's face in the dirt.

Tom, breathing hard, said, "I think we found our missing person."

CHAPTER 26

Dani's phone rang. She left the room to answer it.

Tony said to Sonia, "Did Rob give any indication of where he was going when he left here?"

"No, he just got in his Land Rover and drove off at speed."

"Do you know the number plate of the Land Rover?"

She shook her head. "It was his dad's. Part of his inheritance, along with that bloody house."

"How about the colour?"

"It's blue. A blue Defender."

Tony resisted the urge to sigh with frustration. A psychotic would-be killer was out there somewhere, and all they had to go on was that he was in a blue Land Rover Defender. He mentally amended the term would-be killer. Rob might have already killed. What had happened to Eric? His car was at Miller's

Dale, but the man himself was missing. It wasn't looking good.

"He's taken a girl," Dani said, coming back into the room. "From the Co Op in Bakewell."

"Shit," Tony said, closing his eyes and saying a silent prayer. He wasn't usually a praying man, but he knew what Robert Gibson was capable of. He also had a feeling that James Gibson had killed his victims almost immediately, and Rob was likely to do the same.

"Where will he take her?" Dani said, looking at Tony for an answer.

"The house at Miller's Dale, of course," he said, standing up. "But he can't take her there because of the uniforms checking the Lexus and the woods."

Dani nodded and pursed her lips. "So where will he go?"

Tony tried to think. In theory, Rob could take the girl anywhere, but in reality, his psychological makeup limited his choices. He was doing all of this for a reason; to carry on his dead father's work and make his father proud of him. So, he wouldn't just kill the victim at any old place; it would be somewhere that meant something to both Rob and his father.

He turned to Sonia. "Was there any place where Rob and James went together? A place that was special to them?"

"No," she said, shaking her head. "Rob barely ever saw his father. There isn't anywhere like that."

On one hand, that was good because it limited the number of places Rob might have gone, but on the other, it was bad because it made it impossible to predict where Rob was going.

There had to be a place that linked father and son. They hadn't connected in life but now, Rob wanted that connection.

"Eric drove up here for the funeral," he said, thinking aloud. "Was James buried? Is there a grave?"

"Yes," Sonia said. "It's in the churchyard up the road. Not far from here."

Tony looked at Dani. "It's the grave. Rob will take the girl to his father's grave. What better way to show his old man that he's becoming the son he always wanted him to be?"

"Are you sure?" Dani asked.

He nodded; certain he was correct. "It's the grave."

They went out through the front door. "That way," Dani said, pointing at a church spire a couple of streets away. As they ran along the pavement, she dialled a number on her phone and said, "I need officers at Hatherfield churchyard. We think that's where Robert Gibson is going."

I just hope we're in time," Tony gasped. His lungs were already burning, but he increased his pace. Dani, who was obviously much fitter than him, was at least ten yards ahead, and increasing that distance with each stride.

When he reached the churchyard gates, Tony wanted nothing more than to rest, but he had to put that aside for the sake of the girl Rob had with him. Besides, a blue Land Rover Defender was parked by the gates, with its boot open. Rob was already here. There might not be much time.

As he entered the cemetery, he saw Dani some distance away. She had her hand raised in a halting motion, as if beckoning someone to calm down. Standing in front of her was a dark-haired man in a blue checkered shirt and jeans. In one hand, he held what looked like a knife. His other arm was wrapped around the throat of a teenage girl with long, dark hair.

Tony got closer and realised the girl was bound and gagged with duct tape. She was on her knees, as if she too scared—or too weak—to stand.

Knowing Robert was suffering from psychosis, Tony realised this was a crisis situation. The fragile threads of Rob's psyche that still had a tentative hold on reality were about to snap.

"Stay back," Rob said as Tony joined Dani, "or I'll kill her."

"You're going to kill her, anyway," Tony said. "There's nothing we can do to stop that, is there, Rob?"

Dani shot him a look, but Tony ignored it. She was just going to have to trust him.

"At least you're aware of how useless you are," Rob said.

"Is that your dad's grave you're standing on?" Tony pointed at the gravestone behind Rob.

"Yes, it is."

"James Andrew Gibson," Tony read aloud. "Father and brother. Not much of an epitaph, is it?"

Rob looked confused. "What do you mean?"

"Well, it's not very personal. It doesn't say loving father, or beloved brother. Usually there's something like *Sadly Missed*, but it's not on there. Because no one misses your father. He wasn't loving, or beloved by anyone. He was a nobody, really, wasn't he?"

"He certainly was not."

"Yes, he was. Killing young girls didn't make him special. It made him sad and weak. Are you the same as him? Sad? Weak?"

"No, I'm not, and neither was he."

"So, what's this all about?" Tony gestured to the girl, who was staring at him with fearful eyes.

"It's what he wanted."

"Oh, really? What about what you wanted, Rob? I'm sure you wanted a mother, but he took that away from you, didn't he?"

"I don't know. He said she left us."

Tony snorted. "You know that's not true. Deep down, you know she's in the cellar with the others.

He lied to you. Has he been lying to you lately as well? Telling you how proud you can make him?"

"Shut up."

"Did he tell you to do this?"

"No, I'm doing what he wanted me to do when I was a young boy. I disappointed him then, but I won't do that again."

"Oh, I think he's very disappointed in you, Rob. You've destroyed his life's work by taking two girls out of the cellar. And now, all his dark secrets are going to be brought out into the light. The police will take away every single body from the cellar. All because of you."

Rob faltered. "What? No, that's not right."

"Wasn't it you who removed Daisy Riddle and Joanna Kirk from the collection and took them to Temple Well?"

"Yes, but at the time, I wanted to hurt him for what he did to me."

"What did he do, Rob?" Tony could hear cars pulling up at the gate, the sounds of footsteps and voices behind him.

Rob seemed unaware that the police team Dani had summoned had arrived. "He laughed at me when I didn't kill that girl. He never mentioned it again, but I saw disappointment in his eyes every single day as I was growing up."

"That hurt, didn't it? And you wanted to hurt him back. That's totally understandable. You certainly achieved your goal. Your actions have made sure his entire collection will be taken away."

"No, I didn't mean to do that." A look of panic entered Rob's eyes.

"Of course, you did. You just told me you did."

"Stop trying to confuse me."

"I'm not trying to confuse you, Rob, but you do sound confused. On the one hand, you say you want to be like your dad, but on the other, you ensured the destruction of everything he held dear."

"No, I didn't do that."

"Of course, you did. If he was disappointed in you when you couldn't kill one girl, imagine how disappointed he is now that you've made sure his entire collection will be dismantled. He couldn't *be* more disappointed."

Tony saw the rage building in Rob's eyes. "Get ready to grab the girl," he whispered to Dani.

Turning his attention back to Rob, he said, "Could a father be any more disappointed in his son? I don't think so. As disappointments go, you've really taken it to a new level." He stepped a little closer to Rob, presenting himself as a target. "There should be a picture of you in the dictionary, under the word disappointment."

Rob roared and pushed the girl aside so he could get to Tony. He crossed the space between them quickly, the wicked-looking knife blade glinting in the sunlight.

Tony stepped back, meaning to lead Rob into the waiting arms of the officers who surrounded them, but the back of his shoe connected with something solid on the ground and he felt himself falling backwards.

He landed on his back, the air leaving his lungs in a loud "Ooof" sound that exploded from between his lips. As he struggled for breath, he saw Dani rush over to the girl and drag her away. A shadow fell across his face and he looked up to see Rob standing over him.

There was no mistaking the murderous rage in Rob's eyes. If Tony didn't do something to protect himself, he was going to die here, on someone else's grave.

He kicked out, his foot connecting with Rob's chest, sending the man flailing backwards. The uniforms moved in as Tony scrambled to his feet.

Rob hadn't hit the ground, as Tony had hoped. Instead, he'd moved back to his father's grave. The difference was that now, the girl was safe. Dani had taken the tape off her legs and mouth and was moving her away from the area.

"Stay back!" Rob shouted, swinging the knife in wild arcs as the officers moved in on him.

"Give it up, Rob," Tony said. "There's nowhere to go from here. Let us get you the help you need."

Tears were streaming down Rob's face. He

pointed at the earth beneath his feet. "He wanted to see blood. He wanted me to make him proud."

"No, Rob, he didn't want any of that. He's gone. It was all in your head."

Rob shook his head violently. "No, no, no. He spoke to me."

"Come on, now. Put the knife down and you can tell me all about it on the way to the station."

Rob's eyes darted around the officers circling him before meeting Tony's. He turned the knife around in his hand so that the blade pointed at himself. Then, with both hands, he plunged it into his own stomach.

Staggering backwards, he slid down his father's gravestone, reaching out to touch it with one bloody hand before collapsing in the dirt.

"Shit!" Tony shouted. "Get an ambulance! Now!"

CHAPTER 27

"Put your foot down!" Battle told the officer driving the patrol car. The siren was blaring and the lights flashing, but it felt to the DCI that they were driving through molasses.

"I'm going as fast as I can, sir," the officer said. "These streets are quite narrow."

They were in the village of Hatherfield, making their way along a residential street that was lined on both sides with parked cars. Battle supposed the officer was doing his best but he needed to be at the churchyard now. Sitting in this car made him feel helpless.

"It's just there, sir," the driver said, pointing at a small church at the end of the street. Half a dozen police cars were parked outside the gate, and Battle could see blue lights flashing from somewhere within the churchyard.

He yanked his seatbelt off and was out of the

door before the officer had brought the car to a complete stop. Rushing through the gate, he saw two ambulances parked near the graves, rear doors open. The scene was chaotic. DI Summers had her arms around a teenage girl and was leading her to one of the ambulances, while two paramedics were sliding a stretcher in the back of the other.

A number of uniforms were watching the proceedings while others were gathered around one of the graves, bagging what looked like a knife.

Battle went over to the ambulance which DI Summers and the girl were climbing into, under the watchful eye of a paramedic.

"Summers, what happened?" he asked the DI.

"I'm taking Marcy to the hospital," she said. "Her parents are going to meet us there."

The teenage girl, who had a blanket wrapped tightly around her shoulders, looked like she was in a state of shock. Battle could understand why. If Summers and Sheridan hadn't followed their instincts and chased down the Gibson lead, she'd be dead.

"And who is this?" Battle enquired, pointing at the stretcher in the other ambulance.

"That's Robert Gibson, boss," Tony Sheridan said, appearing from the chaos and leading him away from the ambulance with a firm hand on his back. "He's the man who abducted Marcy from the car park in Bakewell."

"Is he our killer?" Battle looked back at the stretcher. The man strapped to it looked too young to have taken Daisy or Joanna.

"Not exactly," Sheridan said. "He's probably *a* killer. His uncle has gone missing, and I don't think he'll be found alive. But he's not the man you're referring to, no."

"Then where is he? Where's the man who took Daisy?"

The psychologist pointed at the grave where the uniforms had bagged the knife. Upon seeing the DCI, they'd all suddenly become busy, and had vacated the grave area to return to their vehicles.

"He's buried there."

Battle looked at the gravestone. *James Andrew Gibson. Father and Brother.*

He was too late.

Like the families who suddenly realised their loved ones weren't coming home, Battle understood that he was never going to bring Daisy's killer to justice. That had been taken out of his hands.

He walked to the grave, followed by the psychologist.

"I need a moment," he said.

Sheridan nodded. "Of course." Turning, he made his way back to the ambulances.

Battle looked down at the dirt beneath his shoes. Six feet beneath him lay a man who had haunted his nightmares for fifteen years. A man he had vowed to catch but failed to do so.

With the resurgence of evidence in the case—particularly the discovery of Daisy's body—he'd felt a quiet optimism that finally, after all these years, the man responsible would be put behind bars to rot in a cell for the rest of his life.

That was never going to happen.

He hadn't cried in a long time. In fact, he couldn't remember the last time he'd shed a tear. But he did so now. Hot, stinging tears welled in his eyes and rolled down his cheeks, falling onto the grave.

The DCI cried for all the girls who had been taken over the years and their families, who would never know justice.

CHAPTER 28

St Edmund's Church Burial Ground
   Castleton, Derbyshire
   Five Weeks Later

TONY DROVE into the car park of the 12th Century church in Castleton and got out of his Mini. It was a warm, Spring day, and the early morning sunlight that touched his face felt good. He saw Battle's green Range Rover parked near the church, the only other vehicle here.

Tony had come to the burial ground at the church because Dani had told him that the surly DCI—who was getting surlier by the day—came here every morning to visit Daisy's grave. The psychologist saw nothing wrong with that behaviour, and knew it was part of a process Battle was going to have to get through, but he wondered if the DCI was beating himself up internally every time he came here.

There was something he had to tell his boss.

Admiring the architecture of the church, he walked around the building, following a cement path to the graves.

The hulking figure of DCI Battle stood with his head bowed among the gravestones. Tony approached him slowly and stood a couple of feet behind him.

Daisy Riddle's grave was adorned with flowers, teddy bears, and tea light holders. The gravestone itself had a picture of the girl attached to it. She looked happy.

"Tony," Battle said, lifting his head. "What are you doing here?"

"I came to see you, actually. And pay my respects to Daisy, of course." He placed a bouquet of flowers, which he'd brought from the car, among the others on the grave.

"What do you want to see me about?" Battle said, wariness in his voice.

"I want to talk about Daisy. About when she went missing."

"If you've got any information, add it to the report."

Tony had seen the report, which had been written since the search of James Gibson's house and the exhumation of the bodies in the cellar had been carried out. Gibson's work records—which were part of the accumulated junk in his house—had revealed that he'd been working at the Marston family home, where Daisy's friend Sylvia lived. That was where he'd seen Daisy, and that was how he'd known she'd be on the street, walking from the Marston place back to her own house, at the precise time she'd been abducted. Gibson had either followed her out of the house, or he'd been waiting for her in his Land Rover outside.

But what Tony had to tell Battle wasn't anything to do with that. It wasn't a detail about the girl's disappearance; it was something regarding James Gibson's psychological makeup that the DCI needed to know.

"This isn't for the report," he said. "This is for you."

Battle frowned at him. "What are you talking about?"

"I've read the sections of the report that refer to what happened when Daisy was abducted. You searched for her at the train station. You thought she'd run away. I think you partly blame yourself for what happened."

Battle said nothing.

"I need to tell you that there was absolutely nothing you could have done that would have made any difference. While you were searching for Daisy, she was already dead. She was dead by the time you first heard her name."

"You can't know that."

"I do know that. James Gibson killed his victims straight away. He didn't leave them tied up in that cellar for days, or weeks on end. That wasn't what he was about. He dispatched them and added them to his collection. That was what it was all about for him, the collection of bodies in the cellar. There's no way you could have saved Daisy. Or any of the others, for that matter."

Battle took in a deep breath and let it out slowly. "Do you know what really rankles me, Tony?"

"No, what's that?"

"Gibson died before I could get my hands on him. Where's the justice in that?"

"Our job isn't to deliver justice. It's to shine a light into the dark corners and reveal the bad things that are hiding there. We did that with James Gibson. His victims are in the morgue now, and they'll soon get the proper burial they deserve, just like Daisy."

Battle thought about that for a moment, and then nodded. "I suppose you're right."

"Anyway," Tony said, turning away. "I have to go. There's somewhere I need to be." He set off down the path towards the car park.

"Tony," Battle said from behind him.

Tony turned to face the DCI.

"Thanks," Battle said.

Tony smiled and nodded and walked back to his car. When he got in, he waited a moment before starting the car, reflecting on the fact that Battle wasn't the only one who was going to have mental scars thanks to James Gibson.

Yesterday, he and Dani had visited Colleen Francis to tell her that one of the bodies from the cellar had been identified as that of her sister, Mary Harwood. As Tony had correctly guessed, Mary's skull had been marked with a single X. She'd been the first victim to make up the collection.

But not James Gibson's first victim. As well as the collection of girls, a skeleton with an unmarked skull had been exhumed from the cellar. It had been buried beneath the grave from which Rob had dug Daisy's body, and the extra talus bone had belonged to this skeleton.

There was no doubt in anyone's mind that this unmarked victim was Penny Gibson. James had disposed of her so he could begin his series of murders. Tony had delivered the news to Rob, who had recovered from his self-inflicted stab wound, thanks to a capable paramedic team, and was currently residing in Kingsway Hospital in Derby. Rob had simply shrugged upon hearing that his mother's body had been found, but Tony was sure the *laissez-fare* attitude was simply an act. Or a result of the drugs they were pumping into Rob at the hospital.

Yet according to the research they'd done on the man, there might have been another victim even before Penny. A girl named Sarah Rundle had disappeared from James's school, years before, and the circumstances—the victim's coat found by the river to suggest drowning—were similar to Mary Harwood's. That case had now been reopened, meaning that another family would probably be affected by Gibson's actions.

And Tony's fears regarding Eric Gibson, James's missing brother, had been confirmed when the uniforms Dani had sent into the woods had found a grave partially hidden beneath a pile of dead leaves. Eric's body had been buried there. Bizarrely, there had also been an Action Man buried in the dirt beneath the body.

Tony started the car and reversed out of the car park. As he'd told Battle, there was somewhere he needed to be.

CHAPTER 29

The morgue at Chesterfield Hospital was a hive of activity. As Tony walked along the corridor that led to Alina's office, he was passed by various medical staff and even a reporter being ejected from the premises by a security guard.

The Gibson case was the big news of the moment. Since the house at Miller's Dale had been virtually torn down, and the cellar ripped up, the case had been on the front pages of the newspapers every day.

Britain's New House of Hell
Police Find Horrors in Killer's Cellar

The fact that so many bodies had been recovered from the house meant that Tony's date with Alina had never happened. She'd been called out to the house and had been snowed under with work since. They'd spoken on the phone a couple of times, but so far, their work had kept them apart.

That was about to change.

The door to the mortuary office was open. Tony poked his head in and saw Alina standing at the edge of the room, peering through a microscope on the counter. She looked up and saw him.

"Tony!"

He entered the room and held up the paper bag in his hand. "I was wondering if you were hungry."

"What is this? You have brought me lunch?" She went to a sink and washed her hands. "I can take a quick break. It is so busy here, I might actually go crazy." She led him out of the office. "The eating area is down here. Come on."

He walked next to her, the smell of food drifting tantalisingly from the bag in his hand.

"You made that yourself?" she joked.

"Straight from MacDonald's. To me, this is gourmet cuisine."

She laughed. "Oh, Tony, I have so much to teach you."

He smiled. He'd like that. He'd like that a lot.

THE END

Get your copy of the next book in the series HERE

MURDER FORCE BOOK THREE
REMAINS
OF THE
NIGHT
FROM THE AUTHOR OF SILENCE OF THE BONES
ADAM J. WRIGHT

BY THE SAME AUTHOR

EYES OF THE WICKED

SILENCE OF THE BONES

REMAINS OF THE NIGHT

HOUSE OF THE DEAD

ECHO OF THE PAST

ALSO BY ADAM J. WRIGHT

DARK PEAK (DCI Battle)

THE RED RIBBON GIRLS (DI Summers)